DEFENDER OF THE REALM

King's Army

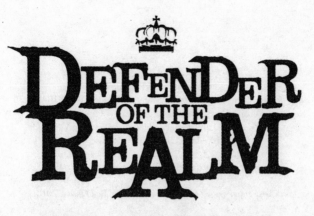

King's Army

MARK HUCKERBY & NICK OSTLER

■SCHOLASTIC

Scholastic Children's Books
An imprint of Scholastic Ltd
Euston House, 24 Eversholt Street, London, NW1 1DB, UK
Registered office: Westfield Road, Southam, Warwickshire, CV47 0RA
SCHOLASTIC and associated logos are trademarks and/or
registered trademarks of Scholastic Inc.

First published in the UK by Scholastic Ltd, 2018

ISBN 978 1407 18666 5

A CIP catalogue record for this book
is available from the British Library.

Printed and bound by CPI Group (UK) Ltd, Croydon, CR0 4YY

Papers used by Scholastic Children's Books are made
from wood grown in sustainable forests.

1 3 5 7 9 10 8 6 4 2

www.scholastic.co.uk

CONTENTS

FOR ELLIOT AND ZACK AND FREYA

I

THE WHITE CLIFFS OF DOVER

Their lives were in her hands. Nine men, thirteen women and eight children. There were no babies, because babies cry and crying gets you caught and getting caught, well, the less said about that the better. Thirty pale faces squinted into her torch beam, all looking to the anxious teenage girl standing before them for some sign that everything was going to be OK, that they hadn't made a terrible mistake leaving their homes and coming here tonight. They wore their warmest clothes and carried no bags, as instructed, though she'd had to confiscate a couple of rucksacks at the entrance. Hayley didn't blame them for trying; she knew how hard it was to leave behind everything you've ever known. When the

1

world around you suddenly changes, you cling to what's familiar, no matter how small.

They stared at her, waiting. She should say something.

"It's not far now. When we make the beach, I'll go ahead. Wait till I give the all-clear. Watch your step. No talking, please."

Hayley trudged on through the steel-lined tunnel, not so fast that she risked losing one of the group shuffling through the darkness behind her, but not too slow either – the longer they were on the move, the greater the chance of discovery. As they descended deeper into the earth beneath the cliffs, her torch picked out graffiti from World War Two scratched into the walls. A stick man running from a flying artillery shell, scrawled names, dates, a slogan that read "Russia bleeds while Britain Blancos", whatever that meant. The first time Hayley had ventured down here she'd found an old needle and thread still connected to a piece of khaki material stuffed behind a rusty, iron bunk bed. She'd thought about the young soldier who'd left it behind, perhaps called above ground to serve his shift on the gun battery, or to keep watch for an invasion that never came. What would he have felt if he'd known the war he was fighting would be won only a few months later? She was happy for him. He had been on the winning side. She hoped he'd had a good life.

But for the sorry rabble who had returned to these damp tunnels seventy years later, the invasion had been only too real. This time it was undead Vikings, along with people's own friends and neighbours turned berserk by dark magic, who were the enemy. And the war was already lost. All that was left now was survival.

That's why tonight was so important – Hayley might have felt scared, but she felt excited too. This was the start of their fightback.

At the end of the long march, she signalled for complete silence and released the heavy iron bolts of the outer door the way she'd been shown. A gale of icy air hit her face as she edged the door open. She stepped on to the beach. A thick carpet of snow reached all the way to the sea, matching the famous white cliffs of Dover that towered above her. A heavy band of unnatural, green-grey freezing fog sat just offshore, as it had around the length of Britain's coastline every day since Professor Lock had seized power; every day since Alfie had been – no, she couldn't go there, not right now. There was work to do.

Hayley flicked her torch on and off. Further down the beach a dim light flashed in reply. She hurried back to the tunnel entrance and waved the families out, counting heads till she reached thirty, then secured the door behind her. To the naked eye it was undetectable, just a natural part of the rocks at the foot of the cliffs. She led the shivering group crunching and sliding down the beach. There was no way to keep this part quiet, so it was better to be fast.

A small black fishing boat waited for them by the jetty. The captain reached out a dry, salt-cracked hand to each nervous passenger as they stepped onboard. His beard was whiter than usual with a night's worth of frost. Hayley wondered if any of them would have been surprised to learn he was in fact a beefeater – Chief Yeoman Warder Seabrook. A few months ago he might have been giving them a guided tour of the Tower of London, telling tales of bygone years and cracking well-tested jokes. Tonight he was their ferryman, charged with transporting them the twenty-one miles across the cold waters of the English Channel to France.

Seabrook nodded at Hayley as she embarked, then turned to the wheel and started the engine. There was nothing left to discuss. They had been planning this for weeks. Opening up the tunnels of the Fan Bay Deep Shelter, finding a boat, picking a route, testing it on the water to make sure the fog bank could be sailed through. Then they'd had to choose their first passengers. This was the most dangerous part, as any one of them could have informed the authorities about it. But no one did. All were happy to accept the chance of a new life somewhere different. They clung to each other now, packed together like seals on an ice floe as the little boat left Britain behind and was swallowed by the cold embrace of the fog. A small girl coughed into her sleeve and was hushed by her mother. The air tasted bitter in Hayley's mouth, like the stink bomb a boy had once set off in school. *Ha, school!* That felt like a lifetime ago now.

After a few minutes the boat reached the end of the fog and they emerged on to a calm, millpond sea beneath a star-filled sky. The icy breeze was gone, and far ahead Hayley could just make out the twinkling lights of the French port of Calais. For the first time she allowed herself to feel hope. If this worked, then they would drop their passengers and return straight away to do another run the following night. They already had more families ready to make the crossing. In France the new arrivals would be refugees with nothing, at the mercy of other people's kindness. But better that than prisoners in their own country. Hayley felt the engine stop. Alarmed, she looked to Chief Yeoman Seabrook.

"What's wrong? Is it broken?" she whispered.

They were towing a small dinghy behind their boat in case of an emergency, but it would take several trips with it to get everyone back to shore.

"Engine's fine," said Seabrook, scanning the water ahead. "I thought I saw something."

Hayley squeezed past the passengers to the bow of the boat and gazed across the idle surface of the sea. Nothing stirred; there was barely a ripple. She turned back to Seabrook and shrugged. He stroked his thawing beard, nodded and restarted the engine. The boat bobbed forward and they were underway again. But before Hayley could retake her place, she heard a gasp from the woman next to her who gripped her arm and pointed.

"What's that?"

A hundred feet dead ahead of them a monster was rising from the water. Eyes the size of dinner plates filled a snake-like head at the end of a long neck. Higher and higher it rose, its long tongue hanging stiffly from open jaws. Then Hayley saw that it wasn't a living creature, but the carved wooden prow of a ship. A Viking longship. The towering figure of Guthrum the Viking Lord stood at the bow, his death-blackened face leering at them across the waves. Twelve more undead Viking draugar sat at the oars. Seabrook gunned the engine and the boat veered away, the passengers shrieking and holding

6

fast to their terrified children. But another longship burst from the depths, blocking their route. Then another and another, until there were more than Hayley could count: an armada of death arrayed against them. She'd heard rumours that Lock had used his knowledge of Norse magic to raise the Swanage wrecks – the legendary Danish fleet lost in a storm off the south coast of England in the time of King Alfred the Great, which was said to number well over a hundred ships – and now she knew it was true. There was no way past them. She reached into the hold and pulled out her bow and arrows, to the protests of the passengers around her.

"We should surrender," cried one man.

"Maybe they'll let us go home," pleaded an elderly woman.

Seabrook killed the engine, took the bow from Hayley, set it down and placed her hands on the wheel.

"I'll draw them away. You get them back to the tunnels. Don't stop for anything. Good luck."

And with that, he picked up his sword and leapt into the dinghy they were towing.

"No, Seabrook, wait!" cried Hayley.

But he cast off from the boat and motored straight towards the Viking fleet without looking back.

Hayley pushed the throttle forward as far as it

would go. The engine roared and she steered back towards the fogbank. If she could reach it first, then they might have a chance. Smoke rose from the whining engine as they thumped across the waves. Behind her she could hear Seabrook's battle cry as he neared Guthrum's longship. Just before they reached the fog, Hayley chanced a look over her shoulder. The Viking fleet was following them, converging as one like an arrow rushing towards its victim.

Speeding on blindly, Hayley expected to see Vikings board them at any moment, but a minute later they cleared the fog and for a few moments it looked as if they had shaken off their pursuers.

But like a pack of hunting dogs breaking from the woods, the Viking fleet flew from the mist, gaining on them fast. Ignoring the jetty, Hayley pointed the boat straight at the beach, in line – she hoped – with the secret entrance to the tunnels.

"Get down! Hold tight!" she yelled and threw herself on to the deck.

The boat beached itself at full speed, lurching to the side and coming to a rest in the shallows at a harsh angle. Hayley looked to the shocked passengers, but apart from a few bumps and scrapes, everyone was in one piece. She swung a small boy on to her shoulders and dropped over the side, landing waist deep in the water.

"Follow me – don't look back!"

They tumbled from the boat one after another, gasping at the icy water that met them, pulling each other on, pushing shaking limbs forward till they hit the stones of the beach. The excited yells of the axe-wielding Vikings rose up close behind, as the draugar leapt from their own ships and waded after them. Hayley wanted to stop and help the stragglers from the water, but she knew it was more important to reach the cliffs first. She had to find the door. By the time she reached the rock face, the muscles in her legs were burning from running uphill through the snow. She lifted the trembling boy from her shoulders and told him to keep hold of her jacket. Her torch was gone and she had to run her hands over the chalky cliff face till she found what she was searching for – a crown-shaped stone hidden beneath the seaweed slime and barnacles. She turned it hard and felt the mechanism click. Wrenching the door open, she pushed the boy through and waved the others after him, counting them in. *Five, ten, fifteen.* The animal growls of the chasing draugars were growing louder. *Twenty, twenty-five, twenty-nine.* One short. Had she miscounted? Had someone drowned in the sea, or stumbled and been caught? She strained her eyes against the dark, but all she could see were the hulking frames of the undead thundering up the beach towards her. *CLANG*. An axe embedded itself in the rock by her ear. She had to close the door, she had to save the others, but how could she leave someone out here with them?

"Here!" she cried. "The door's here!"

A small figure flew from the darkness and brushed past her legs as a young girl ran into the tunnels. *Thirty!* Hayley dived inside and heaved the door closed. She secured the bolts and fell to her knees, lungs on fire. The tunnel shook as axes smashed against the cliff face outside and dead fingers clawed the rock. But they could not find the entrance. Hayley and the others were safe, for now. And yet she felt nothing but despair. The great fightback was over before it had even begun.

2
RESISTANCE

"You will not defeat me. Try your worst, evil fiend. I shall prevail!"

The Lord Chamberlain's face was stern and resolute. Keeping his eyes fixed on his enemy he reached out a single craggy finger ... and pressed the "Start" button. The microwave stared back at him, unmoved. Frowning, LC stabbed the button again. Nothing. He opened the door. The bowl of cold baked beans was still inside. He closed the door, wiped his brow and pressed all the other buttons one after another, to no avail.

"Infernal contraption!"

He thrust his hands back into the pockets of his cardigan and tried to calm down. There was no use in getting angry with the blasted device, he would only end up breaking it just like he had the bread-toasting machine.

"Don't fret, dear," called Hayley's gran from the living room. "I expect Hayley will be back from the shops in a jiffy."

LC had long since given up explaining to the elderly lady that her granddaughter had not gone shopping, but was in fact engaged in a top-secret Resistance mission. Not that he minded looking after Gran, even when she mistook him for her deceased husband, which could be rather awkward. It was his duty – nothing like the responsibilities his high office used to entail of course, but his duty nonetheless.

Truthfully, LC was also glad of the company. Even though she could not hold the thread of a conversation for long, Hayley's gran would laugh heartily over the smallest thing, enough to lift LC momentarily from the gloom that had settled over him like a heavy coat. Not a day went past without him dwelling on the loss of his young king. Had he pushed Alfie too far when he urged him to confront his brother? After all, they were both still teenagers, and it was unfair to place the burden of a nation's fate on such young shoulders. He should have looked after both Richard and Alfie better after their father's death. Little did he know back then that one of the twins was already lost to the seductive promises of Professor Lock, just as the other soon would be to the cold waters of the North Sea. For LC it was a devastating low point in a very long life that had seen more than its fair share of tragedy.

Being trapped in the cramped quarters of Hayley's old flat was its own kind of torture, and the only one who was more fed up than LC with their current accommodation was Herne. The grey dog lay in the corner all day, sighing and every so often whining. He had given up pestering LC for walks and had not touched the contents of his food bowl for days. LC opened the cupboard and glanced for the third time that morning at the sorry contents – three more tins of beans, a bag of lentils and a "Pot Noodle", whatever that was. If Hayley did not return soon, he would have to go on a supply run himself. He shuddered at the thought. He had never been cut out for everyday life outside the walls of the palace or Keep, let alone a perilous excursion on to a Watford housing estate under Viking occupation.

It had been this way ever since Lock seized control of the country with his masterstroke – using the Raven Banner to magically reawaken the Viking blood that had lain dormant in the veins of one in thirty of the population for generations. He never could have done it with just Guthrum and his small band of undead "draugar" Vikings – even though they had caused rather a lot of damage by themselves. But with a couple of million freshly created berserkers at his command, it had not taken Lock long to overrun the entire country from within. Being distant descendants of the Norse people, rather than true Vikings like the draugar, the berserkers tended to be uglier, stupider and slightly shorter than their undead cousins. But they still struck fear into the hearts of the remaining, unaffected population.

Attacked from inside their own ranks, the police and army had fallen into disarray. Within days most people were virtual prisoners inside their homes as squads of berserkers, each led by one of Guthrum's draugar commanders, had taken control of every city, town and village. Where pockets of rebellion persisted, the mere shadow of the Black Dragon soaring through the winter storm clouds overhead soon brought people into line.

And then the snow came: arctic blizzards, the likes of which hadn't been seen for decades, drawn south by the pull of the Raven Banner's Norse magic, further trapping the terrified population in a tomb of ice. Those foolish enough to venture out to find food or search for missing loved ones were soon driven back by the bitter cold. Some said many had frozen to death before they'd even made it a mile.

At the end of that first day, Lock appeared on television, announcing to a shell-shocked nation that King Alfred the Second was dead and his brother, Richard, was now king. What's more, the new King Richard the Fourth had appointed him Lord Protector to "advise and guide him in these dark times". Brazenly, Lock claimed that the Defender and government had failed to protect the country from the Viking invasion, therefore the Crown had made a pragmatic peace with them "for everyone's protection". That was the last broadcast the people of Great Britain would see for some weeks. Straight after Lock had finished speaking, all television and radio stations ceased to transmit. Phones and the internet were cut off. Airports and docks were emptied as all foreign travel was banned. Lock's berserkers took control of the "burghs" – the early-warning system that monitors the magical ley lines for any supernatural intruder entering the kingdom. Within hours the wall of sea fog had surrounded the country and Lock's newly raised phantom Viking fleet was patrolling the waters, scaring away any vessel that came within five miles of the coastline. Britain was an island of prisoners.

At first the outside world had tried to send help, with various countries attempting to liberate their own citizens who were caught up in the chaos and to aid their ally against the bizarre supernatural assault it had suffered. But after the first US submarine was sunk by the longships and a squadron of French jets was blasted out of the skies by the Black Dragon, all Britain's friends had backed off. Three months on, the Vikings had shown no sign of advancing beyond Britain's icy borders, and although there were pockets of similar unrest in Scandinavia, the outside world had now settled into an uneasy state of "watch and wait".

Desperate to get her gran off the streets during that first chaotic night, Hayley had taken her, the Lord Chamberlain and Herne to the place she knew best – her old estate in north London. On the way there they had worked out the story she could tell the neighbours about why they'd been away and who the curious old gentleman in the old-fashioned suit with them was – a distant relative from abroad, maybe – but in the end they didn't need it. No one cared; everyone was too busy dealing with their own problems – homes smashed up by family members who'd turned berserker, friends who were missing, relatives they couldn't contact. Their old flat was yet to be cleaned and reassigned, and Gran still had a spare key in her handbag. The Lord Chamberlain took one look at their small, bare flat and for the first time he began to appreciate how strange the world of palaces and secret underground bases must have been for Hayley.

"You forgot my tea again, dear," said Gran as she watched LC come into the living room empty-handed.

"I regret to say we are experiencing another power cut, ma'am," said LC, picking up the blanket that had fallen to the floor and laying it back over her knees.

"Ooh, hark at you with your airs and graces. 'Ma'am'. You silly billy." Gran hooted with laughter and pulled the blanket higher with quivering hands.

LC reminded himself to tell Hayley what he had observed: her grandmother was becoming weaker. With little else to occupy his time, LC had taken to noting down the amount of time she spent asleep – as he suspected, it was increasing. Her "memory moments", as he called her absent-minded episodes, were also more frequent. She had started to become distressed for no reason and even snapped at him from time to time. In some ways he was pleased Hayley had not been there to see her gran's deterioration over the last week.

His thoughts turned to Dover – he knew there was no sense in worrying about it, but he prayed twice a day for her safe return. He couldn't bear the idea of losing another brave youngster.

"It's on the blink again, Lawrence," she sighed, passing him the TV remote control.

Lawrence was Hayley's grandfather, LC had learned. But he didn't correct Gran. Rather he made a show of trying the buttons on the remote, knowing that it wouldn't work. Even when the flat had power, the television stations no longer transmitted, except for the occasional "official broadcast" from the new regime.

"I'll call an engineer to come and take a look," he replied with a reassuring smile.

Back in the kitchen, LC was just about to remove the beans from the microwave and force himself to eat them cold when the machine suddenly sprang back into life.

"Ha! I should think so too."

"Hayley's on the telly!" Gran called from the other room.

LC chuckled and shook his head as he marvelled at the bowl going round inside the microwave.

"Of course she is, Mrs Hicks. . ."

But when he walked back into the living room, what he saw on the television made him drop his beans all over the carpet in surprise. An old school photo of Hayley was on the screen. A caption read "Hayley Hicks, 14, wanted for hostile acts against the Crown".

An announcer spoke in a serious tone: "If you have information on the whereabouts of the suspect, alert your Community Earl at once. God save King Richard."

Gran was beaming with pride.

"My little Hales on the telly. Hasn't she done well?"

In truth, Hayley wasn't doing very well at all. On the first night after her narrow escape in Dover she had been sheltered by one of the families from the aborted crossing. Viking patrols had hammered on the doors of every house in the town searching for her. She had hidden in a concealed cellar all night, praying they wouldn't find her – she couldn't bear to think what they would do to the family upstairs if they did. After that, she had trekked for two days and nights through the snow across Kent, heading for London. With only herself for company for hours on end, her thoughts turned to Alfie. Sometimes she laughed when she remembered him – the idea that the best friend she'd ever known had been an actual king seemed ridiculous now. But it wasn't, it was real and the pain of his loss still stabbed at her chest like a knife. The worst part was that she'd never had the chance to say goodbye, never got to tell him what he meant to her.

Was that why she always kept herself so busy these days, to stop herself thinking about Alfie? She recalled how, a couple of weeks after the Viking invasion, with the weather showing no sign of improving and all but the most essential movement outside banned, people had begun to accept that things were not going to go back to normal. Buried under thick drifts of snow, schools and offices were not going to reopen, supermarkets were not going to be restocked, buses and trains would not be running again. This was their life now. Some, driven by hunger, volunteered to work for the regime, keeping order on the streets and enforcing curfews, in exchange for extra food and clean water.

Others took greater advantage of the situation, robbing from those weaker than them or relishing the chance to exercise power as one of the new "Community Earls", who each commanded a handful of berserkers. When Hayley saw who had become the earl on their estate she knew she needed to keep a low profile. Her old enemy Dean Barron, whose family had run the newsagent, clearly loved his new status. He'd found an abandoned Rolls Royce somewhere and must have kept a personal petrol supply for himself too, because he would drive it round the estate, stopping to shout orders at anyone he found on the street, threatening to set his berserkers on them if they dared to disobey him. Hayley was astonished, and briefly amused, to see that his chief berserker was Turpin, one of the agents who had finally caught her and her gran just before the Raven Banner's magic swept over the country, transforming him into a slobbering, muscle-bound freak. But Hayley knew that if Dean saw she was back, she would be in trouble – there was no way he would have forgiven her for stealing (and wrecking) his car on the day of Alfie's coronation.

So she had agreed with LC to keep her presence a secret. She would only go out at night, using the fire escape to reach the street unseen and sticking to the quiet alleyways and rat runs where she used to play as a little girl. One industry that was thriving in the new Dark-Age Britain was the black market as people pawned every treasured relic of their old lives for a few tins of food. At first Hayley would just bargain for what she could afford, then hurry home. But before long she couldn't resist messing with Dean's berserker patrols, setting booby traps for them, stealing their weapons, letting the air out of his car tyres – that one really made him mad. The more nights Hayley spent outside, the more like-minded people she met – people from all walks of life, all ages and backgrounds, but who all had one thing in common: they hated Lock's regime and they wanted to do something about it. The others began to follow her lead, sabotaging Viking checkpoints and tagging walls with anti-Viking graffiti. She thought LC wouldn't approve, but he surprised her by encouraging her activities, within reason; she was not to risk being captured.

"What you have started, Miss Hicks, is called the 'Resistance'. It's what many brave French people did during the Nazi occupation in the War," he had told her.

"Yeah, but it's kind of lame at the moment. It's not like we're going to free the country by annoying Dean Barron," Hayley had replied.

"Mighty oaks from tiny acorns grow," LC had said, forcing a smile.

When Chief Yeoman Seabrook made contact late one night, it seemed that the Resistance might indeed be ready to grow. Hayley jumped at the chance to do something bigger – to actually get some people out of the country and to safety. Once the outside world heard the truth about what was happening, surely they would send help. LC had taken much more persuading – a little local sabotage was one thing, but a mission miles from home and across the sea? That was another level entirely. In the end, however, he could see that Hayley would not be discouraged.

Now as she stood on the south shore of the River

Thames, she wished she had just stayed home. Poor, brave Chief Yeoman Seabrook was presumed dead and she was far from out of trouble herself. She pulled her coat tighter against the harsh blizzard that was blowing upriver and prodded her toes against the exposed ice. The river had not frozen solid like this since the impromptu "frost fair" of 1814, when Londoners partied on the Thames for days and someone even walked an elephant across – or so the stories said. But then the current Defender, King George the Third, had driven out the Frost Giant that had caused it, and the river thawed. Sadly this didn't stop people thinking the king was mad – a "perception curse" placed on him by a powerful sorcerer, the French Emperor Napoleon Bonaparte.

Hayley decided that the ice seemed thick enough to support her weight, and crossing here was sure to be less risky than trying to make it over one of the bridges nearer the city centre. But if she fell through, there would be no one to pull her out. And then there was the small matter of exactly how to get across. She could try to walk, but that might take hours; she'd be sure to be spotted. It wasn't like she'd packed ice skates – not that she'd have known how to use them anyway. Foraging through the wreckage of a nearby café, she found a large solid metal tray. Any food left in the kitchens had long since been scavenged by someone else, but she also pocketed a hammer and a screwdriver she found under the counter. Back at the river, she placed the tray on to the ice and lay down on it. Then she took out the tools she had found and, holding one in each hand, dug them into the ice and pulled herself forward. At first she just slid from side to side like an ungainly duck caught out by a sudden freeze. But the further she pulled herself from the shore, the smoother the ice became and the faster she began to move. Soon she found a rhythm with her improvised oars and was zipping across the river like the funny-looking luge riders she remembered watching on TV during the last Winter Olympics. She was so happy it was working that she even momentarily forgot that if anyone spotted her out here then she could find herself captured by some very angry Vikings. For a few minutes it was just her, the scraping sound of the tray against the ice and the rushing of the wind in her ears. She was actually having fun. Right up to the moment she clipped a rock on the far shore, flew off the ice ... and landed in the berserker's lap.

A berserker, Hayley had come to realize over the last few months, could be almost more of a threat than a draugar. The original undead Vikings might be a little smarter and much fiercer, but if you saw them they tended to be on their way somewhere else, under orders from their lord Guthrum, no doubt to put down some local revolt. But the berserkers, unless they were under the command of a Community Earl, would tend to hang around causing trouble, chasing people for fun, sometimes biting them to see if they tasted better than the rotten meat they scavenged for on the streets. If they didn't accidentally kill you with their oversized fists, they would certainly make enough noise to attract attention, and then you'd really be in trouble. So when she looked up from her crash-landing on the shoreline to see the purple-tattooed face of a drooling blonde berserker with a rotten fish's tail hanging from her mouth, glaring down at her, she knew it was bad news. The berserker roared into Hayley's face, the sour stench of her breath worse than anything she had smelled before. Hayley rolled off, grabbed her metal tray and slammed it into the startled berserker's face. That bought her enough time to get to her feet, but the shore was uneven and covered with ice, and she stumbled badly as she made for the nearest staircase that led up to the embankment. Luckily the berserker was no better at keeping her balance and lost her footing completely, tumbling on to the river ice with a crack. Hayley looked back to see that the berserker had broken through the surface and was now thrashing around, howling as the freezing water rose up to her waist. Hayley got up and made for the steps. But then she stopped and looked back at the pitiful sight. If she left the berserker like that she would drown and, although she didn't look like it right now, that poor creature was probably someone's wife or sister or mum. Finding a length of rope, Hayley tied it round a post and threw the other end to the berserker, until the dumb thing realized it might help her, grabbed on to it and started to heave herself out of the water. Satisfied, Hayley climbed the steps to the street, unaware that she had just saved the life of former Prime Minister Vanessa Thorn.

3

LONG LIVE THE KING

The Lord Chamberlain couldn't sleep. Something had clearly gone badly wrong with the mission. What could have happened? Were the refugee families safe? What about Hayley and Chief Yeoman Seabrook? He tried to console himself with the fact that the regime was broadcasting Hayley's face, so at least that must mean they had not captured her.

A click from the hall. A door handle, turning slowly.

LC sat up in bed. Was it Hayley? Or had someone told the authorities that Hayley had been staying at the flat?

Low, grunting noises, coming from the kitchen. Definitely not Hayley. Edging along the hallway, he leaned into her gran's room and grabbed the walking stick that was resting by the door. It wouldn't be much use against a berserker goon, much less a Viking draugar, but if this was to be the end he would go down fighting.

LC could see a shadow moving in the kitchen at the end of the hall. He stepped in and swung the stick around the corner at head height, but it bounced off the wall and he dropped it.

"Not exactly the welcome home I'd hoped for, LC."

The old man looked down to see Hayley crouching by Herne, tickling the dog's belly as he snuffled and grunted with pleasure.

Later, after Hayley had checked on her gran and made sure the curtains were drawn in every room, she collapsed on the sofa next to LC and told him everything that had happened. They agreed that Seabrook's sacrifice would be properly honoured once Lock's grim reign had been brought to an end, though neither admitted how unlikely it now felt that that would ever happen. Herne trotted in and put his head gently on Hayley's knees.

"He's looking thin," said Hayley, stroking his ribs.

"Still off his food, I'm afraid," said LC.

"I'll head down to the market later, after the patrols have passed through. I can swap the microwave for a couple of weeks' grub."

"No great loss."

"She's getting worse, isn't she?"

"Your grandmother? Alas, I fear she is. I have kept a record if you would like to review it?"

Hayley took it and scanned the tightly written notes, sniffing back tears. She'd made it all the way back here without losing it; she wasn't going to start blubbing now. LC was fidgeting with his cuffs.

"I don't need a hug, LC; don't worry."

"Actually, I was going to offer to leave the room while you composed yourself."

She laughed, closed the book and laid back, her toes rubbing Herne's neck as he settled at her feet.

A siren was wailing. Hayley opened her eyes and realized she'd slept straight through till morning. The Lord Chamberlain was dressed and peering through the frost-covered window down at the street below. Hayley rubbed her eyes and joined him.

"What's going on?"

Outside the block of flats Dean Barron was ordering about a team of berserkers. Bizarrely, they'd cleared a large space in the snow and were arranging trestle tables into long rows, and covering them with plates and cups. Nearby others were hanging bunting from the lamp posts.

"It seems," said a puzzled LC, "that we are to have a street party."

The siren stopped and Dean unhooked a loudhailer from his belt.

"Residents!" he yelled through a high-pitched whine of feedback. "You are hereby ordered to attend the celebrations to mark the glorious Coronation Day of His Royal Majesty, King Richard the Fourth. Attendance is compulsory. You have ten minutes."

"Not so tight!" Richard snapped.

He was standing in the candlelit antechamber of Westminster Abbey preparing for his coronation while the draugar servant, very much the meek runt of the undead Viking litter, fussed around him, adjusting the heavy, crimson royal robes with bony fingers.

"What are you, brain dead?" muttered Richard, loosening his stiff collar.

"Technically he no longer has a brain," said Lord Protector Lock, marching in and shaking the snow from his coat. He inspected the new young king and bowed respectfully. "You look just the part, Majesty," he said.

Richard sighed. He knew Lock was lying. Gone

were the days when Richard's looks turned heads. The truth was he looked awful – pale and drawn. The urge to scratch his face was maddening; dragon scales itched beneath his skin like infected boils. They'd had to cover them with thick make-up today, which only made Richard look even more waxy and ill.

Lock gave a thin smile and shooed the Viking servant away, taking over with the robes. "It's quite a crowd out there; bigger than for your brother by far. Street parties are being thrown up and down the country. Your subjects are ready to witness the glory of their new king," he said.

"Mind my back!" Richard hissed as Lock tightened the robes.

The dragon's wings now formed a permanent bump between Richard's shoulder blades, giving him a hunchbacked appearance. Like the scales on his face, the monstrous wings felt like they were just under the skin, coiled and ready to burst out whenever he got angry.

"Apologies, Majesty." Lock said, putting the finishing touches to the robes. "There. You are ready."

The Viking servant shuffled over carrying a full-length mirror. But Richard, wincing with pain, stood as upright as he could and pushed the mirror away without looking at his reflection.

"I look like the last King Richard," Richard muttered.

He meant Richard the Third, the villainous, hunchbacked king who had lived five hundred years before.

"He was a fine monarch," Lock stated, proud.

"Didn't he kill his nephews and bury them in the Tower of London?" Richard asked.

Years ago, when he and Alfie were very young, they'd been given a private tour around the Tower by the beefeaters who delighted in scaring them with the story: how Richard the Third had murdered his nephews so he could become king, and how the ghosts of the two princes supposedly haunted the Bloody Tower.

"Not personally. He hired a goblin assassin, as I recall. Anyway, he did what was right for his kingdom, and that is not always a pleasant task," Lock said, stern. "You won't look this way for long. After you're crowned king everything will be better. You'll see."

Lock threw open the inner doors to the abbey. There was no fanfare and no choir. Richard stepped into the hallowed place to an uneasy silence. And as he proceeded down the vast central aisle of Westminster Abbey, he saw that Lock had lied again. The great church was barely half full of press-ganged citizens and bored-looking berserkers, several chewing their hymn books. The smell of incense hung heavy in the air, but it wasn't enough to conceal the stench of rotting flesh that rose off the undead Viking draugar who lined the nave and grudgingly bowed their heads to him as he passed.

But Richard didn't care. He had to focus on what Lock had said – being crowned would make him better. He would no longer be the Black Dragon. Finally he would be the Defender. This needed to be done. He kept his eyes fixed dead ahead.

Blooooo!

The blast from Guthrum's war-horn shook the abbey walls. Richard looked up as dust fell from the vaulted ceiling where not so long ago he had crouched as the Black Dragon, watching Alfie process up the very same aisle to take the throne, *his* throne. It felt like a lifetime ago.

"He did what was right for his kingdom. He did what was right for his kingdom," Richard whispered over and over to himself like a mantra, his heart pounding as he reached the simple wooden coronation chair. He hoped no one could see how nervous he was. For weeks now they'd been trying to make the regalia he'd taken from Alfie work for him instead. But no matter what spells and incantations Lock recited over the Crown Jewels, they didn't react to Richard's touch: the Great Sword of State refused to glow with a deep blue fire, the Ring of Command sat cold and inert on his finger, the *Colobium Sidonis,* the Shroud Tunic, which was supposed to transform into the Defender's magical armour, hung limp over his shoulders. Night after night they'd tried until finally Lock had emerged from the Keep's archives clutching some dusty scrolls and announced triumphantly he'd finally figured it out. They needed to crown him king: it was the act of the coronation that completed the Succession process and would fully release the power that flowed through Richard's veins.

Blooo!

With another blast from Guthrum's horn Richard sat, gripping on to the armrests with white knuckles. Nearby, the guests of honour bowed their heads. The new so-called "Prime Minister", the revolting Lord Mortimer, was there along with his devious son Sebastian, who winked at Richard like they were somehow best friends. Behind them towered Guthrum, the smell of fish and rank meat hanging over him like a cloud. Richard could see that the undead Viking warlord had been dressed up to mark the coronation, squeezed into an oversized grey suit and tie and looking like a giant wrestler at a wedding. Someone had even tied his greasy hair into a ponytail. But he'd dropped some kind of food all down the front of his suit and was drooling.

Richard closed his eyes and tried to block everything out. He just wanted to be crowned king, become the Defender and finally rid himself of the dragon sickness that lurked inside him. Lock stepped forward and faced the sparse congregation.

"Sirs, I here present unto you Richard Arundel, your undoubted King. Wherefore all you who are come this day to do your homage and service, are you willing to do the same?"

"We are!" the timid crowd replied, apart from Guthrum, who bit into a giant turkey leg he'd brought along, swallowed it whole and let rip with a giant burp.

Lock turned to Richard. "Will you solemnly promise and swear to govern the people of the United Kingdom of Great Britain and Northern Ireland and her Commonwealth of nations according to their laws and customs? To punish the wicked and to protect and cherish the just?"

"Yeah, yeah. Now get on with it," Richard hissed.

Four undead Vikings shambled forward carrying a golden canopy, which they held over the young king. Now hidden from sight, Richard let out a contented sigh. This was it, soon he could forget everything he'd done – the lies, the betrayals, the murder – soon he would be king. Lock poured the strange-smelling sacred oil from the golden flask on to an ornate spoon. Leaning close, he flicked it over Richard's head.

Cold washed over Richard like an arctic wind, numbing his fingers and burning his cheeks. The abbey seemed to disappear around him and he was left hanging in a black void. Then, out of the dark, shimmering apparitions began to float towards him: a parade of former kings and queens. But as Richard watched wide-eyed, the spirits twisted and warped, and their faces snarled. These were not the kindly, good Defenders of the past that Alfie had seen, but the very worst monarchs that had sat on the throne and ruled over the kingdom. The mad jabbering face of the hopeless King John loomed, cackling from the darkness; the blood-drenched figure of the terrifying Mary, Queen of Scots lurched past with a shriek. Richard waved his hands, trying to bat them away, but the ghouls kept coming, and not just past monarchs now, but the sneering traitor Oliver Cromwell, and the cruel-eyed usurper Roger Mortimer dancing and capering around him like they were welcoming him into the fold. Finally, the ghost of a thin, hunchbacked king with a pinched face rushed at Richard like a bottled spider, thin arms ready to embrace him. It was him, Richard the Third, and the smile on his face was blank and full of madness—

Richard screamed. All at once, he was back in the abbey and looking up into the shocked face of Lock.

"The oil burns! Get it off!"

Lock wiped the oil from Richard's skin then jammed St Edmund's crown on to Richard's head. He waved the Viking canopy holders away and turned to the congregation.

"Well, come on, then!" he shouted.

"God save the King!" the crowd shouted, as Lock hurried a shaking Richard away and out of sight. The coronation was over.

Later, back in the privacy of the Keep, Richard was in a rage. Lock watched impassive as priceless relics were thrown against walls, the beefeaters' former desks smashed and tapestries torn from the walls.

"Why won't it work, Lock? WHY WON'T IT WORK?!" Richard screamed in frustration.

After they'd returned from the coronation and Richard had recovered from his terrifying visions, Lock had placed the Shroud Tunic over Richard, but the armour still didn't appear.

"The Succession is an ancient and mysterious process," Lock said. "You cannot expect it to work overnight. There must be something I've yet to discern—"

Richard slammed Lock up against a wall. His eyes flickered red and his voice raged like fire.

"Then you'd better find out what it is, fast. I don't

know how much longer I can keep this *thing* inside me under control."

Richard released his grip and slumped back as Lock brushed himself down and straightened his suit.

"Allow me to tell you a story," said Lock.

Lock strode across the hall towards his chambers. Richard sighed and followed. What choice did he have?

Lock had occupied LC's old room and filled it with ransacked scrolls, books and parchments from the Archives. "When I was a history student, not all that much older than you, I was always strapped for cash. I tried working as a waiter at a pizza place, but I kept getting the orders wrong, so they sacked me."

Richard sniffed with derision and wondered where this was going. Lock was in full-on lecture mode, as if he was back at Harrow, giving Richard a tutorial in his office.

"I needed to make money – fast. And one day, as we excavated a Roman villa near Bath, it struck me."

Lock rummaged on his desk, found something small and tossed it to Richard. It was a coin, dull with age, the makings on it barely visible.

"Artefacts. Treasure. Saxon jewels. Medieval glass. People pay good money for old coins. . ."

Richard's eyes narrowed. "You stole them."

Lock's smile was sly. "As a lover of history, I comforted myself that I was following in the footsteps of a wonderfully ignoble tradition: tomb robbing. I became very well known in certain circles and my student debt went like that." Lock snapped his fingers.

"Anyway, there was a dealer I knew in London called Samuel Weal. He lived in Bloomsbury as it happens, right under the nose of the British Museum – ha! I'd brought him some very fine Roman mosaics I'd liberated, but he hadn't any cash, so we agreed to make a trade. He offered me many things – Egyptian statues, Phoenician burial pots. But I chose this."

Like a stage magician, Lock removed a velvet cloth from his seeing mirror with a flourish. Except this was no trick. Months earlier, Lock had shown Richard his own coronation in the mirror's dark surface long before it had ever happened. And later he'd witnessed Lock speaking to the mirror when he thought he was alone. It might not look much, with its chipped and dull silver frame, but Richard could sense the power contained within. It was like looking at a nuclear bomb.

"Old Weal said I'd gone mad. He didn't think much of the mirror. It had been found in the wreck of a galleon off St David's Head and passed around various dealers over the years. But I knew I had to have it when she started talking to me."

"Who?"

Lock lit a black candle and beckoned Richard closer.

"She who lives in the mirror. I kept it by my bed at night. Her voice was soft at first. She told me the true history of kings like you, urged me to find out more. Talk to her, you'll see."

Richard was about to reply when a strange droning sound sang out from the mirror. It was like a million bees buzzing, their wings whirring. Lock's study seemed to grow dark as the mirror glowed and Richard's own reflection faded to be replaced with stars, like he was looking through a window into a galaxy. It reminded him of summer holidays at Balmoral in the Scottish Highlands when he was very young. Sometimes he and Alfie were allowed to go camping in the gardens. They'd run around, pretending to be explorers. But the best part was when they would lie under the stars, he'd never seen so many—

"Speak."

Richard was snapped out of his memory by the voice from the mirror. The stars had disappeared and now the mirror's glass seemed to ripple like water over fathomless depths. It didn't feel like he was looking through a mirror, it was more like he was staring through a window at a dark, limitless ocean. But instead of the sound of waves, there was the buzzing drone of flies.

A face formed in the water (was it water? It was so hard to tell) in front of him: a woman's, one half in deep black shadow. The side he could see was beautiful and beguiling, her skin snow-clear and eyes as green as emeralds.

"Who are you?" the woman demanded. Her voice was at once sweet and very, very old.

"I'm ... Richard. King Richard."

The woman laughed, long and mocking. "You are no king. Not while your brother still lives."

Confused, Richard glanced to Lock – the professor's gaze was dark and heavy.

Richard turned back to the mirror, fists clenched. "My brother is dead. I killed him!"

"Don't lie to me, child," she replied.

Richard cast his eyes to the floor.

"It's as I feared." Lock had joined Richard as he too stared into the mirror. "The regalia will not work in Richard's hands while Alfie lives."

"NO!"

Richard slammed his fist on the desk causing ripples to spread across the surface of the mirror.

The half of the woman's face he could see was still smiling; it was maddening. Richard could feel his throat tightening and the dragon wings stirring under his skin, itching to get out. Who was this woman in the mirror? How did she know his brother was alive? Why didn't she show herself properly? How dare she tell him—

"Good! Be angry. Let the fire grow inside you." The woman's eye stared at Richard with fearsome intensity. "Maybe this time you can actually finish the job, little lizard."

Richard screamed and in an instant transformed into the Dragon. His wings unfurled and knocked over the desk in an avalanche of scrolls and parchment. The beast lurched out of the study, crashed through the Keep into the Arena, and with one flap of its massive wings, took off into the night's sky above London.

In the study, Lock approached the mirror nervously.

"Mistress, I'm sorry—"

"You promised me a *king*." Her voice was icy.

"I thought Alfie was dead," stuttered Lock. "He must have escaped somehow. He must have had help."

Hel's face rose closer to the surface of the mirror, revealing its other side. It wasn't in shadow after all; it was carpeted with thousands of crawling black flies, the sound of their wings droning hypnotically. As one, the flies parted to reveal what was underneath. The other half of her face was a leering, pure white skull.

"Find him," she hissed.

4

ATHELNEY

The magic hour.

That was what Alfie's dad used to call the time of the day when the sun set the earth aglow with its softest, dying rays. King Henry had loved taking photographs of them all in the walled gardens of Buckingham Palace with a bulky camera that used old-fashioned film. Richard would always throw up bunny ears behind Alfie's head and Ellie would pose up a storm, even when she was tiny. Magic hour always provided the best light for family portraits, he would say.

Back when we were a family. Alfie tried to block the sad thought from his mind by taking in the spectacular view. To the north of his mother's remote

Wyoming ranch, the snow-covered peaks of the Grand Teton Mountains glowed golden, casting long shadows over the steep, pine-covered foothills that ranged below. Everything in America seemed bigger to Alfie, from the cars to the trees, to the landscape. You just didn't get views like this in the English countryside. Suddenly Alfie felt very far from home. He pushed away the feeling of shame that had been nagging at him for weeks. The shame of a runaway.

Alfie shivered and zipped up his coat. His mum had said it would snow soon and once that happened they'd be stuck here until it thawed in spring.

Good. Being left alone was just how Alfie wanted it.

In the paddock a pair of glossy, nut-brown horses whinnied and chased each other playfully. Alfie spent a lot of time out here perched on the rough wooden fences watching them. His mum kept telling him he should take one of the mares out and ride the local trails; there wasn't another house for miles around. But Alfie didn't want to, so he claimed his injuries were still tender. Truth was, his body wasn't hurt; it was his soul that was bruised. Riding would just make Alfie think of Wyvern, his own magical horse who was lost at sea during his battle with the Black Dragon. And that would make him think about Richard, and thinking of his brother would lead to

LC and Hayley and Ellie and, before too long, the thought of everyone back home in Britain he'd either let down or lost would pile on and crush him. Nope, Alfie preferred to just stay right where he was with a clear head, out of the world's way.

With a *gronk*, Gwenn flew in and settled next to Alfie. The Tower of London's tamest raven had hardly left his side since they arrived at the ranch after their long journey across the ocean. The other ravens kept their distance, but Alfie would sometimes hear them in the morning, circling and calling before splitting up for the day, each taking to a different corner of the ranch as if they were sentries on guard duty. Gwenn, however, liked to stick close to her exiled king. With a deep, affectionate croak, the raven nibbled at Alfie's hand, prompting him to stroke her beak.

"Take it easy," Alfie said, as she stared at him with her coal-black eyes. "Wish I had a pea brain like yours. That way I wouldn't have to think about anything— Ow!"

Gwenn pecked his hand, indignant. Yeoman Eshelby, the Ravenmaster, had always said the birds understood more than you realized and were as smart as chimps. "Trust me, if ravens ever develop thumbs, the world's in big trouble," he used to joke.

Alfie wondered where the Ravenmaster was now.

46

Hiding? Rounded up by the Vikings? Did he even survive the battle at the Tower?

"How's our little Hamlet doing out there?" Brian asked. "Talking to any skulls yet?"

"No. Just his bird," Tamara replied, gazing out of the kitchen window across the yard to where her son sat brooding. Behind her stood a long pine table strewn with bullets, springs and gun parts. Brian was cleaning his service pistol for the hundredth time. Tamara knew that as soon as the gun was back together and night fell, Alfie's bodyguard would be outside, restlessly patrolling the perimeter of the ranch.

"I still say we're sitting ducks out here," Brian said, without taking his eyes off his work. "And when that snow comes. . . We should have started heading back to the UK weeks ago."

"Alfie needs more time to recover."

"He's had enough R&R if you ask me, ma'am."

"Has *your* brother turned into a monster and tried to kill you recently? You've got zero idea how he feels," Tamara said. "And enough with the whole 'ma'am' garbage, please, Brian." She walked back over to the sink to deposit her coffee mug, then returned to her vigil.

Brian snapped the last piece of the gun together

and slid it into his shoulder holster. He sneaked a glance at the former queen in her flannel shirt, jeans, sturdy boots, and her hair piled up messily. He could see the close resemblance to Alfie in her fine features. To Brian, she was still Queen, hence calling her "ma'am". She was smart, proud and determined, with only the dark circles under her eyes hinting at the secrets she kept and the toll they'd taken.

He joined her at the window. Outside, the sun was disappearing behind the hills and the light was fading fast. "All I'm saying is, we need at least to be planning our return." Brian's voice had softened. "Qilin will have completed his border recce soon, and we'll know more—"

With a snap of air that popped Brian and Tamara's ears, Qilin, AKA Tony, appeared right on cue, knocking over a chair.

"Waffles. I need waffles," Tony moaned.

"Ugh, I still can't get used to you doing that!" Brian sighed as his heart rate returned to normal. But he was smiling, glad that Tony had made it back in one piece.

The red-robed superhero flicked a tiny golden lever on his belt buckle and his robes were instantly sucked into it like dust into a vacuum cleaner. He removed his leering mask and spun it on his palm, shrinking it to the size of a button, which he stuck on to the buckle like a magnet. Finally he flipped his green hover disc deftly into the air with one foot, where it too shrank until it was minuscule and flew to join the other ornate components of his belt buckle. The whole process took less than two seconds, revealing a weary-looking Tony, who collapsed on to an oversized sofa by the wood-burning stove, flicked his black fringe out of his eyes and adopted a pleading look.

"And please say you have maple syrup? And bacon. And ice cream either on the waffles or on the side of the plate but not touching the bacon," Tony finished.

"I'm on it," Tamara said, sliding a cast iron skillet on to the stove.

Brian pulled up a chair. "What did you see?"

For the past three weeks, Tony had been painstakingly blink-shifting the four thousand miles from the ranch in Wyoming to the shores of the UK and back, surveying the locked-down country's defences and searching for a way in. Although Tony could teleport from one spot to another with ease ever since he was a child, his power was limited. He could only "blink-shift" to somewhere he could see, which meant he had to make the journey in a series of hundreds of jumps. The more jumps he made the more tired he became, which increased the chances of making a mistake and jumping into a dangerous situation he couldn't escape. Crossing the ocean was the most risky part. At first there would be enough ships and buoys and oil rigs to make good progress, but after a while he might have to wait hours or even days for the next ship, which meant hiding from crew members who would understandably be rather freaked out by the sight of the bright red superhero hovering around their vessel. All the time he had to remember to conserve energy for the return journey. It was like running ten marathons in a day.

"It's not good news, folks, I'm sorry to say. I must have jumped to every boat in the Atlantic and the Irish and North Seas and I still couldn't get close to land. That winter storm is a permanent fixture. Snow, hail like beach balls, lightning, and fog without a single gap. There's no way ashore that I could see. This one Irish fishing boat I hitched a lift on got too close and was sunk by one of Lock's longships. I just managed to shift them all back to the mainland in time. Boy, were they happy I turned out to be on board! They insisted on taking me to the pub and then they made up a song about me. Want to hear it?"

Brian and Tamara's disappointed expressions told Tony that maybe now wasn't the time for the "Ballad of the Red Spirit Sailor".

"Maybe later, then. Ooh, can I have some green

tea? No wait, orange juice. Cola. All of the above," Tony continued. Blink-shifting long distances always made him ravenous too.

Brian sank into a seat at the table. "So we're not getting home that way," he said, rubbing his temples. "There must be a better way in than just sailing through that fog and hoping for the best. . ."

"Where's Alfa-bet?" Tony asked from the depths of the sofa.

"His usual spot," Tamara said, frying some bacon.

"I'll cheer him up," Tony said, getting up, suddenly full of beans. He peered out of the window at Alfie's silhouette on the paddock fence, flicked his belt lever and whipped his mask and robes back on. "That's one mission I never fail!"

"Wait, Tony!" Tamara pleaded.

But with a whump of air, Tony teleported out of the kitchen . . . and only a few moments later reappeared back inside and removed his outfit, looking glum.

"Er, he said some very bad words to me. Mission not accomplished."

Tamara handed Tony his waffles. "I'll go talk to him."

In the paddock, Alfie was trying to calm a horse as it paced restlessly, snorting, its ears pinned back.

"Easy, girl. . ." Alfie said, reaching for the horse's

nose, but she flicked her head away and kicked out her legs.

"They don't like it when Tony blink-shifts," Tamara said as she approached the horse, keeping her body low. "Something to do with the change in air pressure, maybe. I've got this. . ."

Alfie stepped aside. His mum had always had a strange connection with animals, and sure enough, moments later she'd calmed the creature down enough to lead it back into the stables, Alfie trailing behind.

Inside, it smelled of wet straw. Tamara passed Alfie a shovel and together they mucked out the last stall.

"I really could have used you when I was learning how to ride Wyvern," Alfie said.

Tamara looked up sharply. They'd been arguing a lot recently. Full-on, sparks-flying, hundred-decibel rows. About how Tamara knew Alfie was going to be the Defender and have his world turned upside down but never told him. About how she'd abandoned them all to come to this ranch in the middle of nowhere. About how Tamara wasn't there for him when he needed her the most and how it wasn't good enough to just say she "had her reasons". But for the past couple of days Alfie had felt his anger slipping. It was like losing your grip on a ledge; you couldn't hold on to it for ever.

"I didn't mean it like that. Do I get the lame joke thing from you or Dad?"

Tamara laughed, relieved. "Your dad. Definitely."

"Let me guess, you've been talking to Brian and he thinks I'm a wuss hiding out here."

"He would never say that." Tamara shrugged. "Besides, you're not the first English king to go into hiding. A thousand years ago, when the Vikings drove Alfred the Great into exile, he lay low on an island in a swamp called Athelney. At least you've got hot showers and satellite TV."

Alfred the Great. There he was again, casting his shadow like an overbearing relative, making Alfie feel childish and small by comparison. Tamara watched her son as his face clouded over. She put her hands on his shoulders and drew him close.

"You're right. I should have been there for you. But I had other things I needed to take care of."

Alfie shook off her hands, anger pricking his cheeks again. "Do you have any idea what I had to deal with after you went away? The horrible things the newspapers said, everyone gossiping and laughing at me, the bullying. . ."

"I'm so sorry."

Tamara put her hand to her mouth. For a moment, Alfie thought she was going to cry.

"Mum?"

"There's nothing I can say that will make up for what you went through, Alfie. But perhaps there is a way I can help you understand. I've protected you from the truth for too long. It's time you knew the real reason your dad and I split up."

5

THE PLAGUE GODDESS

"I knew I'd never fit into the Royal Family, even before I married your father," said Tamara.

They were in sitting in the wood-panelled den, where comfortable leather sofas faced a roaring fire and a neat stack of logs. Alfie could sense Brian and Tony's nerves as they watched him listening to his mother. Clearly they knew what was coming, and it was big.

"Apart from being an outsider, there was just so much to learn," she continued. "Dress codes, diplomatic etiquette, the right way to address everyone. Your dad did his best to teach me, but I was stubborn too, and if I'm honest I liked the looks on those stuffy Brits' faces when I broke their rules. No offence."

"None taken, ma'am," said Brian.

"But no matter how hard it got – and boy, did it get ugly when the press turned on me – what kept us strong was our number one rule. No secrets. So when he became king it took me about five minutes to bust him. At first I thought it was just the pressure of the new job, then I thought maybe he was ill. But in the end I knew there was something he felt he couldn't tell me."

"The Succession," said Alfie. "He'd just found out he was the Defender, but he wasn't allowed to tell you."

"Yeah. Well, that lasted about a week. Then your father finally gave in and showed me everything. The Keep, the regalia, Wyvern, bless her. The works. The Lord Chamberlain practically blew a fuse when he found out."

"Been there, done that." Alfie laughed, remembering the night he'd introduced Hayley to LC. He thought the old man was going to have a heart attack.

"Anyway, LC got over it, kind of. Put up with a civilian hanging around the Keep, and an American at that, asking all these dumb questions. But after a while, I started trying to organize the Archives. I mean, you've seen them, right? Total bombsite. I figured the least I could do was alphabetize them."

Alfie smiled again, thinking of Hayley installing Wi-Fi and LC believing it was some ancient magic spell.

"But your dad backed me up and I got to work. What I didn't expect was to get so into the history. I kept getting sidetracked, finding out about a battle here, a monster there. I mean, dragons causing the Great Fire of London! Who knew? But then I went back further, to around the year 1350 and I started reading about something else, a disease called the Black Death."

"Blaaaaack Deaaaaath!" Tony said in a low voice, like he was doing a voiceover for a movie trailer.

"It killed between seventy-five and two hundred million people," said Tamara.

"I am a very bad person," Tony squeaked, reddening.

"Anyway, as I was learning," Tamara continued, "just like every other part of British history, there was an untold story behind the Black Death. And it was a whopper."

She leaned down to the fire and pulled a log from the pile. With a clunk and rattle of chains, the fire snuffed itself out and the whole wall slid across to reveal a secret room beyond.

Alfie gawped. The concealed study was crammed full of scrolls, ancient books and parchments – just like the Keep. "If you're trying to make me feel more at home, it's working," he said.

Alfie could tell by their lack of surprise that Brian and Tony had already been in here, which bugged him.

His mum gestured for Alfie to sit down at a desk. It was covered with old books sporting elaborately carved leather covers.

"You see, it wasn't rats and fleas that spread the plague, it was this Norse Goddess." Tamara opened one of the books to an ancient woodcut depicting a woman; half her face was radiantly delicate and beautiful, but the other side was a nightmarish glistening white skull. "Her name is Hel."

The hairs on the back of Alfie's neck stood up.

"As in Hell?" he asked, pointing to the floor.

"Sort of, but with only one 'l'. It's probably where we get the word from though. Hel was always bad, even by the brutal standards of the old gods. Every evil thing that happened in those ancient times was down to her. So, aeons ago, the other gods banished her from earth. Centuries later, after they too became tired of living in the mortal realm, the last of the gods left and mankind became the top dog."

"Including a few blue bloodlines the gods had created by mingling with humans while they were here, if you catch my drift," added Tony with a cheeky wink.

Tamara frowned at him and carried on. "For hundreds of years nothing was heard from Hel. But she had been busy plotting her way back. Finally, around the time Edward the Third came to the throne, she succeeded. Hel's return unleashed a plague designed to wipe all but her tiny number of devout followers from existence. Millions died before the Defender was finally able to send her back into the pit she'd crawled out of. They called it the Hundred Years War."

Alfie rubbed his forehead. He was getting a headache. "This is all terrific as far as scary bedtime stories go, but what's it got to do with you and dad breaking up?"

"I'm getting to that, geez," sighed Tamara. She rooted around in the same book to find another ancient etching that depicted the Defender, astride Wyvern, holding Hel by the throat and pushing her down into a black pool ringed with metal. The page was so faded it was hard to tell. "The Defender trapped Hel in an enchanted mirror, where she was supposed to remain for eternity."

Alfie noticed other knights in the picture looking on – all in different types of strange, exotic armour and carrying various odd-shaped weapons.

"Who are those guys?" he asked, pointing at them.

"Edward the Third couldn't defeat Hel alone; he was backed up by an alliance of blue-blood superheroes from all over the world. He named them the Order of St George."

"AKA, the Knights of the Garter," Brian added. "So called, according to legend, because the king returned a garter which had fallen from the leg of a dancing countess at a royal ball."

Tony smirked, but was silenced by a glare from Brian.

"Yeah, I've heard of them," said Alfie. "I've seen their banners hanging at Windsor Castle. But I assumed they were ancient history. You'd think I'd have learned by now."

Tamara smiled. "I thought Hel was ancient history too, when I read about all this in the Archives," she said. "But then I came across an account of how her return in the Middle Ages was preceded by all these weird things: freak climate change, wars, civil unrest – and I started to worry that she might be on her way back again. I mean just look at what's happening in the world right now. It was all too similar. Your dad thought I was on to something, so we started talking about getting the Knights of St George back together, just in case. Then we told LC—"

"And, let me guess, he freaked out?" Alfie said.

Tamara nodded. "He didn't want to know. Banned me from the Keep. All this talk about the ice caps melting and droughts being connected to an ancient Norse goddess. He thought I was paranoid."

"Climate-change deniers. I can't stand 'em either," Tony chipped in.

"Even so, your father and I didn't stop," Tamara went on. "But this time we kept it secret from LC. I started to travel the world with only my trusty bodyguard here for protection." Tamara patted Brian on the hand. "And wow, did the press nail me for that."

Alfie dimly recalled the headlines. "QUEEN T'S NEVER-ENDING HOLIDAY!" What he remembered better was his mum never being around much.

"What I was really doing was trying to recruit new members to the Order. I approached the existing royal houses of Europe first, but they're even more secretive than we are, and it was hard to get to them without attracting attention. After I struck out there, I decided to try to find the old royal bloodlines which were no longer on their thrones – Germany, Eastern Europe, Russia. But it was dangerous work and I was all alone. Your father believed in my theory that Hel was stirring, but he had his own duties to attend to and couldn't guarantee my safety. So we faked a divorce. I moved out here to the ranch to take some heat out of the situation and carried on my research. Borrowed a fair few things from the Archives, as you can see." Tamara said, nodding at the shelves groaning with books and scrolls.

Alfie's head was spinning. He couldn't believe what he was hearing.

"Wait a second. You left Dad – us! – and moved out here all based on some crazy theory?"

"I know it sounds bad, honey. But we were so sure we were on to something and nobody else was doing anything about it. And look, it paid off big time. I got a lead in China about a former royal dynasty that led me all the way back to London, where I found this little marvel." Tamara pointed at Tony, who waved at Alfie, like it was the first time they'd met. "We pulled a few strings to get Tony into Harrow, and Brian became your Close Protection Officer so they could both watch over you. What we didn't realize was how close the threat was, and how advanced his plans were."

"You mean Professor Lock?" asked Alfie. "You think Lock has got something to do with Hel?"

Tamara nodded. "What he's up to exactly, we just don't know yet. But if we're right, if this is what he's been planning the whole time – to bring back

Hel – then the world is in big, big trouble." Tamara pointed at the woodcut of the Defender wrestling with Hel, forcing her down into a mirror. "Lock must have figured out that, as it was blue-blood magic that imprisoned Hel, only blue-blood magic would bring her back."

"OK, say you're right," said Alfie, trying to understand. "Why didn't Lock just grab me and feed me, or however it works, to this plague goddess? Why kill Dad; why replace me with Richard?"

"We're not sure," said Brian. "But we think that for the ritual to work, maybe the blue blood has to be given willingly. He must have realized he could use Richard's jealousy of you to his advantage. Now he's given Richard what he always wanted, he'll be easier to manipulate."

Tamara sat heavily, suddenly overwhelmed. "I should never have gone away. I thought I was doing the best thing by leaving, but all I did was hand you over to that monster to do his work. . ."

Brian nodded at Tony and they both withdrew from the room, leaving Alfie and Tamara alone. Alfie didn't speak for a long time. It was all so much to take in. He thought his parents had split up because they didn't love each other any more. He thought his mum had left because she was selfish and didn't love him and his brother and sister enough to stay. But while the world sneered at them and judged them, his parents had been fighting a secret battle to save them all. Alfie thought he had a pretty good idea how that must have felt. Finally, he sat next to his mother and took her hand. "I still wish you'd told me sooner, but ... none of this was your fault, Mum. I see that now. I forgive you."

She looked up at him with tears in her eyes. "Your father and I spoke so often about how to protect you – we just felt like we'd landed you with this curse from the moment you were born and there were all these vultures circling, waiting to pick you off. First the politicians and the press, and now Lock and his evil. And even if he doesn't get what he wants from Richard..."

Alfie realized with horror what she meant.

"Ellie ... he has Ellie too."

G

THE PRINCESS
IN THE TOWER

Ellie had never liked being alone. As a young child she would spend her days chasing her big brothers, Alfie and Richard, through the endless hallways and grand ballrooms of Buckingham Palace. Sometimes they would get fed up with her and tell her to "go and play with her dolls", but Ellie was not a "dolls" kind of girl. If she wasn't harassing her brothers, then she was tugging at her father's arm, demanding to be spun round in the air again, or swinging from the branches of an oak tree while her mother lay reading in the shade. At school, the boisterous, red-headed princess had eventually found "her gang" – the rough-and-tumble sporty crowd who were all business on the hockey pitch and all play off it. She drew energy from being surrounded by others, and if she was honest it also helped take her mind off the car crash that her family had become – Mum gone AWOL, Dad dead and buried, Richard a moody recluse, and Alfie unreliable as ever, despite the fact he was now the king. If there was one thing Ellie was not designed to handle well it was being kidnapped by a giant, undead Viking and thrown into solitary confinement in the Tower of London's dungeons for weeks on end.

Aside from that rather startling turn of events, Ellie knew nothing about what had happened to the country since Lock had seized control. She had spent the first couple of days shivering in the bleak confines of her small stone cell, cold and in shock, trying to process the impossibility of what she'd witnessed at Wimbledon. The only light came from a small bulb near the ceiling that would sometimes go off without warning, plunging her into pitch darkness. Twice a day the Yeoman Jailor would open a hatch in her door and slide through a meal – soup and stale bread usually, a dried chicken leg if she was lucky.

At first she had thrown her food back at him and screamed, "Why am I in here? Where are my brothers? What's HAPPENING?!"

But he never replied, or even looked her in the eye. After a while she gave up and took the food without a word. One morning she woke up with a searing headache to find that someone had been in her cell. Her supper must have been drugged. She was lying on a fresh mattress in a proper iron bed. Soap, a towel and a bucket of water were arranged next to her. The water was icy cold, but she used every drop to try to wash the dead Viking stench from her skin. There were new clothes too – an awful flowery dress she never would have chosen for herself – and a book, some romantic rubbish, which she could only enjoy by adding in car chases and ninja fights in her head as she read it. But she was pleased to be reasonably clean and comfortable for the first time in weeks. Had the Jailor taken pity on her at last? Or was there someone more powerful looking out for her?

Late one night, desperate to talk to someone, she uncovered the small grate through which she had heard the strange whispers from the next cell during her first hours in the dungeons. The odd voice of the prisoner next door with his old-fashioned words had made her feel woozy, like he was putting her under a trance, so she had stuffed a blanket over the grate to drown him out. Talking to him again was a risk, but if she was careful perhaps she could get some useful information.

"We meet again, Princess," came his hushed greeting, before she had even uttered a word.

"Who are you?" she asked.

"My name is Colonel Thomas Blood, loyal subject of King Charles. Or 'Father of all Treasons', depending on who you ask."

"Treason? Is that why they locked you up? What did you do?"

"Nothing improper, my fair young maid, I assure you! Although I may have vexed my sovereign when I purloined his regalia."

"You mean you stole the Crown Jewels?!"

"Borrowed, if you please. His Majesty's jewels were in a state of utmost poverty; it was a veritable stain on the nation's honour. My scheme was in truth merely to melt them down and refashion them into treasures that would befit the glory of a monarch! But alas, matters went awry in the process. A curious magic of which I was unaware resided in the regalia and as they were disassembled it had a most intense and permanent effect on me."

"What did it do to you?"

"Something unspeakable. The point of the matter is that I would not have you think me a common thief. Nay, I am a master in the finest art of all – the art of deception!"

Ellie thought Blood's voice carried a slight Irish lilt to it – was that what made it so mesmerizing? He had only spoken for a minute and yet she could feel herself falling under his spell already, like she could listen to him for ever, do anything he asked. She shook her head and focused.

"Do you know what's going on out there? Why have they put me in here?"

"Alas, I regret that I have been alone in the dark longer than Your Highness. But I do know that one's circumstances can change in the blink of an eye." His voice was suddenly dark and spiteful. "One moment you are a princess, the next a lowly prisoner, left to rot like so much spoiled meat. . ."

Ellie grabbed the blanket and began to stuff it back over the grate.

"Forgive me!" cried the voice, making her head swim again. "I shall bother you no further, except to say this. All is not forsaken. Not every cell need be a tomb."

Ellie sat poised with the blanket, ready to muffle him if she felt herself being hypnotized again. But here was where she did learn something that could be of use to her, as Blood regaled her with stories of all the prisoners who had escaped from the Tower of London over the centuries. From the bishop who shimmied down the walls on a rope smuggled inside in a wine barrel, to the priest who had written notes to fellow conspirators in invisible ink made from orange juice. From the earl who slipped past the guards dressed as a woman, to the traitorous Earl Roger Mortimer, who escaped on a ladder held by supporters on the other side of the moat. The Tower of London might be a fortress that many had failed to break into over the centuries, but plenty of people had succeeded in busting out.

Ellie did not sleep that night. Instead she pulled the mattress off her bed and prised several of the iron bedsprings loose. Using all her strength she bent and twisted the springs until she had moulded them into a rudimentary knife. It would take time to sharpen it. But then time was the one thing she had plenty of these days. Her bed would never be as comfortable again, but that didn't matter, because she wasn't staying. She was going to escape from the Tower of London.

Ten days later, Ellie lay curled up on her bed when the door hatch opened and a small tray slid inside. A bowl of thin, grey soup and a hunk of rock-hard bread. Perfect. She tipped the soup on to the floor, leaving the bowl on its side, and tore the bread in half.

Reaching under her mattress, she retrieved the now scalpel-sharp knife and slid it up her sleeve. She lay down on the cold floor, turned her head away from the door and waited. An hour later she heard the hatch slide open again. She knew that the Jailor would be able to see her lying there. But would he fall for it? Would he think she had choked on the bread?

Clunk. Bolts being opened, a key in the lock! Ellie slid the knife down her sleeve into her hand. Footsteps – one, two, three – he was right by her. He was bending down, a hand on her shoulder, rolling her over. NOW! Ellie sprang up, knife aimed at the Jailor's throat.

Except it wasn't the Jailor. A strong hand batted the knife from her grasp, sending it spinning on to the floor. Ellie looked up into the face of the person standing over her. It was Richard! She jumped up and hugged him.

"Rich! How did you find me? Come on!"

She grabbed his hand and tried to pull him towards the door, but the Jailor was standing just outside. Scowling, he slammed the door in her face. Puzzled, she looked up at Richard. His face was pale and drawn in the dim light from the bulb. His hand was cold and clammy. He pulled away from her.

"What's going on? Are you a prisoner too?" asked Ellie.

"No," replied Richard.

He wouldn't meet her gaze, instead darting

his bloodshot eyes across the paltry collection of possessions in the cell.

"I wanted to come and see you sooner, but things have been . . . difficult."

Ellie laughed in disbelief and grabbed his arm, forcing him to look at her.

"Difficult? I've been locked up in here for MONTHS! What's going on out there? Where did those monsters come from?"

"It's complicated, but we can't do anything about it now; we just have to get along with them as best we can. It's better that way."

"Better? Better for who? How come I'm banged up in here and you're not?"

"It's for your own safety. I have to keep you safe. I have responsibilities now that I'm king—"

"King? What are you talking about? Alfie's king."

Richard shuffled uneasily from foot to foot.

"No. He's gone."

"Gone? What do you mean? Richard, tell me."

"Alfie's dead."

He felt bad lying to her, but their brother would be dead soon enough anyway, so there was no point getting her hopes up.

Ellie felt her knees give way. She gripped on to the bed, eyes searching Richard's face for some sign that this was just a sick joke.

"How?"

"I don't know. It happened in the fighting. I'm sorry, I thought they would have told you by now."

Ellie couldn't think straight. Tears blurred her vision. Her head was pounding.

"Why would someone do that to Alfie? He wasn't a threat to anyone, he was just . . . our stupid brother. What happened?"

"There was nothing I could do. I couldn't stop it."

Ellie stared at him, confused.

"You were there, weren't you? Why didn't you do something?"

She could see an odd look in Richard's eyes – not sadness or regret. Guilt. She gasped.

"You wanted to be king! Alfie humiliated you at the coronation and you wanted to get your own back."

"No, it wasn't like that, Ellie, I swear."

He backed off, but she flew at him, furious, fists pummeling his chest.

"They killed Alfie and you let them do it! How could you?"

She struck him across the cheek, disturbing the thick make-up that covered his scaly skin.

"NO!"

Richard clutched his face and lashed out at Ellie, throwing her against the wall. She held her side where he had hit her, weeping. A red fire burned in Richard's eyes. His voice was low and rasping.

"Don't you see, I'm trying to protect you?"

Richard was standing at the cell door. It was open again. It occurred to Ellie that he looked stooped and grey, much older than his years.

"I'm sorry. I'll come back when I can," he said.

Before she could say anything, he had gone and Ellie was alone again.

Richard pushed past the Jailor and made for the staircase. He'd done what he needed to do. Ellie knew that Alfie was history. There was nothing more he could say that would make her feel any better. All he wanted to do now was get out of the dungeons. A shadow filled the staircase ahead of him and Lock descended, barring his exit.

"The princess is comfortable enough, I hope," said Lock.

"What do you care?" sneered Richard.

"You're right, I don't, especially. But I admire your brotherly loyalty."

The eavesdropping Jailor grinned at Lock's dig.

"I was just checking on her. Now I have to find my brother. . ." said Richard.

Lock held up a hand, stopping him from passing.

"No need."

He circled the large globe of long, glowing keys that hung at the centre of the chamber, studying them. The Jailor eyed him nervously.

"Please don't touch them, my lord. They are a devil to untangle."

"No doubt," replied Lock with a wry smile. "Nevertheless, I need to speak with Colonel Blood. Release him."

The Jailor looked at Lock like he'd spat in his porridge. "Impossible! You'd never catch him again, he's the worst kind of—"

"I know what he is," snapped Lock, gripping the Jailor by the scruff of his neck and pushing him towards the key bundle. "Now unless you'd like to live out your days in one of your own cells, do as I say and let the colonel out."

Trembling, the Jailor ran his fingers over the keys and pulled one out from deep inside the bunch. He pushed it through the cobwebs that coated the lock of Colonel Blood's cell and, using all his strength, turned it to the side. There was a heavy click and the sound of rushing air, as if from the seal on some long unopened tomb. The door swung open. Richard stepped back, eyeing Lock. He hoped the professor knew what he was doing. The prisoner emerged. But what came out of the dark cell was not a man, but a cloud of red mist that flew around the chamber like a swarm of bees. Startled, Richard thought he could smell copper as the red cloud settled before them, hovering in mid-air.

"I am much obliged to you, my liege," came the colonel's voice from the red mist itself.

"Lord Protector Cameron Lock, pleased to make your acquaintance."

"That stuff is Colonel Blood?" asked Richard.

"Indeed, yes," replied the red mist, "Though I am less than half the man I used to be."

He tittered with laughter, sending the blood mist twirling round like a miniature tornado.

"I hear," continued Lock, "that you are capable of occupying another's body. A demonstration, perhaps?"

"It has been a while, but very well," said Blood with glee.

The Jailor, realizing what was coming, bolted for the stairs, but the blood mist shot after him, spiralling round his body.

"No! Get off me!" cried the old Yeoman.

Richard watched with horror as the red mist blasted into the Jailor's ears and up his nose and disappeared. The Jailor suddenly stood upright and returned to them, inspecting his own arms and feeling his own beard.

"Oh no, no, this won't do at all, such a crabby old

fellow," came the colonel's singsong voice from the Jailor's mouth.

"I'm sure you'll find better vessels on your journey," said Lock, with a sly smile.

The possessed Jailor peered at him, eyes alive with intrigue.

"And where might I be going, pray tell?"

"I have a task for you. An assassination."

"Not really my expertise, though I have slain my fair share on the battlefield," replied Blood. "But what would I have to gain from this bargain?"

"It is my understanding that you can only inhabit a host body for a short period of time before you must move on," said Lock. "Do this for me and my mistress will give you a permanent solution to your . . . situation."

The possessed Jailor scratched his chin and smiled.

"Very well. Who is the unfortunate target?"

Lock reached into his jacket and pulled out the Orb – part of the regalia that the Defender used to scout out the land ahead of him. The Jailor's eyes lit up as he took the precious object in his hands.

"The Orb has an urge to find its master," said Lock. "Once you are close enough, it will lead you to him. You're to set off at once for America."

Blood gasped with delight. "The New World! I have heard wondrous things. I accept your proposal!"

And with that, the rest mist exited its host body the same way it had entered. The Jailor shook his head and swatted at the air, groaning. Colonel Blood's mist caught the Orb before it hit the ground and drifted away up the stairs, through a window and across the moat. On the street, a dim-witted berserker watched as the Orb floated towards him and rested in his hands, before the red mist carrying it flew up his nose and into his ears.

"Ye gads, I do hope they have more agreeable bodies where I am going," said Blood as his host body set off at a gallop, bound for the airport.

7
ZEMI

Britain looked dead.

From the snowy roof of the tower block, Hayley had a good view across night-time Watford. What was once a sparkling, vibrant universe of street lights and car headlamps was now dark and empty. The electricity supply, patchy during the day at best, was totally out by night. Occasionally, someone with a candle or a torch would pass by a distant window, a mum tucking her cold children into bed maybe, or scavengers checking abandoned flats for something they could trade for food.

Hayley pulled her coat hood tighter against the icy wind and looked to the south, towards the centre of London. There was light in the sky over that way all right, but it wasn't natural. The clouds pulsed blood red, lit up from below. She couldn't see Big Ben or the Houses of Parliament from here of course, but she knew somewhere beneath that horrible red glow was the Raven Banner, pumping its dark curse out along the ley lines of Britain like a diseased heart. Its magic had created the berserkers and now controlled them, as well as keeping the snowstorms blowing and the foul fog bank wrapped around the coastline.

Hayley's eyes narrowed and she could feel her heart racing as anger surged through her. This was *her* country, *her* home. *Look what they've done to it.* She couldn't stand it any more. Gran had always said count to ten when she felt like lashing out, and Hayley got to six before she kicked an air vent as hard as she could and stomped towards the stairs.

"LC. We've got to do something."

The old man was attempting to make tea by candlelight when Hayley stormed into the kitchen. He looked ridiculous wearing an old bobble hat and two jumpers over his dressing gown, but then, it was bitterly cold in the flat.

"Your resistance activities have made you the most wanted person in this once great country." LC sounded tired. He barely looked up and continued to dunk the teabag up and down in the cup methodically. "I'd say you were doing enough."

"Enough? We haven't done anything!"

"You've only just returned from your last mission, Miss Hicks. By the skin of your teeth, I might add."

"Yeah, a mission that achieved nothing! And even if we'd got a few people out, so what? It's a drop in the ocean. It's USELESS!"

"Shhh. Your grandmother is sleeping," said LC.

"I don't care. I can't hack another day of this. We have to do something else, something . . . BIG!"

"And what do you suggest we do?" LC sighed, wrung the teabag out and dropped it in the bin.

"How should I know? You're the Lord Chamberlain. You're supposed to be the one with the clever plans, but all you do these days is mope around staring into space and making cold tea!"

"It's ex-Lord Chamberlain, I think you'll find. The ravens have fled, the Tower has crumbled, the king is. . . He's dead." LC muttered like he was reciting a super-depressing poem.

LC started to leave the room, but Hayley blocked his way, fighting to hold back her tears.

"So that's that, is it? Game over. They win. We give up and sit here waiting to freeze to death?"

"Hayley, please. . ."

But she pulled him over to the window and flung open the curtains, pointing at the red glow on the horizon.

"See that? That's the Raven Banner. It's only twenty miles in that direction and without it Lock doesn't have his berserker army, or his endless winter. Can't we, I don't know, tear it down or blow it up or something?"

LC scoffed and pulled the curtains closed. "Preposterous. I suppose we shall have to start calling you Hayley Fawkes from now on." He tittered to himself, then immediately regretted it as he saw Hayley's eyes light up.

"Guy Fawkes. Yeah . . . yeah! Gunpowder, treason and plot and all that November the fifth stuff."

Hayley remembered learning about the Gunpowder Plot at school one November. A man called Guy Fawkes had famously tried to blow up Parliament way back in the year 16-something-or-other. He and his fellow plotters had smuggled barrels of gunpowder beneath the Palace of Westminster. He'd come close to pulling it off too, but was discovered at the last second. That's why people let off fireworks on November fifth, to remember it. Gran had always loved that night, tucked up in a blanket, urging Hayley to push her wheelchair closer to the bonfire. Hayley could take it or leave it, but the fun for her was watching her grandmother's face light up with pure joy at every bang and blast. If she found a way to blow up the Raven Banner, maybe one day they'd celebrate "Hayley Hicks Day", in honour of the girl who gave freedom back to the UK!

"Why not, LC? Let's blow it up!"

LC looked at her like she'd just turned cartwheels across a lawn with a "Keep Off the Grass" sign on it.

"Absolutely not. Impossible. Plots against the Crown have rarely worked in the past—"

"I'm not plotting against the Crown! Lock and Richard stole the crown and everything else. We have to take it back!"

"Even if I agreed with you. . . We'd never get close enough for starters. The Palace of Westminster is crawling with dead Norsemen."

"Yeah, but I bet you know a secret way in. A tunnel or a magical portal or something." LC's eyes darted away from her and she pounced. "You *do* know a way, don't you?"

"Stop it!" LC towered over her, trying to look commanding, but the bouncing bobble on his hat was kind of ruining the effect. "You can't go around wrecking Britain's greatest buildings on a whim, Hayley Hicks."

"I just want to blow up the banner, nothing else. No one would get hurt!"

"Hayley!" Gran's voice croaked from her bedroom.

LC gave Hayley a "told you so" look. But suddenly there was a crash from the hallway.

"GRAN!" yelled Hayley, as they both rushed to the hall.

Hayley's gran was lying on the floor. They rushed to prop her up, but she was delirious, her skin cold and pale. There was a long gash across her forehead.

"Oh my God, Gran!" cried Hayley. "She needs a hospital!"

It took them twenty minutes to carry Gran down the stairs to the ground floor. The lift would have been faster, but the power was out. By the time they reached the bottom of the stairwell, they were both exhausted and sweating despite the cold. Nevertheless, Hayley raced straight back up to the flat and returned a few minutes later with her gran's wheelchair. Gran moaned as they eased her into it and wrapped a blanket around her.

"We can push her to the hospital. It's only a mile," Hayley said.

"But the curfew," said LC. "Berserker patrols everywhere. You're a wanted criminal."

"I don't care."

Hayley was about to push open the fire exit when LC stopped her.

"Wait!"

Dean Barron's Rolls Royce had pulled up outside the block of flats, music thumping. The new Community Earl got out of the car and perched on its bonnet like he was starring in a hip-hop video. He was holding a chain attached to his pet berserker Turpin, who drooled and hooted along with the music.

"You can't go, Miss Hicks, he'll see you."

"I have to—" Hayley said but LC stood in her way.

"It doesn't help your gran if you're caught. Leave this to me. Meet me at the hospital when you can sneak out."

Before Hayley could answer, LC was through the door and pushing the wheelchair purposefully across the icy car park. Dean was busy laughing at his dancing berserker and with the awful music turned up so loud, LC thought he might be able to just walk right past—

"Oi, where do you think you're off to?" Dean shouted at LC. But the old man kept walking. Dean leapt off the bonnet of the car, yanked Turpin's chain and strode in front of LC, blocking his way. "Curfew. K-U-R-F-O-O. You know what that means?"

"This woman is ill. She needs a hospital."

Dean gave the old woman a cursory glance.

"Old Mrs Hicks. Blimey, is she still alive? Go in the morning," he sneered.

"This is an emergency, young man."

LC tried to push the wheelchair past, but Turpin

snarled and slapped a powerful hand on the back of it, making Gran groan.

"Listen to me, you mad old moron—" said Dean.

"NO, YOU LISTEN TO ME!" LC rose up to his full height and his eyes flashed with a pure anger that made even Turpin take a step back. "This woman has had a stroke and needs urgent care. You and your thugs wanted power and you've got it. Congratulations, the country is yours. But with that power comes a responsibility to its citizens, however young or old."

Dean shuffled awkwardly, not wanting to meet LC's fierce gaze.

"Now, you're an ambitious young man, everyone can see that. Smart, as well," LC continued.

"Yeah, that's right."

"Just the kind of up-and-coming fellow our new masters would want to see promoted because of his excellent relations with the community." LC smiled at Dean. "Play your cards right and you'll come out of this a hero. Maybe get a better neighbourhood to rule over."

Dean nodded. He could see what the old man was saying. It couldn't hurt his prospects to do a good deed.

"Fine. You can go." Dean said, trying to sound like he'd just had the idea himself.

"I was rather hoping you could give us a lift," said LC, glancing over at the Rolls Royce.

Half an hour later, Hayley, hood pulled low, hurried through the crowded Accident and Emergency Department of Watford General Hospital. She'd watched with amazement as LC had talked Dean into giving him a lift. As soon as the Rolls Royce had left the car park, she was out of the door and running. There was a crowd of berserkers near the hospital entrance jumping up and down on an abandoned ambulance, but she just joined the throng of people and slipped inside.

"Excuse me, I'm looking for a patient, my gran?" Hayley asked a nurse, but it was like she barely registered her as she ran past with an armful of bandages.

The hospital was in chaos. There was light here, at least, probably from generators, but it kept going on and off like some kind of nightmare disco strobe. Desperate, Hayley turned around, unsure which way to go. A man with blood pouring down his face was being helped to a chair by his wife as she shouted for someone, *anyone* to help them. Patients on trollies lined the corridors. Someone shouted for water. Screams. A baby cried. Machine alarms beeped. The lights dimmed then came back on again—

A hand fell on Hayley's shoulder.

"Miss Hicks." It was LC. "Thank goodness you're safe."

"Where's Gran?" Hayley pleaded.

"This way," said LC, leading her down a maze of corridors filled with yet more patients.

"What's going on here?" asked Hayley.

"I talked to a porter briefly. It's been like this ever since the Vikings took over. There aren't enough doctors, the nurses are overstretched, beds full, drugs running out. . ." LC muttered, disgusted.

"Sounds pretty normal to me," muttered a man on crutches who had overheard them as he hobbled past.

They turned a corner to find Gran on a trolley, being attended to by a young doctor.

"Gran!" said Hayley.

But her gran's eyelids kept fluttering and closing; she was barely awake.

The doctor took her stethoscope off Gran's chest and turned to Hayley and LC. She looked like she hadn't slept for days, but despite the black bags that ringed them, her eyes were kind. "Family?"

Hayley nodded for both of them. "She takes heart pills, and she has dementia. Is she going to be OK?"

"I'm sorry," the doctor replied. "If I had an Intensive Care bed we might be able to stabilize her – for a while, at least – but even then. . ." She placed a hand on Hayley's arm for a moment and smiled. "I really am sorry."

And with that she was gone, hurrying off to the next patient. Hayley watched her go, devastated.

"Wait!" she cried. Then turned back to Gran and hugged her. "Oh, Gran."

"I don't know if she can hear you," LC said.

"Shut up, LC. I can hear the girl just fine." Gran said, her eyes flicking open.

Hayley laughed and cried at the same time, and hugged her again for the longest time. After a while, Gran's breathing grew short.

"We've been through the wars, haven't we?" Gran whispered, her voice quiet again, so low Hayley had to lean in to hear her.

"I love you, Gran." It was all Hayley could think of saying.

"Saw one of them Vikings from the taxi. . ." Gran said and faltered, taking a deep breath. Hayley looked alarmed but Gran seemed to rally again. "Phoo-ee, they stink. Someone should really kick their butts."

Hayley laughed through the tears. "That's the spirit."

"I'm proud of what you're doing. You know that, petal? Your mum would have been as well." Gran fumbled with her necklace, trying to take it off, so

Hayley slipped it over her head for her. On the end of the silver chain hung a small wooden carving of a woman's head with a fierce expression on her face. Hayley had never really looked at it before. "Zemi. That's its name. They say it holds the spirit of our ancestors. You wear it now, love. And when I'm gone . . . you take me back home . . . back to Jamaica."

"Don't talk like that, Gran, you're going to be fine. I'll find that doctor. . ."

All the strength seemed to drain out of Gran. Her eyes went back to fluttering again and her breathing became shallow and came in fits and starts. LC put a hand on Hayley's shoulder.

"I know it's hard. But you should say goodbye now," he whispered.

Hayley grasped her gran's hand. It felt like a bunch of straws that could snap at any moment. "I'll do it. I'll take you home, I promise. You can go now, Gran. It's OK. I love you."

Hayley stood by the trolley and watched her gran's face until no more breaths came. She didn't need a doctor to tell her; she could see it clearly. Her gran was gone.

8

QUEEN'S GAMBIT

The attractive young stewardess in the lilac uniform stood in the shadow of Denver International Airport's peaked white mountaintop roof. She smiled so wide it cracked her make-up as she gazed at all the strange people in their curious clothes and the incredibly shiny cars that carried them to and fro at such speed. In a few jerky steps, she had reached the front of the cab rank queue. But when she showed no sign of getting in, the cab driver, a balding man wearing a white T-shirt stained with that morning's breakfast, lowered his window and raised a weary eyebrow at her.

"You getting in, or what?" he barked.

The stewardess looked down at him and smiled. Colonel Blood's journey thus far had been a long one, through thirteen different states and twenty-two different bodies, but the thrill of travel after so long in a cell was keeping his spirits high.

"I beg your pardon, my good fellow?" said the stewardess.

"Oh, you're a Brit, huh? Say, were you on that flight outta London I heard about on the news? Your lucky day, huh?" He jumped out and opened the rear door. "Your carriage awaits, my lady!"

"Thank ye verily, good coachman," she said, getting in.

"No luggage, miss?" asked the driver, frowning. Something in the stiff way she moved unnerved him a little. It reminded him of a marionette. *But maybe that's just what English people are like*, he thought.

"Just this," she said, reaching into her handbag and pulling out the Scout Orb.

The cab driver stared at the golden, jewel-encrusted sphere, open-mouthed.

"That's quite the souvenir; you must've been somewhere exotic. So, where to?"

"Ah yes, our mysterious destination," she said. "One moment."

She placed the Orb on the seat and they both watched as it slowly rotated to the right and stopped. The woman pointed in the same direction.

"What's that way?"

"Um . . . the mountains?" said the perplexed driver.

"Then the mountains it is!" she declared. "On second thoughts, I do believe I would like to try driving your horseless carriage myself."

"Come again?"

Colonel Blood's cloud of red mist shot from the stewardess's ears, flew round the inside of the cab, then rocketed up the startled driver's nose. Once the screaming young woman had fled, Blood used the driver's foot to step on the pedal and the cab jerked away from the kerb, veering across three lanes of traffic, before settling into a route north, towards Wyoming.

"I don't know what's gotten into them tonight," said Tamara, stroking a mare's nose to calm her down.

Brian and Tony were trying to help Tamara stable the horses for the night, but they were skittish, whinnying and pulling at their reins.

"Probably our friend here jumping around too much again," said Brian, looking at Tony, who was being pulled around in circles by a lively foal.

Gwenn flapped on to the roof of the stables and let out a throaty *gronk*.

"Spooked by your overgrown blackbirds, more like!" cried Tony.

*

Inside the ranch's kitchen, Alfie was thinking about Hayley. One minute he'd been taking a drink out of the fridge, the next his eyes had alighted on a tub of ice cream and he was back in Buckingham Palace the night he'd first taken Hayley there. Creeping through the long, dark corridors, laughing at the look of disbelief on her face as they crossed a gilded ballroom, and sitting together in the kitchens, taking a scoop each from every ice-cream tub they could find. There was so much he missed about England, and he was desperately worried about Ellie, but he realized at that moment that it was Hayley, his plain-speaking, smart, funny friend he missed most. So much that his stomach ached.

The dull drone of the TV news barely registered with Alfie, whose thoughts had strangely now jumped to Edinburgh. The dark tunnels beneath the castle, and the fiery cavern where he saw the Black Dragon before he knew the creature was really his own brother. He could feel the heat of the rekindled volcano from below, prickly against his skin, the thick smell of smoke in his nostrils. He coughed. Smoke. . . A shrill alarm split the air, startling Alfie out of his daydream. Thick smoke was pouring from the oven. The dinner! Tony appeared from nowhere, hurried past Alfie and turned the oven off. Tamara burst in and heaved the oven door open, pulling out the blackened carcass of a pork belly.

"Alfie, I thought you were watching it!" she said.

Alfie held up his hands, "Sorry!"

Brian waved a towel around, silencing the smoke alarm.

"Maybe you're more like Alfred the Great than you think," he said, laughing.

"What, a lousy chef?" asked Tony, who was opening windows.

"Don't tell me you've never heard the story of King Alfred and the cakes?" asked Brian.

Tony shrugged. "I don't know. Did they make a movie out of it?"

Ignoring him, Brian continued. "He was hiding in some peasant family's hovel while he was on the run from the Vikings, and they'd left him to watch the cakes that were cooking. But I suppose he had other things on his mind, because they burnt to a cinder. And when she came back, the peasant woman gave him an earful, king or no king. . ."

"I get it," said Tony. "See, Your Alfie-ness, you take after your ancestor after all."

But Alfie wasn't listening. He was watching Gwenn, who had just arrived on the windowsill, hopping up and down and tapping the window with her beak.

"What is it, girl?" Alfie said, opening the window and stroking her beak.

She hopped inside and flew round the kitchen ceiling.

"Not in the house, I've told you, Alfie!" said Tamara, swatting the raven away.

As the smoke cleared, Tony saw something on the TV news that made his eyes bulge in their sockets and his tongue loll out.

"Wowee. Who's that?" he purred.

Gwenn finally flew back out of the window, allowing Alfie to see what had caught Tony's eye. It was the familiar, elegant figure of the young Queen Freya of Norway. She was being greeted at the White House by the President and First Lady. *What's she doing over here?* he wondered.

Thud, thud, thud, thud.

The ground shook and pots and pans rattled where they hung. Everyone stopped what they were doing and looked at each other, confused. Alfie opened his mouth to shout GET DOWN! But before he could form the words, the wall next to him caved in and the troll smashed her way inside.

A tornado of flying wood and metal erupted around them as the ten-foot-tall, angry green troll bulldozed through the table, chairs and work surfaces. Tamara pulled Alfie to the corner as the ceiling began to fall in chunks, ripped away by the troll's flailing fists. Brian levelled his gun at the intruder and let off two shots, which merely ricocheted off her tough skin. Holgatroll swatted Brian aside with the back of her hand and bore down on Alfie and his mother.

"WHERE IS IT?!" she roared through thick ropes of yellow drool.

Tamara's scream was interrupted as Tony, who had whipped on his Qilin outfit, popped out of the air next to her. The next thing they knew, Alfie and his mother were lying outside in the dirt next to Qilin, a hundred yards from the ranch. Tamara's finished her scream and looked bewildered at the boys.

"What about—?"

"On it!" shouted Qilin.

He vanished again and was back two seconds later with a stunned Brian. They watched in shock as tiles rained from the roof of the ranch house and windows shattered.

"What is that thing?" gasped Tamara.

"That is Holgatroll," said Alfie. "She's a friend. Sort of."

Alfie had met Holgatroll, Queen Freya's nocturnal alter-ego, during his first state visit to Norway before the Viking takeover. She'd been friendly enough to lend him the Raven Banner. But as another wall came down and Holgatroll continued her rampage from room to room, Alfie figured she wasn't feeling so sociable this time.

"If she's your friend, why is she wrecking my ranch?" cried Tamara angrily.

"She probably wants her Raven Banner," said Alfie, wincing. "I was going to give it back, honest!"

"Well you can apologize once she's calmed down," said Brian, reloading his gun. "But for now, we could do with putting a little distance between us. Tony?"

Qilin looked around – it was a cloudy night and there was no moon, nor any other artificial lights to illuminate the landscape around them. He shook his head.

"Too dark, chief. I could wind up shifting us all into a tree at a thousand miles an hour. Not wise."

Another roar shook the house.

"WHERE IS IT?!"

The oven flew out through the roof and spiralled past them. Brian pointed at the pick-up truck parked by the stables.

"Let's go," he said.

"Keys are in the house," said Tamara.

Qilin took a breath.

"On it, AGAIN," he sighed and blink-shifted back to the house once more.

The others hurried towards the truck.

"There's no point," said Alfie, "She'll catch us. You should see her when she jumps."

"Driving's better than running," replied Brian.

A crash came from the house and what was left of the roof exploded as Holgatroll leapt out, flew over their heads and landed on the truck, flattening it like it was a tin can.

"Looks like we're running," said Tamara.

They turned and ran back towards the wreckage of the house, but the enraged troll stamped after them. Suddenly Qilin reappeared and threw a handful of silver balls at her, which erupted into bright purple fire on impact. Holgatroll yelled and stumbled to the side, taking out a water-pump windmill.

"I didn't know you had those!" Alfie said to Tony.

"I'm full of surprises!" Tony replied with glee.

He blink-shifted from spot to spot all around Holgatroll, dropping more fireballs that blew her back and forth as she snarled and tried in vain to grab him.

"I'LL BITE YOUR HEAD OFF, YOU LITTLE FIREFLY!" threatened the troll.

She jumped and stamped on the ground, sending Qilin off-balance as he reappeared, making him drop a silver ball, which erupted next to him. Holgatroll caught Qilin as he flew backwards and covered his eyes with her mighty hand.

"HA-HA! CAN'T DO YOUR DISAPPEARING TRICK NOW, CAN YOU?" she gloated.

Alfie pushed past Brian and ran towards them.

"Don't!" shouted Brian.

But Alfie was already in front of the troll, waving his arms to get her attention.

"Stop it! You've made your point!"

Holgatroll snarled at him and prepared to bite Qilin's head off.

"YOUR MAJESTY, PLEASE!" Alfie pleaded.

The troll paused, thinking it over, then tossed Qilin to the ground. He wiped the slimy troll sweat from his face and blink-shifted wearily to the others. Holgatroll towered over Alfie, a huge finger pointing at his face and roared at him in a gale of meaty breath.

"I WANT WHAT'S MINE, BOY!"

"And you'll get it," said Alfie, soothing. "But can we talk about it like civilized people?"

Holgatroll snorted with derision, then, looking at the wrecked ranch house and the carnage around it, shrank back into the human form of Queen Freya. The emerald necklace she wore shone brightly for a moment, then dimmed. She looked like she had just come from a state banquet (which she had); there was not a golden hair out of place, not a crease in her flowing green ballgown.

"Very well, but don't expect me to apologize," said Freya in her softly lilting accent.

Tony's eyes grew wide as he took in the radiant beauty of the Norwegian monarch.

"Now *that* is my kind of troll," he gushed.

Tamara clipped him behind the ear. "She's just totalled my home!"

While Brian helped Tamara retrieve what she could from the gutted house, Alfie explained to Freya what had happened to the Raven Banner – how his brother had stolen it from him and how Lock had used it to create an army of berserkers and take over the country.

"I warned you it might not behave the same way on British soil," snapped Freya, still clearly in no mood to be mollified.

"I know. I messed everything up and I'm sorry. But what else could I do? We had to try to stop the Vikings somehow," said Alfie.

"What good does that do me? Now MY kingdom is under threat. Remember that cave full of Viking draugar you saw beneath Geirangerfjord? Well a few weeks after you failed to return, those lovely boys began to wake up. Now they have overrun half of Norway, and without my banner I have no way to stop them!"

Tony was watching her rant and rave with a big smile on his face.

"And if your friend doesn't stop smiling at me like that I may bite his head off after all," the queen hissed.

Tony hurried up to her like an over-excited puppy and extended his hand.

"I'm Tony, AKA Qilin. I'm royalty too, you know, from China."

"This is not a cocktail party," she sniffed.

Tony ploughed ahead undeterred, "Sorry, I wouldn't have thrown all those fireballs at you if I'd known you were, you know..."

"What, a woman?"

"So pretty."

"Listen, you little squirt, I was going easy on you. You're lucky you still have a head left to spout nonsense from."

"Golly, I love your accent," said Tony, doe-eyed.

Alfie winced and beckoned Brian over. "Emergency evac needed. Could you airlift Tony out of this conversation, please?"

A cold wind whipped down from the hills making the pine trees moan. Freya shivered and rubbed her arms. Tamara came over and offered her a coat.

"Not sure if this is your style, honey, but the rest are still buried in there, I'm afraid."

Freya took the coat, sat down and looked guiltily at the wreck of the ranch house.

"My temper can be difficult to control when I am ... my other self. You don't happen to have another house somewhere?"

"Nope, that was it," said Alfie's mum, sitting next to her.

"How did you find us, if you don't mind me asking, Your Majesty?" said Brian.

"I followed your king's scent," she answered.

Alfie blushed as Tony laughed and dug him in the ribs.

"Stinky Al!"

"Honestly, where did you pick up this half-wit?" said Freya, much to Alfie's amusement. "Trolls have a very keen sense of smell. They can track almost anything, given enough time. And if I found you, then others can too. You're not safe here."

"So you *do* care!" beamed Tony.

"Won't your people be missing you back in Washington?" asked Brian.

"Let them miss me," Freya scoffed. "I have already been criticized for fleeing the crisis in my homeland. I no longer care what people think of me. But I do care about what happens to them."

She got up and dusted herself down.

"Anyway, I suppose it's not entirely your fault. I should never have lent you the banner."

Alfie stepped forward.

"Then help us get it back for you."

The others looked at him, surprised.

"Do you mean it, Alfie?" asked his mother.

"Yes," he replied. "I've been away from home for too long."

"It won't be easy to get past that Viking navy," said Tony.

"We'll find a way," replied Alfie.

"And there's no guarantee we can get the banner back even if we do," added Brian.

"I will retrieve the banner of Odin even if I have to slay a thousand Vikings," declared Freya.

Brian nodded, "That might do it."

Alfie turned to his mother. "I promise I'll find Ellie, and I'll do everything I can to save Richard too."

"No need to promise," said Tamara. "Because this time I'll be right by your side when you do."

"You're coming?" asked Alfie, surprised.

"Sure," she replied, "I've hidden long enough too. Plus," she said, looking back at the wreckage, "my house is kind of trashed."

Alfie smiled, "That's settled then. I just hope there's a country left for us to save when we get there."

9

THE WATFORD ARCHIVES

Hayley rolled her gran's tiny Zemi figurine between her palms, concentrating on every ridge and point in the hard wood, letting the silver chain run through her fingers. She wanted to focus her mind on something small and easy to handle, not the terrible events of the last twenty-four hours. Herne must have sensed that she needed the company and was curled up asleep on the bed next to her. After they had returned from the hospital, she had gone straight to her gran's cold bedroom and begun to pack away her things. By first light the bed was stripped, the framed photographs from the bedside table wrapped and placed into boxes. The clothes from the wardrobe that still smelled of her gran were folded and put into bin bags. She dusted every surface and washed the windows, until she was exhausted. She hadn't noticed that the Lord Chamberlain was watching her from the doorway until he came in and sat with her.

"I thought if I put all her stuff away then I might not think about her every single second," said Hayley. "But I can't get her out of my head. Lying there like that... Anyway, you might want go 'cos there's going to be more crying."

But Hayley was surprised when LC reached over and laid a comforting hand on hers.

"I know you think I don't understand all this emotional business – family and loved ones and so forth," he said. "But you do not reach my age without having experienced certain attachments."

"You had a family?"

LC cast his milky eyes to the window, as the sun struggled to rise above the freezing fog.

"Yes. Very long ago now. But I can still recall the joy I felt when I was with them, and the sadness afterwards..." He withdrew his hand and composed himself. "I chose to devote what time I had left to king and country. I know that must sound terribly old-fashioned to you, but it is a devotion that has been just as rewarding in its own way."

Hayley opened the chain and hung the Zemi

around her neck. It felt strange and bulky against her skin.

"When I knew they were sending Gran to that home, it wasn't just her I was worried about. It was me too. I'd spent all my life looking after her, then all of a sudden she was gone. But then Alfie turned up and it felt like it was meant to be, know what I mean? I had a purpose again."

She stood up and closed the final box, looking round at the bare room. "Alfie's gone. Now Gran too. What's the point? Why carry on with any of this?"

LC stood and straightened his jacket. "The point, I believe, is to honour what they stood for. To honour them."

"How?"

"Before last night I had not realized how truly dire things were out there. Perhaps it is a time to, how did your grandmother put it? To kick some Vikings in their butts?"

"Close enough, LC," Hayley said, smiling. She hung the Zemi round her neck, tucking it under her T-shirt. "Gunpowder, treason and plot, eh?"

"If there is a chance to destroy the banner and loosen Lock's grip on the country, then we are duty-bound to seize it," said LC, warming to the idea. But then he frowned. "There is a problem, though. Without access to the Keep Archives, I'm not sure I can remember enough about the layout of the Palace of Westminster. We don't even have your newfangled internet to look it up. . ."

"You know, Watford has some pretty good archives of its own," replied Hayley.

That night they stood on the snow-covered pavement outside a large, faded red-brick building. LC cast his eyes over the broken lettering above the door.

"Watford Public Library?" he said, unable to mask his distaste.

"Give it a chance," said Hayley, handing Herne's lead to him and looking for a window she could force open. "Gran brought me here every Saturday when I was little."

They had waited till dark and crept out of the flats via the basement. Travelling in a group was risky, as it was more likely to get them spotted by the Viking patrols, but the time for caution was over. Herne strained at his lead, whining, and pulled LC towards the main doors, which suddenly glided open.

"Did you see that?" said LC, astonished. "The entrance is enchanted!"

Checking no one on the street had seen them, Hayley took his arm and pulled him inside.

"Exactly how long is it since you lived in the real world, LC?"

Inside, candles were burning, making it look more like a church than a library. People huddled in every corner, some reading by candlelight, others sleeping. A young couple soothed a restless baby in a cot in the biography section. A line of stooped figures were handed soup from a large pan that sat amid darkened computers. The whole scene reminded Hayley of the refugee camps she used to see on news reports about wars in far-away places. A small, middle-aged woman pushing a trolley that was stacked half with books and half with brand-new toothbrushes, sponges and nappies, stopped and peered at them over her glasses.

"You look lost," she said.

"Um, no," said Hayley, "Just surprised you're open."

"Ah yes, we used to shut at six on Wednesdays," she replied, patting Herne on the head as he sniffed the trolley.

"I was thinking more of the whole undead Viking invasion thing," said Hayley, feeling silly.

"It would take more than a few hairy old bath-dodgers to close the libraries," she scoffed.

Hayley noticed a group of people warming themselves by an electric fire.

"You still have power?" she asked.

"Yeah, rigged up our own generator. But we keep the lights off at night so as not to attract too much attention," said the librarian, fishing out a tin of dog food from the bottom of the trolley and handing it to a bemused LC. "So, what are you looking for?"

"British History, if you would be so kind, madam," replied LC.

"Follow me," she said, abandoning the trolley and marching towards the back of the library.

An hour later, Hayley was still holding a candle for the Lord Chamberlain as he pored over a table covered with open history books. Some were tattered with yellowing pages: old accounts of the Gunpowder Plot and the tumultuous reign of James the First. Others were newer: guidebooks to London's top tourist sites, with glossy photographs of the Houses of Parliament. The librarian had brought them some sandwiches and a bowl of water for Herne, who was now asleep under the table. But LC hadn't touched his food; he was too intent on his research. Hayley swapped the candle to her other hand and flexed her sore wrist.

"Do try to keep the light steady, Miss Hicks, my eyesight is not what it was," said LC.

"I'm trying," replied Hayley. "Are you getting anywhere, or what?"

LC opened a page showing a floor plan of the Palace of Westminster, the oblong of huge buildings and towers that housed Parliament.

"Slowly but surely," he said. "The cellars where

Guy Fawkes planted his gunpowder aren't there any more. They were destroyed in a fire."

"I thought he was caught before he set off his gunpowder?"

"Yes, yes. This fire was much later. A petulant witch with a penchant for inferno spells, as I recall. Besides, Guy Fawkes was targeting the House of Lords. We need to destroy the Raven Banner, which is located in the House of Commons, here."

He pointed at the long chamber in the middle of the map.

"The beefeaters still check the cellars before each State Opening of Parliament." LC looked briefly despondent: "That is, they did before they were scattered to goodness knows where..."

Hayley nudged him, bringing his attention back to the floor plan.

"So, how do we get down there? Is there a secret tunnel or something?"

"Oh yes, lots. It's like a rabbit warren beneath that part of London. The only problem is I don't know which of the entrances are still in operation. I do know they closed down many of the subterranean routes over the years – too much of a security risk."

"Smart, but not much use to us right now." Hayley put the candle down and flicked through a guidebook. "There must be some way of finding them?"

"There is – a picture of St Edward's Crown indicates an entrance. Not very subtle, I'm afraid. But there is something to be said for hiding in plain sight. If only I knew where to start looking..."

Hayley closed the book, frustrated. But the cover caught her eye. It was a photo of a red phone box standing on the pavement in the shadow of Big Ben.

"A crown? Like this?"

LC peered at the picture. Sure enough, above the door to the phone box was the symbol of a crown.

The old man sprang to his feet, clutching the book.

"The phone boxes! That's it! Bravo, Miss Hicks."

The librarian shushed them from her desk. Hayley stifled a laugh.

"Explains why they still bother having phone boxes, I suppose," she smirked.

All of a sudden, a growl erupted from beneath the table. Herne stalked out, eyes to the ceiling, hackles raised.

"What is it, Herne?" said Hayley.

An answer came in the form of a scream from one of the tables near the windows. They rushed over to find a mother comforting her young daughter and others staring outside, pointing fearfully at the sky. Hayley squeezed through to the window and looked up to see a dark-winged shadow sweep over the rooftops. Moments later, it passed by again, this time issuing a jet of flames that illuminated the frightened faces at the window. The Black Dragon was flying over the city.

"Might I suggest you all come away from the windows?" said LC.

The rattled inhabitants of the library didn't argue. They'd seen enough.

"Do you think they know who the Dragon really is?" whispered Hayley.

"No," replied LC. "They believe that young King Richard is doing his best to maintain peace with the Viking occupiers. I doubt they've made any connection with the beast. And yet, it is odd that he is still. . ." LC trailed off, gazing into space.

"What?" replied Hayley. She knew that look – there was something LC couldn't explain and it was bothering him.

"Nothing." LC shook his head, back to business.

"So what now?" asked Hayley. "We know how to get in, but it won't be much of a Gunpowder Plot without any gunpowder."

LC smiled. "Now that is something I do believe I can provide."

"Really? You know where to get explosives?" asked Hayley, surprised.

The librarian bustled up to them. She spoke nervously, checking over her shoulder.

"I'm not prying; I don't want to know what you're up to, but we have families here and if there's a raid. . ."

Hayley looked around. Eyes were peeking out at them from behind countless dark shelves, people pointing at her and whispering to each other. She had been recognized. It was easy to forget that she wasn't just some random teenager any more. She was Britain's "most wanted" – famous and hunted – and it wasn't a nice feeling. *Is this what life was like for Alfie?* she wondered. *Everyone knowing who he was the whole time. . .*

"You have been most helpful," said LC, taking her hand and bowing to kiss it.

The flustered librarian tucked a loose curl of her hair behind her ear.

"If there's anything else I can do? I would like to help."

"As a matter of fact, there is," said LC. "You don't happen to know anyone with access to transportation?"

The librarian led them outside and around the corner into a narrow, icy side street. A row of black cabs were parked up in a line. Canvas shelters had been rigged up next to them and the drivers warmed themselves by a firepit.

"Ged?" called the librarian, waving at a portly

driver, much to the amusement of his friends, who nudged him and pushed him over towards them.

"All right, love? People will talk," said Ged, giving her a peck on the cheek.

"I wish you'd come inside where it's warm, dear."

"What, and let some berserker foul up my cab? No chance. What'll I do for a living when all this blows over if that happens? Besides, you know I ain't much of a reader."

"In that case, I have a fare for you," she said, scowling. "Unless you'd rather hang around with your friends all night."

The cabbie looked LC and Hayley up and down.

"Where to, folks?"

"It's a somewhat delicate matter," replied LC. "I have a consignment of barrels I need to move. They're in Woolwich."

The cabbie sucked in air through his teeth and stroked his chin.

"South of the river, during an undead Viking occupation? That's gonna cost you, guv."

The librarian clipped her husband round the ear, which sent his friends into fresh gales of laughter.

"All right, no charge," the cabbie muttered, shame-faced. "But if you're who I reckon you are, then I dare say this might take a spot of planning," he said, and grinned.

"How do we know we can trust you?" asked Hayley.

The man looked offended.

"I'll have you know I am a fully licensed driver of hackney carriages. And if you can't trust a London cabbie, who can you trust, eh?"

10
ROAD TRIP

"Emergency, emergency!" Tony yelled, pawing in the darkness for the window button. He calculated he had about three seconds before everyone inside the speeding four-by-four would choke to death on the poisonous gas.

"Hurry!" Alfie yelled from the middle seat, holding his nose. "I'm dying here!"

Gasping for breath, Tony finally opened his window and took a deep lungful of cold night air.

"Oh, grow up, it's not that bad." Freya said, rolling her eyes. "It's my inner troll, what can I do?"

"Maybe cut down on your meat intake, sweetie?" Tamara suggested from the front passenger seat, waving her hand in front of her nose as Freya glared at her.

They'd been cooped up in Tamara's old jeep for nearly two days now, their destination a little fishing town called Alsea, nine hundred miles away on the Oregon coast. That was where they'd find the submarine that would carry them on the four-day voyage back to the UK for who-knows-what. Battles. Fire. Blood. Alfie tried to block the scary thoughts from his head, but it was like trying to forget about an upcoming appointment at the dentist, only a million times more important and worrying. First they'd all have to get into the UK undetected, then they'd have to somehow recover Alfie's missing regalia so that he could be the Defender again. And even if they managed all that, there was Guthrum and his undead army to defeat, Lock to confront, Ellie to rescue and the not-so-small matter of Richard. Could he save his brother? He didn't know, but he had to try. And this was before he had even factored in some old Norse goddess called Hel who wanted to wipe the world clean and start again.

"How do you eat an elephant?" Tony had asked when Alfie had confided in him earlier about the daunting size of the challenge that faced them.

Alfie shrugged, baffled about what elephants had to do with it.

"One bite at a time," Tony said, smiling. "One bite at a time..."

Alfie knew what Tony meant – they just had to go step by step; it was easier to deal with that way. And weirdly, when he did manage to stave off the thoughts of the future, he was kind of enjoying this road trip. It was less like a preparation for an invasion and more like the weirdest family holiday ever.

"Are we nearly there yet?" Tony whined, tapping his foot on the seat in front of him.

"Ugh, you're such a child!" snapped Freya.

"I am not," said Tony. "Hey, let's play I-Spy!"

Freya sucked in her cheeks like she'd just bitten into a lemon. "How long did you say this trip was, Brian?" she asked urgently.

"Another couple of hours," Brian said, glancing in the rear-view mirror as he drove. "Let's cut the chit-chat and stay alert, please, folks."

The bodyguard had been in a tense mood ever since they'd set off from the ranch. He'd taken them down lesser-used roads, twisting and turning through the hills at breakneck speed and he hadn't slowed down even when Alfie complained he was feeling carsick. They'd crossed through Idaho and sped into Oregon and all the while, Brian kept checking his mirror like a nervous meerkat scanning for predators.

Half an hour later, Brian pulled the jeep off a quiet stretch of road next to a meadow, fringed with dark pine trees, and turned to the back seat.

"OK, people. Potty stop. You've got exactly three minutes before we hit the road again. Don't wander off."

When the three minutes were up and they were returning to the jeep, Freya lingered, eyeing the distant woods hungrily. "I need to eat. Just a couple of rabbits will do."

Brian shook his head. "Sorry, no time to go troll again tonight. Back in the jeep."

The Norwegian queen glared at Brian with icy blue eyes; she wasn't used to being bossed around.

"You forgot three words, driver: 'please' and 'Your Majesty'," she said, haughtily.

"When we're safely in the sub they'll be time for all that. But for now, get your royal derrière back in the truck right now or I'll leave you behind chasing furry little woodland animals. . . Your Majesty." Brian held her glare.

Alfie and Tony stared at each other, wide-eyed, wondering if it was all going to kick off, but the young queen broke first and huffed her way back into the jeep. For the next hour you could have cut the tension with a knife, but eventually Tamara had produced some roast beef sandwiches from a cooler and soon Freya had started breaking wind again. At least she seemed a little happier.

"Is this, like, one of your secret powers?" Alfie

groaned, covering his nose again.

"Engage TROLL WIND!" said Tony, putting on a video game voice.

Their laugh was interrupted when Brian suddenly killed the headlights and pulled the steering wheel hard to the right.

"HOLD ON!" he yelled.

Everyone screamed as the jeep careered off the road and bounced through a field. Alfie felt like he was inside a bottle of ketchup that was being shaken up and down. Finally the jeep fishtailed around and stopped behind a small stand of trees.

"I think I bit my tongue," Tony stammered.

"Who taught you to drive?" Freya said to Brian, annoyed.

"Shut it and stay still," Brian barked. He drew his pistol and spun round to watch the road. "We're being followed."

They sat in tense, unbearable silence, the only sound the wind rushing through the pines outside and the ticking of the jeep's engine as it cooled down. After a few moments, a cone of headlights swept past and Alfie caught a glimpse of a yellow car as it sped by. All was silent again.

"Right, everybody out. We're doing the rest of this trip on foot," said Brian.

A chorus of objections exploded from the back seat.

"What? How far is that?" asked Freya.

"Just because of a car?" said Tony.

Tamara raised her hands, hushing them, and turned to Brian. "What's got you spooked?" she asked.

"Taxi," Brian replied.

"Don't think you'll get one out here," Alfie said, trying to make a joke and immediately wished he hadn't when Brian gave him a death stare.

"Did none of you see that?" the bodyguard snapped. "That was a taxi that passed us back there on the road."

"And your point is. . .?" Freya asked.

"I might not have any superpowers like you, Your Majesty, but I *was* trained in counter-surveillance. You look for anything unusual in your surroundings and question it. For instance, what's a yellow city taxi doing out here in the middle of nowhere?"

Tony put his hand up. "Oh, I have a theory! What if somebody missed their connection at the airport and hired a taxi to take them home out here in Oregon. That makes sense . . . doesn't it?"

They left the jeep where it was, shared out the bags and started to trudge across the fields.

Freya sniffed the wind, taking in big draughts of air and rolling it around her mouth like she was tasting a fine wine back at her palace in Norway. It was impressive and disgusting at the same time. Finally she stopped and nodded. "Brian's right," she pronounced. "There's something out here. And it's not of this world."

"Stay close. Stay alert," Brian said, and everyone fell into watchful silence as they hiked into the dark woods.

"I have two questions. One: do you get bears out here?" Tony whispered after a while, glancing behind him at eerie shapes of the tangled trees. "And two: why do I have to go last?"

"Because you're expendable," Freya hissed back.

"Oh, ha, ha, smelly Norway Queen. You're so funny—"

"Aieeeeeearghh!"

The unearthly scream echoed through the trees. Brian pulled his pistol as everyone instinctively formed into a circle, ready to fight. The beam from Brian's torch played around the trees and stumps, making everything look like a snarling, monstrous face looming out of the dark. Alfie forced himself to control his breathing and wished he had Wyvern to call upon. He could do with being on top of a fierce ghost horse with an attitude problem right now.

"What was that?" he said after a while.

The scream came again, half-animal, half-human,

closer this time. Tamara burst out laughing. Everyone looked at her in alarm – was she so terrified that she was losing her mind?

"It's just a loon," she said.

"There's a crazy person out here with us?" Tony asked, still worried.

"It's a bird. A red-throated loon. You get them on the lakes round here."

A couple of hours later they emerged from the woods, scratched from the trees and weary from the trek. They were looking down on a lonely, all-night gas station that glowed bright and polished like a star nestled against the dark, tree-lined road. Beyond the gas station, the lights of a town twinkled and, further out still, the flat Pacific Ocean stretched to the horizon.

"That's the port of Alsea," Brian said. He punched a code into his phone. "The sub will surface in T-minus ten minutes on the dock. Get ready to move fast. I'm going to bag some supplies, we've got a long voyage ahead of us. Any special requests?"

"Meat," Freya said.

"This is going to be such a fun trip," Alfie said, scrunching his nose.

"Wait here for me. Anything kicks off, head straight to the sub," Brian said and marched off down to the gas station.

From their vantage point, they could see it was deserted, except for a sleepy-looking teenager with his nose in a comic, manning the cash register. Brian moved efficiently up and down the aisles, throwing stuff into a basket.

"Think he's gonna struggle with getting our five-a-day in there," Tamara said. "Little health tip for you: never eat in the same place you fill up your car."

Alfie was just about to say he could use a bit of junk food when the sound of a car engine echoed down the road.

"Everybody down!" Tamara ordered and they ducked behind the trees.

"Taxi!" Tony squealed, peeking out.

Sure enough, a yellow taxi lurched on to the gas station forecourt, ground its gears and came to a jerky stop. Before any of them could react, the pot-bellied, bald driver got out, glanced around and headed inside. Brian was at the till paying for the food and the cab driver was standing behind him.

"I don't like the look of this. We should be down there," Alfie said, getting up, but Tamara stopped him.

"It's OK, Brian's got this. Look."

In the mini mart, Brian had finished paying and was headed for the exit with two large bags of food.

He barely even glanced at the cab driver. Once outside, he looked around like he couldn't remember where he'd left everyone.

"See," Tony said. "Told you there was nothing to worry about."

Tony stood up and Brian smiled, waving them down. Alfie shrugged at his mum and together they walked on to the forecourt. Only Freya stayed crouched behind a tree, sniffing the air.

"I hope you guys like microwave noodles," Tony said as he rummaged in Brian's shopping.

Alfie could hear tapping coming from somewhere nearby. He followed the sound to the back of the cab parked on the forecourt. *Tap-tap, tap-tap.* Curious, he inched open the rear door and the Scout Orb rolled out, landing at his feet. Puzzled, he picked it up.

"Hey, that's weird," said Alfie. "This looks just like. . ."

"So I guess he was nobody to worry about after all?" Tamara said to Brian, pointing at the cab driver who was standing in the mini mart, looking like he'd just woken up from a deep sleep and couldn't decide if he was still dreaming.

"No, a mere vessel, my good lady," Brian said in a high clipped voice that wasn't his own. "I bring a message."

Tamara stared in dumb shock at Brian as he un-holstered his pistol and pointed it straight at her son. Alfie froze, all the spit in his mouth drying in an instant as his stomach lurched.

"Professor Lock sends his finest regards," said Colonel Blood as he closed Brian's finger on the trigger.

But instead of the bullet hitting Alfie, it was the giant green bulk of Holgatroll that collided with him, pushing him clear.

Tamara rushed to check Alfie for bullet holes, while Holgatroll and "Brian" squared off with each other on the forecourt.

"Oh, a troll!" Colonel Blood trilled, as he waved the gun around in Brian's hand. "I've always wanted to see inside one of those!"

The fine red mist that was Colonel Blood shot out of Brian's ears, wrapped itself around the roaring great troll's head and spiralled up one of her nostrils.

Now free of Colonel Blood, Brian came to and shouted across to Alfie and Tamara: "GET TO THE DOCK!"

Alfie just had time to pick up the Scout Orb, which he'd dropped when Holgatroll rammed into him, before Tamara dragged him to his feet and together they sprinted down the road in the direction of the town. But with a high-pitched giggle, the possessed Holgatroll kicked the empty taxi towards them like it was a football. Alfie squeezed his eyes shut and prepared to become a very flat, ex-King of England. But *whomp!* the air shivered around him as Qilin materialized in a red flash and blink-shifted Alfie and his mother out of harm's way. The tumbling car smashed into a tree with a terrific crunch of metal. In the gas-station window, the confused cab driver and cashier gawped at each other.

"Where am I?" asked the cab driver.

"Alsea..." said the cashier.

"This sort of thing normal round here?"

The cashier shook his head slowly.

"What's got into Holgatroll?" Alfie shouted, still deafened by the gunshot.

"Colonel Blood!" Brian yelled. "And he's supposed to be in the Tower's dungeons!"

Hearing the name, the possessed Holgatroll snapped her head back to Brian. "Indeed, my good man, out here in this fresh air I feel positively liberated!"

Brian rolled out of the way just in time as Holgatroll leapt towards him. Qilin joined the fight, zipping around the enormous troll, ducking under the concrete-shattering punches, appearing and disappearing so fast he was a blur.

"GO!" Brian shouted from the middle of the fray.

Tamara took Alfie's hand again and pulled him along. He felt terrible; he was no use to anyone without his armour, a total sitting duck. They turned off the road and in a couple of minutes they were creeping down an alley between the houses of Alsea.

Some way behind them, the gas station exploded, sending a bright orange mini mushroom cloud into the sky. Alfie stared at it and wondered how it could be that his invasion of the UK seemed to be over before it had even begun.

"The sub. We've got to get you to the sub. That's all that matters," Tamara said, catching her breath.

Across the alleyway and at the end of a rickety-looking wooden dock, the mini submarine surfaced between two medium-sized yachts. With its blue metallic sheen, its chimney-pot periscope and assortment of ornate golden ridges and portholes, it looked more like some overgrown tropical fish than a submarine. But right now it just meant safety – if they could reach it. Alfie and his mother bolted along the dock, but suddenly a barn ahead of them was reduced to driftwood as Holgatroll smashed out of it and stood in their path.

"Sorry, Majesty, your voyage is to be a short one, alas."

Alfie thought how funny the airy voice sounded coming from the drooling cavern of Holgatroll's mouth – or rather how funny it would have been if he were not about to be killed. The troll bent her knees, preparing to leap on to them.

Groooonk! In a swirl of black feathers, Gwenn dived out of the sky on to Holgatroll, pecking at her face.

"Away with you!" Blood yelled angrily.

The troll waved her mighty arms only to find more ravens dropping out of the night sky and attacking her.

"FOUL BIRDS!" cried Blood's voice.

Alfie and Tamara hit the deck as the troll spun out of control through walls and houses in her desperate attempt to escape the whirlwind of stabbing beaks and scratching claws as the frenzied ravens protected their king. Gwenn burrowed her beak into one of the troll's ears and with a sickening pop, plucked out the red mist of Colonel Blood, freeing Holgatroll of his possession. She shook her head and rubbed her face like a dog coming round from an anaesthetic.

The red mist shrieked in anger and shot towards Alfie and his mum – but the ravens weren't done with Blood yet. They circled him, pecking at the crimson particles.

"No! Vile creatures! Stop!" the disembodied Colonel Blood cried.

But his voice was weakening as the ravens split his foggy form into smaller and smaller clouds and harried them into the sky and far away out of sight. Alfie remembered the Ravenmaster once telling him that a flock of ravens was known as an "unkindness", and seeing them go after Colonel Blood, that seemed like an understatement.

"Everyone all right?" Brian said as he and Tony ran up behind them.

Holgatroll had transformed back into Freya. She was rubbing her sore ear, confused.

"What on earth happened?"

"You all saved me, that's what happened. Look, I just want to say thanks—" said Alfie.

"Save the speeches for later. Everybody onboard," Brian ordered and led them down the wooden dock to the submarine.

The ravens had returned and were perched proudly on the small communication mast, preening themselves. Gwenn *gronked* and demanded a pat for her night's work.

"Thanks, Gwenn. How about we head home?" Alfie said and clambered on board.

A few minutes later, on a hill overlooking the town, the mist that was Colonel Blood reformed and watched the submarine sail silently out of the harbour then disappear beneath the waves.

"Fare thee well, young Alfred. We shall meet again."

II

THE SEARCH FOR WYVERN

"God save the King!" the beefeaters bellowed as Alfie entered the bustling Keep.

It felt like a long time since he'd seen them all, but nothing seemed to have changed. Old-fashioned telephones jangled above the low murmur of conversation and LC leaned over the huge ops table map, keeping a check on the country's defences.

"All is well, sir. Perhaps you'd care for a cup of tea?" LC said, idly stirring sugar into his cup without looking up.

"Awesome," Alfie replied.

Come to think of it, he hadn't seen LC in a while either, and it felt so good to be with him again.

Resisting the weird urge to give the old man a hug, Alfie joined him at the map.

"And a slice of cake, if there's any going."

"Oh, I should think so, Your Maj—" LC froze, as if someone had just hit pause on a remote control.

"LC? You all right?" Alfie said.

The Keep suddenly felt very cold. Alfie spun around and saw that all the Yeoman Warders were also rooted to the spot in eerie silence. It was like being in the middle of a bunch of dead-eyed shop mannequins. Was it a spell? An attack? Alfie sprinted to the Arena, weaving his way through his frozen friends. He had to find the regalia and transform into the Defender, but as he threw back the heavy curtain, he found to his horror that the old display case was broken and empty. And somewhere, at the very edge of his hearing, a horse was whinnying. Wyvern! Her snorts and neighs were lonely, desperate, unbearable to hear—

Alfie woke from the nightmare, sat up and cracked his skull against one of the submarine's iron bulkheads. Somehow he didn't shout out. Probably because over the past few days of living below the waves, he'd got used to knocking his head, tripping over and stubbing his toes. The small submarine's interior might have looked luxurious at first glance, like a Victorian wooden yacht, but really it was all for show. The wood panels didn't quite conceal the brass dials and awkward old levers that were just at the right height to give you a dead leg when you walked by.

Alfie rubbed his forehead and stared at the rivets above his old rope hammock. He'd been having these dreams ever since they left America, and the closer they got to Britain, the weirder and more intense they'd become. Ellie. Hayley. Herne. LC. Where were they? Would he see ever them again? Had they survived?

"Owl pellets are actually quite delicious," Tony announced confidently.

But he was only sleep talking, tucked away in his own hammock strung between two banks of dials. Nearby, Tamara was also asleep and the sound of Freya's thunderous snores came from the submarine's only cabin. Its door had a small gold crown attached to it indicating it was meant for the King or Queen of Great Britain, but that hadn't stopped Freya commandeering it for herself.

"You want my help getting rid of your country's Viking problem? Then I need my beauty sleep," she'd announced pretty much as soon as they'd boarded. They hadn't seen much of her since, except for dinner time, when she'd eaten not only her portion but everyone's leftovers as well. *Probably a good thing she has her own cabin come to think of it*, thought Alfie.

Alfie shivered. A chilly breeze swept through the submarine, which could only mean one thing. They'd surfaced to recharge the batteries and the top hatch was open. Alfie swung his legs off his hammock and promptly whacked his foot on the Scout Orb, which sat on the floor beneath his bunk. Stifling a yell of pain, he tiptoed past his sleeping companions and squeezed down a narrow corridor, being sure to mind his step this time. On the bridge, he ducked under the periscope and climbed the ladder up to the conning tower, where Brian stood, gazing out across the sea. The submarine was sailing slowly between the huge steel towers of a silent, offshore wind farm. High above them, Gwenn and the rest of the ravens settled on the idle turbine blades and preened their feathers. Appearing whenever the submarine surfaced, they never seemed to get tired.

"Any idea where we are?" asked Alfie.

"This is the Beatrice Wind Farm," replied Brian. "We're fourteen miles off the coast of Scotland. Welcome home, Your Majesty."

Overhead, clouds swept across a bright half moon, periodically illuminating the sea in every direction, except one.

"Is that what I think it is?" Alfie asked.

A few miles to the south, a sick-looking, green fog churned, reaching hundreds of feet into the air, obscuring any sight of land. A breeze brought with it a familiar, foul reek of rotten fish and spoiled milk. Alfie shuddered as his memories of fighting the undead Vikings came flooding back.

"Somewhere beyond all that filthy cloud is your kingdom . . . not to mention about a couple of million brainwashed berserkers," Brian said and immediately wished he hadn't.

Even in the dim moonlight, the bodyguard could see Alfie clench his jaw and turn white. It had been a long, tiring voyage from the Pacific Ocean, across the icy Northwest Passage and down to the coast of Britain, with cramped, slow days spent under the waves. When they weren't sleeping, they were huddled around maps of the UK, busy planning how to win back the kingdom. An approach up the River Thames from the English Channel seemed to be the best idea, followed by a smash-and-grab raid for Alfie's Crown Jewels at the Tower of London and then an attempt to retrieve the Raven Banner from Parliament and put an end to the berserker curse and the magical miasma that lay across Britain. That was the theory at least; in truth there were a thousand ifs and buts. They didn't know if they could slip in undetected past the Viking longships, they didn't even know if Lock had moved the Crown Jewels from the Keep. The closer they got to the UK, the quieter Alfie had become.

Brian patted him on the shoulder. "Courage, lad."

"I'm not ready," Alfie murmured.

"Rubbish. I've seen you in action against those monsters. You get your armour back and you can take them on, no worries."

"The armour's not enough. I need Wyvern."

"Batteries are fully charged. We should dive," Brian said, ignoring him.

They'd been through this. The plan to take back Britain did not involve searching for Alfie's ghost horse. The precious magical spurs that housed her were lost under the sea months ago during Alfie's oil rig battle with the Black Dragon, and who knew where the current had taken them? They could be anywhere, buried under several tons of North Sea mud by now. It was hard, but Alfie would have to get used to not having Wyvern any more.

"You don't understand," Alfie pleaded, as Brian ushered him down the ladder and pulled the hatch shut.

"Try me."

"I don't like being this useless."

"Never bothered you before, boss," Brian said with a wink.

"I'm serious. Back there when Blood attacked, all I could do was run away."

"Sometimes running away is the smart move," Brian said and pulled the lever that flooded the ballast tanks.

Alfie did his best to ignore the lurch in his stomach as the submarine dived. "Yeah, but not for the Defender. I'm meant to be a leader, aren't I? How am I supposed to win back the kingdom without all my powers?"

"We don't have time to wait for you to feel ready," said Brian, impatient. "The longer we dawdle here, the greater the chance we're spotted. We have to get ashore pronto."

"But we're going to sail right past where I lost her, aren't we?" Alfie said, tracing his finger down one of the maps, along the coast of Scotland to London and the mouth of the Thames. "I know she's still out there, Brian. I can hear her, she's calling for me."

"Maybe horse whispering runs in the family," said Tamara, joining them on the bridge.

"And Alfie *is* king," Tony added, with a yawn, close behind her. "Which means you have to do what he says."

Alfie stepped between Tony and Brian. "Listen,

you're in charge, Brian. If you say it's impossible, I'll accept that. But if there's even the slightest chance we could find Wyvern... I couldn't live with myself if we didn't at least try."

Brian furrowed his brow, sighed and studied the charts on the map table. "I can plot a course that goes via the rig site, in theory. I still say it's a waste of time, but... Very well, Your Majesty." Brian said with a mock bow. "Full steam ahead."

A few hours later and Alfie was squeezing into a bulky, rigid outfit that looked like a cross between a suit of armour and an old-fashioned robot. Brian said it was made from magnesium alloy and was actually called an "atmospheric diving suit".

"I don't want to worry you, Alfie-betti-spaghetti, but it says 'made in 1931' on here," said Tony as he examined the huge helmet with its thick, porthole visor.

"It's old tech, but it's functional," Brian said. "I hope."

"Oh, very funny," Alfie replied.

But his words were lost as Brian screwed the helmet in place. Inside the musty suit, it was exactly the opposite of being in the Defender armour. That was like wearing your favourite old T-shirt, whereas this felt like he had a dishwasher strapped to his back. Every movement was a monumental struggle.

"You'll move easier when you're outside of the sub," Brian said, his voice coming in tinny over a communication link. "Now step into the escape trunk. And good luck."

Tamara watched nervously as Alfie lumbered into the small airlock and the door was clamped shut behind him. In front of him another door unscrewed itself and, with a *whoosh*, everything went black and Alfie was floating down towards the sea floor. Even though the sub was pretty close to the bottom already, the drop felt like it took for ever.

Alfie's breathing came in small gasps as he prayed the old suit wouldn't spring a leak. It was so dark down here, he couldn't tell if his eyes were open or closed.

"Um, guys, I think I should have brought a torch!" Alfie said.

"On it," Brian said over the comms and a powerful headlamp on the top of the suit blinked on, casting a beam of light across the ocean floor.

"Oh wow," said Alfie.

"Have you found the spurs?!" Tony said, his voice filling the inside of Alfie's helmet. "I knew you would. You have, haven't you?"

"No, I mean 'oh wow', as in there's literally nothing here."

Everywhere Alfie looked was just a murky desolation of mud and rocks. It was like being on another planet and a grim and intensely cold one at that. A large crab scuttled for cover as Alfie stamped past.

"Keep heading out. You're now right under the rig site," Brian said.

Sure enough, the further Alfie waded from the sub, the more debris he found. Steel girders were jumbled together in rusting piles. He dug down in the mud and found old plastic safety hats, lengths of pipe and miles of twisted wiring tangled together. Alfie burrowed his gloves into the mud and pulled out clumps of jagged metal, torn lengths of canvas, all of it blackened by fire. Dragon's fire. Alfie shuddered as despair rose up inside him. Brian was right; this was hopeless. There was no way he could find the spurs down here, even if he searched for a year or two or three—

"Call for her, Alfie." It was his mother on the comms now. "Call for Wyvern."

"Honestly, Mum. There's nothing out here."

"You said yourself, you can hear her. Just try it."

In the atmospheric suit, Alfie sighed. What did he have to lose?

"Wyvern?!" Alfie shouted. "WYVERN?"

A curious black fish swam into the beam of the

headlamp and darted away.

"Really? That's how you spoke to her?" Tamara asked.

"When she was trying to throw me off her back, yeah, pretty much."

"Don't talk at her, talk *with* her. Like she's there. Remember what that was like. How she felt. Crouch down, keep your voice soft and slow."

Feeling a little silly, Alfie crouched down like he'd seen his mum do at the ranch and closed his eyes.

"Wyvern ... come on, girl," Alfie murmured and made a clicking noise with his cheek and tongue. But there was nothing out there, just the slosh of water around the heavy diving suit and a weird clomping sound, probably old girders clunking together in the current.

"Sorry, Alfie, I'm calling it. Head back to the sub," Brian said after a while.

"Wait!" Alfie said. The clomping sound was louder and it wasn't girders; it sounded like hooves. And there was something else: a distant whinny and a snort. Alfie spun around, trying to shine the headlamp in every direction at once.

"Wyvern?"

There! Something was burrowing towards him through the mud, churning up sediment, the sound of hooves now unmistakable even through the water.

A crab scurried out of the way as a flash of silver broke the surface of the sea floor, exploded out and arrowed through the air straight towards Alfie. He reached out on instinct and something sharp and hard smacked into his hand. The spurs!

"Wyvern!" Alfie shouted with delight as the sound of whinnying and contented snorts filled the suit. He turned the spurs over in his hands; they were as pristine and clean as if he'd plucked them out of the regalia cabinet in the Tower.

Back on the sub, a whooping Tony jumped up and down and Tamara shook her head in wonder. Even Brian was smiling. He was about to order Alfie back to the sub when a loud *PING* rattled one of the dials. Brian leapt over to the brass console and studied it. A large green blob had appeared on the radar and it was heading straight towards them.

"Incoming! That's a big signal. Alfie, back to the sub!"

On the sea floor, Alfie wrenched his eyes from the spurs and looked around. "Is it on the surface?"

"Negative. Get back to the sub NOW!" Brian shouted.

Alfie turned around in the suit and started the long, slow trudge back.

"Hurry, Alfie!" Tamara said as radar pings started to come faster and louder.

"Going as fast as I can!" Alfie said as he heaved his legs on, one step at a time, conscious of the fact that he couldn't easily turn his head to see whatever was coming up behind him. He was breathing hard now and sweating; it was like one of those nightmares where you're desperately trying to run from something you can't see, but your legs are ten times heavier than usual.

Alfie stopped to catch his breath and glanced back. Big mistake. Now he could see what was heading his way.

"VIKINGS!" Alfie screamed.

A longship was ploughing through the depths, the huge zombie crew pumping the oars. At the prow stood the Viking captain, ripped dead skin and stringy black hair billowing out behind him in the water. He raised his axe and pointed it straight at Alfie. This was just the shot of adrenaline Alfie needed and he picked up the pace. The sub emerged out of the gloom in front of him, light glowing through the portholes, twenty feet away.

"ALFIE!" Tamara yelled.

Ten feet. Alfie couldn't see it but the longship felt very close now. He expected to feel the blade of an axe in his back any second. Five feet, three feet, but no blow fell on him as he hauled himself into the airlock and the hatch swung shut behind him.

"I'm in!" Alfie gasped, just as the longship slammed into the submarine with a crunch and groan of metal.

Alfie lost his balance in the diving suit and fell over, still clutching the spurs.

"Full power!" Brian yelled and shoved a lever forward.

"More of them coming in!" Tamara shouted as she peered out of one of the small portholes.

Two more longships had emerged out of the gloom and were making a beeline for the submarine. They were trapped.

"Fire the torpedoes!" Tony squealed.

"We don't have any!" Brian yelled back.

"What kind of submarine is this?" Tony said to himself.

Freya stormed out of her cabin. "I'm trying to get some sleep!"

SLAM. Another longship rammed into the submarine, shaking the rivets and knocking them all off their feet.

"On the scale of one to ten, how bad is a leak on a submarine?" Alfie said as he crawled from the airlock and pointed at a stream of water gushing between the rivets.

"I suppose I'll have to deal with this," sighed Freya, and before anyone could ask what she meant, her emerald necklace glowed green and her arms began growing like the roots of a Norwegian pine tree filmed in super-fast time-lapse. Freya's neck elongated horribly as a huge, warty nose grew out of her face.

"Gross!" Tony said, staring in wonder, as Holgatroll filled the cabin with not only her size, but her wet earth troll stink as well.

"Cover your ears," grumbled Holgatroll.

She threw back her head and let out a sound that started as a roar so loud it shook your ribcage, rose through the octaves until it was a painfully high-pitched, then dropped down again like whale song. It was a sound none of them had heard Holgatroll make before.

Outside the submarine, the Viking captain laughed as the troll's demented howl shook the water.

"Ekki hræðumsk ek trǫllusǫngva! Drekkit þeim!"*

The longships manoeuvred into position, ready to ram the submarine and split it in half.

Brian looked around the cabin, alarmed. "Tony, can you blink shift us out of here?"

"Not all of you," Tony said. "Besides, we're too deep, the pressure would..." He mimed his head exploding.

---

* "I am not afraid of troll music! Drown them!"

"What you asking the squirt for? I told you, I'm handling it," grunted Holgatroll.

Just then, another strange sound reverberated through the water, piercing the hull of the sub. High-pitched, eerie and echoing.

"Is that a whale?" Alfie said.

"Even better," said Holgatroll through her fangs, and she laughed, sending gusts of hot meaty breath around the sub. "It's Selma."

"I don't get it," said Tony.

"No way! Nessie?" Alfie shouted happily.

Outside the sub, the longships reached ramming speed just as the great sea monster appeared, answering Holgatroll's call. Three times their size, Nessie shattered the first Viking boat with a lazy flick of her scaly tail, scattering the crew in the water. Wrapping her huge neck around the second like a boa constrictor, she squeezed and snapped its rotten timbers, then head-butted the third longship, crushing it to pieces. Helpless, confused zombie Vikings wandered the seabed like lost tourists. Her work complete, Nessie swam alongside the sub, escorting it away. Inside, Holgatroll transformed back into Freya and put her palm against a porthole, where Nessie's giant eye appeared, peering in. The others looked on, astonished.

"That's my girl," Freya said, as Nessie swam away, back into the depths.

Alfie caressed the intricately embossed gold of the spurs in his hands. He could feel Wyvern sleeping, peaceful and content. "Freya, I don't know how to thank you," he said.

"You can thank me by keeping it down, please. I'm going back to bed."

And with that, the Norwegian queen turned on her heel, strode back into her cabin and slammed the door.

12

GUNPOWDER, TREASON AND PLOT

"Wake up! Princess Eleanor! Wake up!"

Ellie woke, startled to see the Jailor leaning over her bed, shaking her. At first she thought she was still dreaming. It had taken her hours to get to sleep, as her mind raced trying to understand how Alfie could be dead, and trying to work out why Richard was acting so cold and heartless. He had been like a stranger to her. When sleep came at last, it was filled with disturbing nightmares, so it was only the musty smell of the Jailor's breath that made her realize she was awake and this was real. Gasping in shock, she sprang up against the wall.

"What do you want?"

Over his shoulder she could see the cell door was

hanging open. Ellie leapt off the bed, delivering an efficient punch to his mouth as she went, and ran out. The glowing light from the ball of keys hanging at the centre of the antechamber was blinding after the darkness of her cell. Growls and hoots from the other prisoners filled Ellie's ears as she shielded her eyes and spun around, trying to pick out an exit.

"Hold up, girl!" hissed the Jailor, as he stumbled from the cell. "I'll help you get out, but you have to keep your trap shut, or we'll both lose our heads."

He took out a grubby handkerchief and dabbed his bleeding lip.

"Blimey, you ain't half got a decent right hook for such a scrawny little thing."

Ellie backed away, on guard.

"Maybe if you fed me more than that gruel, I'd be bigger," she snapped back. "Why are you suddenly helping me now, anyway?"

"Sorry, Your Highness, but I couldn't risk it before. I had to keep the professor sweet to make sure he didn't let any of these nutcases out."

A snarl came from behind the nearest door. The Jailor kicked it with his heel.

"Stick a paw in it or I'll dock yer tail!"

"OK, I'm listening," said Ellie.

"After he released our friend the Colonel, I

realized this geezer's going to do whatever he wants anyway. No sense in you getting caught up in it any longer. The Keep should be quiet this time of night – there's a tunnel you can use to get out. Here."

He passed her a crumpled piece of paper with a map of the Keep scrawled on it.

"Aren't you coming?"

The Jailor shrugged. "Nah, my place is here. If they ever got out, the horrors behind these doors would make them Vikings look like a pack of Girl Guides."

"Hey, I was in the Girl Guides. We're tougher than we look," said Ellie. She turned to go, then looked back. "What's your name?"

The Jailor seemed to need to think about it for a moment, as if it had been so long since anyone had asked, that he'd forgotten. "Sid," he said eventually. "Just Sid."

"Thank you, Sid." Ellie smiled.

Sid was right about the Keep: it was quiet. But it wasn't empty. A Viking draugar was slouched asleep over one half of the broken ops table, his rattling snores echoing off the high walls of the Map Room. Ellie checked her map – the tunnel entrance was in the corridor beyond. Padding through the wreckage of the beefeaters' work stations, she tried to stay focused, but she couldn't help taking in the startling tapestries hanging on the walls either side: bizarre images of what looked like the Defender in famous moments from British history. She didn't know it, but Professor Lock had chosen to switch the tapestries to the worst Defenders – monarchs who had chosen to use their powers for evil. There was Edward the First, "Hammer of the Scots", who was posing with a miserable, chained-up Loch Ness Monster. Then there was a drunk King John, holding out one hand to levitate an oak desk and the long scroll of the Magna Carta over a group of terrified barons. On the opposite wall hung the tapestry of "Bloody" Mary the First, who appeared to be attacking a town beneath white cliffs, opposed by plucky townsfolk in striped jumpers carrying burning torches and a banner which read "We wunt be druv!", whatever that meant.

Ellie couldn't understand what all this was doing here, beneath the Tower of London, but she had no intention of hanging around to find out. She held her breath as she tiptoed past the slumbering Viking, in case the stench might make her cough and wake him. She was almost at the door when heavy footsteps and long shadows filled the stone corridor ahead. Ellie backed up, stepping right on the foot of the sleeping draugar.

"Yargh!" he cried, rubbing his eyes as he sat up.

Ellie ducked and crawled behind the table. Hearing the approaching patrol, the dozy Viking heaved himself up and searched around for his axe. Ellie took her chance and darted for the nearest exit, bounding up some steps and out of sight just before the other Vikings stomped into the Keep. She could hear them arguing in a strange language as she crept higher up the cold stone spiral staircase.

The gust of fresh air that met her face as she emerged on to the top of the tower was so welcome after months in the cell, that Ellie nearly didn't see the gaping hole at her feet and the hundred-foot drop to the flagstones below. She gripped the door frame and stepped carefully around the gap, shivering in the biting wind. A harsh snowfall blew across the Tower of London, dusting the walls like icing sugar. But as her eyes adjusted to the dark again, Ellie could see that the once-proud silhouette of the fortress was now jagged and broken, clad in scaffolding like an unruly set of teeth in braces. It was a shocking sight – the central White Tower was almost completely demolished, the outer towers and walls less so. A mixed band of berserkers and human builders were shuffling to and fro in the lanes below, carrying brick hods and pushing wheelbarrows of stone. A Viking draugar thundered up and down the lines of workers, yelling.

"BYGGIÐ ÁKAFLEGRI! ENDA ÞÉR GEFUM VÉR HUNDUNUM!"*

Ellie ducked down as a pair of burly builders hurried along the battlements just beneath the tower.

"He can yell all he wants," said one of them. "The cement won't set and the stone won't hold. This place don't want to be rebuilt..."

Ellie kicked herself for not having called out to them; they were too far away to hear her now. Maybe they would have helped her escape. But then again, maybe they would have turned her in. She was crouched on top of the Devereux Tower at the northwest corner of the fortress, overlooking the outer wall. Ellie was surprised to see that the moat was now full, water lapping amid patches of ice. If she could climb down closer, maybe she could jump in. The thought made her knees go weak. She hadn't been swimming since she nearly drowned last spring, when the Black Dragon attacked the Boat Race. She'd survived the fall from Hammersmith Bridge, with the Defender's help, but she couldn't believe she was contemplating another high dive.

A huge shadow was approaching from across the river. It passed over the darkened, empty Tower Bridge and descended on bat-like wings, whipping

---

* "BUILD FASTER! OR WE'LL FEED YOU TO THE DOGS!"

up tornadoes of snow from the rooftops. Ellie froze in terror — the Black Dragon was coming straight towards her tower. She thought it had been killed in the battle at Alfie's coronation. How could it be here? There was nowhere to hide, and if she ran for the stairs now it would surely see her. She swung herself over the side of the roof. Finding a narrow ledge, she pulled herself down, clinging on to the wet stone with her fingertips. There was nothing between her and the cobbled lane far below and she would be plainly visible to any Viking patrol that passed outside the Tower. The impact as the Dragon landed shook her feet from the ledge and for a moment she dangled by one hand. Heaving herself back against the wall, she could hear the deep, rattling purr of the Dragon as it settled on the roof. It was so close she could feel the heat from its fiery throat.

Meanwhile, only a few miles downriver, a hearse, escorted by four black cabs, was turning into Parliament Square. In the back seat of the leading cab, Hayley was shocked to see the ominous sight of Big Ben up close — a pulsating red beacon, crisscrossed with hideous, glowing scars, pumping out its Norse blood magic. The famous green lawn of the square had turned black, the roads and pavements cracked with the crimson tendrils that spread out in all directions from the base of the tower. Hayley was relieved to see that their target, the phone box, was still in place on the pavement leading to Westminster Bridge. But before they could get close they would have to negotiate one of Lock's new security checkpoints that had sprung up across the city.

The funeral cortege crawled towards the checkpoint, rumbling over rips in the asphalt as it approached a repurposed guardsman's hut. The collaborator guard, a short, bald man, flanked by an especially ugly Viking draugar, stepped into the path of the convoy and raised his hand. To emphasize the point, the Viking shook his axe in the air and let out a long roar.

Hayley lowered the black veil over her face and rested her head on LC's shoulder.

"Talk about hiding in plain sight," she said.

"Last chance to change your minds," whispered Ged from the front.

"The plan is sound," said LC. "We proceed."

"You're the boss. But I'll be expecting a proper tip," said the cabbie.

The convoy came to a halt and the checkpoint guard marched past the hearse and up to the first cab's window. Ged lowered the window and leant out, grinning.

"Evening, guv'nor."

The guard peered into the cab with his angry little red face, brow furrowed all the way up to the top of his shiny scalp. He was wearing what looked like a traffic warden's uniform with a large Viking brooch crudely pinned over the "Westminster Council" badge.

"What's all this?" he barked.

"Funeral, chief," replied the cabbie innocently.

Right on cue, Hayley started sobbing. The guard recoiled for a moment.

"But you can't just... I mean, this is— Where are you going?" he bleated at them, his voice rising an octave.

"That's my fault, officer," LC interjected, talking as slowly as he could. "You see the deceased, my dear departed wife, was in a nursing home in Woolwich, but our church is in Watford – St Barnabas. Do you know it?"

"What? No. Listen, you can't just... It's after curfew!"

Hayley wailed louder.

"My poor granddaughter was too upset to come out of her room, I'm afraid," LC droned on. "It caused something of a delay. I am sorry for the inconvenience."

The Viking pointed at the coffin in the back of the hearse and laughed.

"Grafa þeir líkamar jörðinni eins ok skikkjurakkana! Brenna skyldi þeir bátunum eins ok eðlilegt er!"*

The guard rolled his eyes.

"Fine, but get a move on. And don't come back this way!"

He scuttled off and ordered the Viking to lift the barrier. The convoy drove through, honking a cheery "thank you" as it passed the checkpoint.

Hayley whipped off her veil and dried her cheeks.

"Excellent performance, Miss Hicks," said LC.

"Yeah, you should win an Oscar for that, love," added Ged. "Look lively, here we are."

As they approached the red phone box, the hearse driver cut his engine and glided to a halt. The cabs fanned out behind him, blocking the hearse's rear doors from sight.

"Wish me luck," said Hayley, reaching for the handle.

LC took her hand for a moment.

"If anything goes awry there is no dishonour in retreating. Live to fight another day."

Hayley was touched by how worried he looked.

"Don't worry. Just take care of Gran for me, yeah?"

Hayley's gran had already been cremated and her

---

* "They bury their dead in the ground like lapdogs! They should burn them on boats like normal people!"

ashes were safely tucked away in a box beneath the front seat.

"You have my word, Miss Hicks." LC nodded.

Hayley climbed out. The cabbies had already opened the rear doors of the hearse and were pulling the coffin out. Hayley watched as they eased the lid off, revealing the three large black holdalls inside. She stepped past them without a word and entered the phone box.

At the checkpoint the Viking grunted and pointed at the stationary cars on the far side of Parliament Square.

"What now?" said the guard, putting down his mug and looking over his shoulder.

A jet of weak tea spouted from his mouth all over the Viking's back as he hurried to grab his hat.

The interior of the phone box was dirty and cramped and smelled of something Hayley didn't want to think about. She lifted the heavy plastic receiver and checked the first number she had written on the back of her hand – 871 – "easy to remember", according to LC, because it was the year King Alfred the Great ascended to the throne. She dialled the number and remembered just in time to place her feet as far apart as she could. The floor in the phone box slid away, revealing a dark hole beneath. One of the cabbies wheeled the first holdall into the phone

160

box and towards the hole. For a moment it got wedged in place, until Hayley gave it a sharp kick and it fell through. The cabbie raised his eyebrows at her in relief, and turned to get the next bag.

On the other side of the barricade of cabs, Ged lifted his bonnet and pretended to be working on the engine. The checkpoint official was hurrying towards them, waving his hands.

"You can't stop there! What are you doing?"

Ged intercepted him before he could get past, handing him an oily dipstick.

"Sorry, mate, engine trouble. Reckon it might be the oil level, what do you think?"

The startled official held the dipstick at arm's length as if it were a venomous snake.

"I don't know! If Lord Protector Lock sees all this. . ."

The Viking bent down, sniffed the dipstick and licked it as if it were an ice lolly.

"Ekki illr. . ."* he grunted.

At the back of the hearse, the other cabbies were struggling to pull the third and final holdall out of the coffin. In the phone box, Hayley waited anxiously. Together the cabbies wrenched the bag out, but it clattered against the side of the hearse. The guard

---

* "Not bad. . ."

161

heard it and strained his neck to try to see round the cabs.

"What was that?"

"Just the lads taking a cheeky tea break, probably," said Ged, none too convincingly. "Here, maybe it's the spark plugs. What do you reckon?"

But the guard pushed past him, heading round the screen of cabs. In the phone box, Hayley watched the last holdall fall through the hole, donned a head torch and checked the second number on the back of her hand. LC had stressed the importance of dialling it before she climbed down, as it would close the floor after her. But to her horror, Hayley saw that with all the effort of off-loading the bags, the last two digits had become smudged with sweat. The first was an eight, the second maybe a six or nine, but the third was completely rubbed away. If she got it wrong the floor wouldn't close and they'd all be caught red-handed. It was the end date of King Alfred's reign, but what was it? She stuck her head back out of the phone box and looked to the back of the first cab. But LC wasn't there; he was busy helping Ged delay the increasingly frustrated guard's progress round the cabs. He took the guard's hand and gripped on to it, shaking it warmly.

"I just wanted to thank you for your understanding," blustered LC. "I know a lot of people call your sort rather unkind names like quisling and collaborator, but not me. You've been most helpful."

"Eh, get off me!" said the guard in a shrill voice, pulling his hand back. "Now let me past!"

The cabbies meanwhile were debating the date of King Alfred's death.

"Was it 1066?" offered one in a whisper.

"That was the Battle of Hastings, you numpty," whispered another. "What school did you go to?"

Hayley could see she was going to have to remember herself.

She pressed the first two numbers in – 8 ... 9 – then closed her eyes and focused. 871 to 89. . . 89. . . 899! That was it. She punched in the last nine and dropped through the hole, landing on the soft bags in the tunnel a few feet below.

"You – move them out of the way!" yelled the guard to the Viking.

The undead Norseman pounded forward, heaving a cab aside with each hand, and pulled the hearse away from the curb to reveal ... the undisturbed coffin, rear doors closed and three cabbies sipping tea from their thermos mugs next to the empty phone box. The guard marched forward, looking at them suspiciously, then jumped as Ged slammed his cab bonnet shut.

"All fixed! Tea break's over, lads."

The cabbies got back in their cabs and started their engines.

"Sorry for the trouble!" called Ged.

The breathless guard watched as the convoy pulled away and drove out of Parliament Square. As it turned the corner, he saw the dotty old man sitting in the back of the hearse, but he couldn't see the girl with him. The guard spun back to the phone box and pulled the door open. Inside all seemed normal, except for one thing – the receiver was hanging loose. He picked it up, inspected it and replaced it on its cradle.

Six feet below, Hayley waited till she heard the clunk of the phone box's door closing before she dared to move. She unzipped the first bag and checked the black, grainy contents – gunpowder. They had spent the last few nights retrieving it from its hiding place in Woolwich, south of the river. While Ged kept lookout from his cab, his mates had helped them access the secret store beneath a block of luxury flats that stood on the site of the former Master Gunner of England's mansion. LC explained that for hundreds of years this had been where the gunpowder for the king's cannons had been stored and that when it was closed, the then Defender, Queen Grace, decided to leave some there in case of emergencies.

Smart lady, thought Hayley as she zipped up the bag, heaved it on to its wheels and started to pull it down the long, narrow tunnel towards Parliament's cellars. It would take her half the night to make the trip there and back three times, but if she succeeded, then the Raven Banner would be destroyed and the first real blow against Lock's evil regime would have been struck.

13

HUNG, DRAWN AND QUARTERED

One hour earlier, anyone caring to gaze at the dark waters below Tower Bridge would have seen what looked like the smooth, glistening back of a small whale break the ice and bob to the surface. Luckily for the occupants of the mini-sub, there had been no traffic over the bridge for months, and Brian was able to dock at the wharf unseen. Centuries before, the "Pool of London", as the stretch of river between London Bridge and Tower Bridge was known, would have been packed with the tall masts of cargo ships bringing in coal from the north and sugar from the West Indies. There were said to be so many ships that you could cross the river without getting your feet wet.

Tonight there were only five travellers disembarking,

but they made a strange band – a Norwegian queen, the heir to the defunct Chinese throne, the deposed British king and his mother, all led ashore by a disgraced bodyguard and former King's Armourer. The ravens circled, then settled on the wooden posts of the wharf, pecking at barnacles and resting their wings after their long fight. Alfie noticed Gwenn peer at the dark silhouette of the nearby Tower of London's walls, then ruffle her feathers and turn away as if sad – did she think it wasn't her home any more, he wondered? The young king took his first step on to home soil since his exile, slipped on the slimy planks and fell on his backside.

"That can't be a good omen," he said, as his mum helped him to his feet.

"Don't worry, sweetie," said Tamara, brushing him clean. "William the Conqueror did the exact same thing the first time he set foot on an English beach."

"Mum, leave it, I'm fine," said Alfie, embarrassed.

"Actually, it is a good comparison," said Queen Freya, "because like him, we are now the invading force."

She was gazing downriver at the crimson glow thrown into the sky from Big Ben – it reminded her of the spectacular Northern Lights from her homeland, but there was nothing wonderful about this evil counterpart.

"First we take back His Majesty's regalia, then we go for your banner," said Brian, fixing her with a stern stare. "Agreed?"

The others looked to Freya, nervous, but she shrugged. "Fine. Your turf, your rules." She strode off the wharf, towards the Tower, then stopped and looked back at them, arching a long eyebrow. "Come on then; some of us have our own kingdoms to get back to."

As the submarine engaged its autopilot and submerged beneath the ice once more, the invaders crept away from the river.

The riverside was strangely quiet and at first it was easy to pass unnoticed as they picked their way through the streets. But the area around the Tower of London's walls was much busier. The group ducked into an alleyway as a truck ferrying stone rumbled past them. Alfie peeked out to see lines of exhausted builders marching to and fro, flanked by their Viking masters. Some brave market traders had set up stalls in the shadows of the now darkened shopfronts and were selling soup and bread to the workers. Some appeared to be doing a good trade, even if a berserker would occasionally lumber up, scattering the customers and helping themselves, unchallenged.

"We're too conspicuous like this," said Brian, worried. "We need to split up."

Tamara pointed at a pub on the corner that seemed

168

to be back in use, with market traders, builders and berserkers coming and going.

"Safety in numbers?" she said.

Brian nodded. "You and Her Majesty wait for us there. We'll see if we can get into the Keep through the sally-port." He turned to Freya. "And no, er, 'transformations' unless things go really pear-shaped, if you don't mind."

Freya scowled at him, then took Tamara's arm and headed for the pub.

Brian turned to Alfie and Tony. "Right, boys. Walk like you have a purpose. Not too much, though – like we're just going home, not planning on raiding the Tower, if you know what I mean."

"Determined, but casual?" asked Tony, looking nervous.

"Can we just get it over with?" asked Alfie, pulling his cap low.

"We'll be fine, trust me," said Brian.

The three of them strolled – in a purposeful, yet relaxed way – heading across the square that ran alongside the moat, past the empty ticket office, within inches of slobbering berserkers and stomping Viking draugar.

The Hung, Drawn and Quartered pub was bustling with activity, boorish Community Earls and collaborators enjoying a night off. If it hadn't been for the possessed berserkers crunching on pool cues like breadsticks, and the undead Vikings thumping the tables and singing hearty battle songs in guttural Old Norse, you might have mistaken it for an average Friday night in the city. The young barmaid ignored the pair of berserkers smashing glasses over each other's heads and turned her weary gaze to the new customers.

"No credit cards, no cash. Gold, silver or jewellery only."

Freya's hand slipped protectively over the emerald necklace concealed beneath her shirt. But Tamara smiled, removed a silver ring from her finger and slid it across the bar.

"What's good?" she asked.

"The mead seems popular these days," shrugged the barmaid.

She held Tamara's gaze for a moment, a flicker of recognition in her eyes. But if she knew who the ex-queen was, she didn't say anything. Instead she poured them their drinks and went to deal with the berserker who was bending the beer taps over with his teeth. Freya took a sip from her glass and recoiled from the sweet taste of the viscous yellow liquid.

"Urgh, they really are barbarians round here."

Tamara laughed and downed her drink. "I'd forgotten how much I missed English pubs."

Meanwhile, Alfie was amazed to find that they had made it all the way to the shadows of the Merchant Navy Memorial on Tower Hill without anyone so much as looking twice at them.

"Ha, you were right," he said, relieved. "Guess they're all too busy to care about three more homeless chaps."

"Actually," said Brian, wiping his brow, "I was sure we'd get caught. We got lucky."

He hurried to the concealed tunnel entrance that led under the moat and into the Keep beneath the Tower, and pressed the release stone, but nothing happened.

"What's wrong?" asked Alfie.

"I don't know," said Brian. "It must have been sealed. The professor is no fool."

"So what do we do now?"

"Duck!" blurted Tony, pointing to the sky.

Alfie and Brian followed his gaze to see the Black Dragon flying high over the river and banking in their direction. Alarmed, they pinned themselves behind the wall, but when they peeked out again they saw that the Dragon was not aiming for them. It had landed on top of the corner of Devereux Tower.

Looking at the glossy dark scales of the reptilian beast, Alfie was instantly back on the oil rig months earlier, facing off with Richard, begging him to resist the evil that had infected his body, sure that he could save him. He recalled the swell of horror in his stomach when he realized he had failed and the Dragon opened its jaws and blasted him with fire, sending him tumbling into the sea far below. He still found it hard to believe that trapped somewhere inside that nightmarish creature was his brother.

"Who's that?" said Tony, pointing to the girl who was swinging herself over the tower's wall to perch precariously on a tiny ledge.

"Ellie?" gasped Alfie.

He went to run out from the cover of the memorial, but Brian pulled him back.

"No, you'll never reach her," he said.

"It's my sister! We have to help her!" said Alfie.

Brian turned to Tony. "Do you think Qilin could grab her?"

Tony sized up the tower, rubbing his chin. "Tricky. I can't blink-shift into thin air and there's no room on that ledge. . . But I'll try."

He flicked the lever on his belt buckle and his robe swirled over him as his mask and hover disc deployed.

On the tower wall, Ellie craned her neck to peek

over the battlements at the Dragon. It had its back to her, hunkered down, wings folded, like it was going to sleep. Suddenly, with a strange cracking sound, its limbs began to retract and its scales shrank, transforming into pink skin. She watched in disbelief as the monster transformed into a young man, and as he turned his face she could see who it was – Richard.

"No!"

Ellie screamed and lost her footing, falling from the ledge, arms pinwheeling through the air. Across the road, Alfie, Brian and Tony watched, helpless, as she fell from sight behind the Tower walls, followed a split second later by the dark shape of Richard leaping after her. Then, with a heavy whump of leathery wings, the Black Dragon flew back up, carrying the struggling girl in its claws, before disappearing once more into the grounds of the Tower.

At the memorial, Tony removed his mask. "I'm sorry, there was nowhere to shift to. I couldn't get her."

Alfie pulled away from Brian's grip. He was angry. "You should have let me go!" he hissed.

Brian scanned the street to check no Vikings had heard Alfie, but all eyes were still fixed on the Tower.

"The princess is safe, that's the main thing," he said.

"Safe?!" spluttered Alfie.

"At least now we know where she is," offered Tony, patting Alfie's shoulder.

"Come on, there's nothing more we can do tonight," said Brian. "We need to regroup."

In the pub, Freya was growing impatient. "It's totally sexist, the men leaving us in here while they take care of business."

"Once Alfie has his armour back, you'll have a much better chance of retrieving your banner," replied Tamara, smiling to make their conversation look as normal as possible to anyone spying on them.

"I know he's your son, but I don't need any Defender to help me," scoffed Freya, "Holgatroll could take this lot single-handed."

A thick-set man in a pinstriped suit, with a Viking badge pinned to his lapel, wobbled up to them, spilling half his drink on the floor.

"What did you say about the Defender, love?"

He leaned against the bar, too close to them, breath stinking of stale cigarettes. Behind him, two more suits leered at them with hideous yellow-toothed grins.

"Nothing," said Tamara with a smile. "I think perhaps you misheard us. Have a good night."

Tamara turned away, but the yob spun her back round.

"I know what I heard," he sneered. "And it's no use hoping that poxy superhero will ride to the rescue, sweetheart. He's dead. But if you need saving, look no further."

Freya pushed past Tamara and went nose to nose with the lout.

"What, by you?" she laughed. "Some spineless ex-banker who likes to suck up to Vikings?"

"Oi, you little—"

He grabbed Freya's arm. But instead of heaving her off her feet as he had intended, he found he couldn't budge her an inch. A green glow was coming from the emerald necklace beneath her shirt. When he looked down he was astonished to see that the young girl's arm was growing, bulging with muscles and turning dark green.

"Freya! Don't!" cried Tamara, but it was too late.

She just had time to dive over the bar as the Norwegian queen transformed into the immense Holgatroll, leaving the man in the suit dangling from her tree trunk of an arm.

Outside, Alfie, Brian and Tony were approaching the pub as fast as they could without drawing attention.

"Time to collect the ladies and make a quiet retreat," said Brian.

The front window of the pub exploded as the suited man smashed through it and rolled, groaning, into the road at their feet.

"Maybe it's nothing to do with her?" said Tony, optimistically.

But the ear-shattering troll's roar from inside the pub said otherwise. Panicking customers poured from the doors and leapt through the windows, filling the street around them. Brian's training kicked in as he efficiently diverted Alfie and Tony out of the way of the stampede, pinning them against a wall. Just in time too – as three Viking draugar came hurtling out of the pub, tossed aside one after another by the rampaging Holgatroll. A horn sounded from across the square inside the Tower grounds and Alfie turned to see a fresh troop of Viking undead charge over the drawbridge, axes raised, bellowing their battle cry.

"Shake a leg!" yelled Brian, steering them through what remained of the shattered pub doors.

Inside, Alfie coughed as he was hit by the dust cloud, and stepped across a carpet of smashed glasses, round pulverized tables and over groaning berserkers.

"Mum? Freya?" he called.

"Over here!" shouted Tamara from behind the bar.

Alfie ran over and helped up the dazed barmaid, who looked around at the wreckage and shrugged.

"Rubbish job anyway," she said, grabbing a bottle of whisky and sauntering out.

Brian scanned the bar for exits. "We won't be alone for long. Where's Freya?"

Tamara pointed at a large freshly dug hole in the floor behind the bar. "Our troll friend made her own way out."

"She can burrow tunnels too?" marvelled Tony. "Trolltastic."

Alfie knelt down and peered into the dark abyss of the troll tunnel. It seemed to plummet a long way before levelling out, like a water slide at a fun park, only much slimier and smellier.

"Where do you think it goes?" he asked.

Gwenn the raven flew past the pub letting out a warning "*Gronk!*" The Viking patrol was right outside.

"Knowing Her Majesty, I've got a pretty good idea where," said Brian, booting Alfie up the backside and into the hole.

Beneath the Houses of Parliament, Hayley massaged the feeling back into her fingers. She had lost track of how long it had taken to wheel the three holdalls of gunpowder along in the dark. The floor of the large tunnel was uneven and full of potholes, and LC's warning about the unstable nature of the explosives rang in her ears at every step. She'd had to keep count

177

of the paces she took, so that she would place the bags in exactly the right spot, directly beneath the chamber of the House of Commons. It was hard work, but at least now she was actually DOING something, she thought. Not just sitting in her flat waiting for a rescue that was never going to come. Even so, Hayley didn't relish the idea of the damage she was about to wreak. Parliament and the politicians who worked there before the invasion may not have done much for her, but she hated doing something so violent to such a historic place. She wondered what her gran would have said about it, and hoped she would have understood. Because if it worked, and they destroyed the Raven Banner, no one would be hurt – except a few Viking draugar, and they were dead already – but millions of people would be freed from Lock's berserker curse.

She connected the fuse and wound the wire back down the tunnel as far as it would go. Her arms might have been tired, but her legs were fine, and she was confident she could sprint back to the exit in time. A sudden strange smell reached her nose – a wet, fishy odour – but she dismissed it. *Who knows what's died down here over the years*, she thought, and shuddered. Or it could just be leaking through from the Viking hordes above. She flexed her fingers once more and took out the matches.

One strike was all she needed, and as she lowered the flame the fuse burst into light, fizzing as it burned. It was the light from the burning fuse that gave Hayley her first good look at the troll standing over her. The giant green monster roared at her and stamped the fuse out with its foot. Hayley screamed and stumbled backwards, colliding hard with the wall and falling down. Which was just as well, as Holgatroll's next move was to swing her mighty right fist in Hayley's direction, thumping into the wall instead, sending rocks and dust raining down on both of them.

"BLOW UP MY BANNER, WOULD YOU?" yelled Holgatroll.

Hayley swallowed her shock long enough to get to her feet and take off down the tunnel. The raging troll fell on to all fours and thundered after her. Running blind, arms outstretched, Hayley realized she must have lost her head torch when she fell. If she hit something now it would be game over, but she couldn't afford to slow down. Suddenly she heard another scream, getting closer – someone else was down here, but where?

Bang! From nowhere, a body collided with her in the darkness, sending her tumbling head over heels to the ground. Winded from the fall, Hayley didn't even have time to look up and see who had floored her before she was grabbed by the ankle and hoisted off her feet by Holgatroll.

"Let me go!" shouted Hayley, dangling upside down.

"I'M GONNA SMASH YOUR BRAINS OUT!" bellowed Holgatroll.

Suddenly torchlight blinded Hayley and Holgatroll as more bodies tumbled from the troll tunnel.

"Your Majesty, we had a deal!" cried Brian. "Now put her down!"

The troll grunted and huffed, but dropped her catch and shrank back into the form of the Norwegian queen.

"I'm not used to being made to wait," snapped Freya, tying up her long blonde hair. "And it's a good thing I didn't, or your friend here would have blown the place sky high."

Hayley sat up, rubbed her neck and looked, bewildered, at the group emerging from the dark before her – Brian, Tamara and Tony.

"Brian? Queen Tamara?"

Brian gazed at the fuse leading to the bags of gunpowder. "Kept yourself busy, I see, Hayley," he said, pulling her to her feet.

"I . . . I don't understand," she spluttered.

"Ha!" laughed Tony, "If *that's* blowing your brainbox, wait till you get a load of *this*."

He stepped aside and Hayley saw for the first time the figure that had tumbled into her from the troll tunnel. Dishevelled and bruised, but unmistakable.

"ALFIE?!"

Alfie wiped the mud from his eyes and beamed at her.

"Long time no see."

14

HOMECOMING

Richard couldn't remember what it felt like to be totally human. Now when he transformed back from being the Black Dragon, the impression of scales never completely left his body, but lingered like supernatural acne. The fire burned day and night deep in his throat, and his back ached constantly where the wing tips poked through at the shoulder blades. His fingernails and toenails were thick, sharp and curved, more like talons. His eyes remained flushed with red and yellow, and his tongue had begun to split at the tip like a snake's. His mind was different too. He could no longer shake off the lizard part of his brain that worked on instinct, fuelled by hate and always searching for prey. He was scared that if a cure didn't come soon, he would never be himself again, instead for ever trapped inside the beast. Worse still, Ellie had seen it. She had been the one person he cared about who still knew him as just Richard, her brother. Not any more. He'd seen her eyes, wide with terror as the Vikings dragged her back to the dungeons. She would never see him as anything more than a monster again. He had lost her too. There was no one left for him now.

Richard found Lock in the Keep, covering his mirror, the sound of buzzing flies still fading away. But if he was hoping for a sympathetic ear, he didn't get it.

"Right now we have bigger problems than your body issues," said Lock.

"Why? What's happened?" asked Richard.

"It seems that Colonel Blood failed in his mission."

"Alfie's still alive?"

"Yes. What's more, he's back. There was a disturbance near the Tower last night." He nodded to the mirror. "Our mistress has a certain insight into these things and she has confirmed it. King Alfred has returned to his kingdom. Our enemies are regrouping."

Richard screwed his hand into a tight fist, his rock-hard talon-nails drawing blood from his palm.

"You should have left Alfie to me in the first place," he hissed. "I'll hunt him down."

Lock looked him up and down, impressed. "That's more like it. Rage suits you so much better than self-pity. And when our mission is complete and our mistress resurrected, she will make you well again."

"She can do that?" asked Richard.

"Her power knows no bounds. She will make you the greatest king this world has ever seen."

Hayley had been too shocked to hug Alfie when she first saw him in the tunnel beneath Parliament. Everyone had talked over each other in the chaos – Brian working hard to persuade Freya to wait till they had recovered Alfie's Defender armour before she launched a raid to regain the Raven Banner and instead to burrow them a quick exit back to street level, and Tamara asking Hayley if she had been hurt during her encounter with Holgatroll, while Tony wittered on about how they should get out before the Vikings found them.

It wasn't until they had retreated from the tunnel, leaving the gunpowder where it was, and rejoined the cab convoy outside, that Hayley found her voice again.

"You're supposed to be dead!" she blurted at Alfie, thumping him for good measure.

"Sorry to disappoint you," said Alfie, rubbing his chest. "I thought you'd be pleased!"

"It's been months – we thought you were at the bottom of the sea! Do you have any idea what it's been like here?"

"I've not exactly been on holiday myself, you know. We were nearly killed about five times trying to get back!"

Brian, sitting opposite the bickering pair, nervously scanned the abandoned streets as the cab whistled along with its lights off.

"All right, you two, maybe save the lovers' tiff till we're safe, yeah?"

Alfie and Hayley stared at each other, red in the face, then folded their arms and looked out of opposite windows. In the second cab following close behind them, a grumpy Freya told Tony to shut up for the third time as he pointed out yet another famous London landmark. Later, after a nervous few minutes in an alleyway near Hayley's tower block, waiting for a berserker patrol to move on, the group finally made it to the safety of the flat. But if Alfie was hoping for a warmer reception from the Lord Chamberlain, he was to be disappointed.

"Your Majesty?!" he blurted on seeing Alfie and the others pour inside. "What on earth are you doing here? This is a disaster!"

Before Alfie could reply he was flattened by

a hundred and forty pounds of yapping, licking wolfhound as Herne barrelled into him.

"Good to see you too, boy. OK, Herne, take it easy!" said Alfie, sinking to the floor under the furry assault.

LC was equally shocked to see Brian appear, ushering Tamara, Tony and Freya inside.

"Lord Chamberlain," nodded Tamara, curtly.

LC regained his composure and nodded back. "I can see that this evening is to be full of revelations. Perhaps a round of tea, Hayley?"

"Ooh, yes please, I'm gasping!" said Tony.

Freya handed LC her coat and marched into the kitchen, sniffing the air. "Ugh, tea – you people's answer to everything," she said.

Later, in the living room, they all found seats where they could. Tamara and Brian took the sofa, while Freya (eating her seventh uncooked chicken drumstick) had claimed the only armchair and grudgingly allowed Tony to perch on one arm. Alfie sat awkwardly on a footstool, knees almost reaching his chin. Herne curled at his master's feet, nudging his hand with his nose every time Alfie stopped stroking him.

The Lord Chamberlain paced up and down by the window like a fretting caged bird, pausing every few strides to peek through the curtains.

"Sorry, LC, but isn't it a good thing that Alfie's come back?" asked Hayley. "Even though I'm still mad he didn't call," she added with a smile at Alfie.

"Ha!" was all LC could muster in reply.

"This is no time to keep things to yourself, LC," said Tamara. "You didn't even seem that surprised to see Alfie just now. Why not? Didn't you think he was dead?"

LC turned his attention from the window to the room, mouth pursed tight and eyebrow arched like he had no intention of talking. But after a leisurely throat-clearing and tie-straightening, he did. "Your observation is not without merit, Queen Tamara."

"Wait, what?" said Hayley. "You knew Alfie was alive?"

"Suspected," said LC. "But I did not wish to get your hopes up, Miss Hicks."

"Wow, thanks for treating me like a grown-up," said Hayley, slamming her mug down on a table.

"It was simple deduction," LC said, checking the window again. "Events have forced me to accept that I was perhaps rather hasty in dismissing Queen Tamara's theory about who is behind Professor Lock's campaign."

"You mean Hel?" asked Tamara.

"Who?" asked Hayley.

"Ancient Norse goddess," whispered Alfie. "Seriously bad news. I'll explain later."

"Impossible!" gasped Freya, standing up so fast that Tony unbalanced the chair and toppled off.

"Oh yeah, we probably should have mentioned that to you earlier, sorry," said Tony from the floor.

Freya swatted his hand away, her gaze fixed on LC. "Please tell me this Lock is not trying to revive the plague goddess."

"I'm afraid, Your Majesty," continued LC, "Lock's every move has been one more step towards resurrecting Hel and bringing about the cataclysm that would come with her."

"Just like I always said. Apology accepted, old pal," said Tamara with a wry smile.

LC sniffed. "You may have been in the right, but that does not mean your actions haven't made things worse."

Tamara threw up her hands in exasperation. "You never change, do you?" she exclaimed.

"I still don't understand," said Alfie. "Even if you realized Hel was behind all this, why did that make you think I must be alive?"

"Because she is yet to return." LC sighed. "Lock has inveigled his way into power, seduced Richard into doing his bidding and seized the kingdom. But still he has not completed the ritual and brought his mistress back to Earth. Why not?"

"Blue blood," said Brian in a whisper. He looked at Tamara, horrified as she too realized the significance of LC's words.

"Richard's blood isn't working," she gasped, looking at Alfie, eyes full of fear.

"But . . . mine would?" asked Alfie.

"Yes, only a true king's blood is powerful enough to free Hel from her imprisonment," said LC gravely. He turned on Tamara and Brian. "And what do you do? You deliver His Majesty right to Lock's doorstep! You should all have stayed lost."

With that the air was filled with angry shouts and pointing fingers – Tamara blaming LC for his stubbornness, LC berating her and Brian for their "renegade" activities, while Freya yelled at all of them for bringing the world to the brink of a new Black Death. Hayley finally got everyone's attention by turning the lights off. Only once they had all quietened down, did she turn them back on.

"It's late and I'd rather not get any noise complaints from the neighbours, if you don't mind," she said sternly. "Especially the undead Viking ones!"

Alfie struggled to his feet, which took longer than he'd planned from the footstool.

"Maybe it wasn't the smartest thing in the world to come back, but there are a lot of people who need help – people like my sister – and I'd like to be part of that, if I can." Alfie turned to LC and Hayley. "I'm sorry if you're not pleased to see me here. For what it's worth, I missed you both. A lot."

He sloped out of the room, followed by Herne. Hayley pulled her coat back on and shouldered a rucksack.

"Where are *you* going?" asked LC.

"Shopping," she replied, and closed the door behind her.

At the market, business was slow. Traders lined the walls beneath the railway bridge, blowing on their hands and stamping their feet to keep warm. It was nothing like the thriving market Hayley used to go to with her gran every Saturday morning. Where there had once been long stalls piled high with a rainbow of fruit from all over the world, and racks of vibrantly patterned clothes, there were now scattered cardboard boxes only half-filled with tinned food, many without labels. There were grubby piles of used clothes and furniture broken up for firewood. Those with nothing to exchange begged for handouts, only to be chased away.

How much longer can people live like this? wondered Hayley as she scanned the sorry contents of another box. She knew she should be pleased that Alfie and the others were back – now perhaps the country had a chance. And she *was* happy that Alfie was alive – deliriously, ecstatically happy – so why couldn't she show it? For months she had imagined him walking through the door as if nothing had happened and how she would hug him and tell him he was her best friend and how she'd never given up on him. But the truth was she *had* given up; she had thought he was gone for ever. And now here he was, alive and in the flesh, along with his new superhero mates, and as messed up as it sounded, she just couldn't bring herself to forgive him for the agony his disappearance had put her through.

"You buying, or what?" barked a woman wrapped in a dirty white fur coat, as she lounged in an old deckchair next to her stall, looking Hayley up and down with heavy eyes.

Hayley pulled her scarf higher over her nose. The freezing weather at least meant she could hide her face without anyone thinking it was suspicious. There had been a "Wanted" poster of her on a wall near the estate and she didn't know how many others the Vikings might have put up. She ran her fingers over the woman's boxes, pulling out several old tins with faded labels – beans, peaches, soup – till she had as many as she thought she could fit in her rucksack.

"And how are you planning on paying for all that, love?" sneered the woman.

Hayley took a pair of silver-plated earrings from her pocket and handed them to the woman. The trader cast her eyes over them and tossed them back at her in disdain.

"Bloomin' timewaster. Get out of here," she snapped, clawing her tins back.

But Hayley stood her ground and pulled a sapphire ring from her pocket. It had been her grandmother's, but she didn't think Gran would mind. "Shiny things are for dull minds," Gran used to say whenever they saw something they couldn't afford in a shop window. The woman heaved her lumpy frame out of the deckchair, snatched the ring and inspected it.

"Are we good?" Hayley muttered.

The woman took one tin back from the pile, smiled and waved her away. As Hayley walked off carrying her heavy load, the trader called after her.

"You feeding an army or something?"

Hayley didn't answer and hurried off.

Above the market, unseen on the disused rail bridge, crouched the hulking frame of former government agent Fulcher. She hadn't really minded living out on the streets since the Viking takeover; in truth it suited her more than her old nine-to-five office routine. She was tougher than any wild animal and the day-to-day battle for survival didn't faze her one bit. But what had happened to her partner, what their evil magic had done to him – that she *did* mind, very much indeed. Fulcher shifted her eyes from Hayley back to the market trader and watched as the woman slid the ring on to her finger, then packed up her boxes and hurried through the underpass and up to a passing berserker patrol. She waved her arms as she spoke to their human commander, pointing urgently back towards the market. Fulcher hunkered down, intrigued, as a Rolls Royce pulled up next to the patrol and wound down its window, revealing the face of Dean Barron. The patrol leader leant down and spoke to him, pointing to the nearby woman from the market stall, who smoothed back her greasy hair and waved. Barron stepped out of the car, pulling a berserker behind him on a heavy metal leash. The berserker was short, arms and legs bulging with muscles, grey skin crisscrossed with blue war-paint tattoos. He might have changed, but Fulcher recognized him at once. It was Turpin, her partner.

15

THE ENEMY OF MY ENEMY

It was cold in the flat when Hayley got back. The central heating hardly came on at all these days, and ice was beginning to claw its way inside through the rotten window frames. She found LC, Brian and Tamara hunched over some plans in the living room, deep in conversation.

"I agree a full-frontal assault is too risky, but we'll need a distraction and I reckon the lass will be up for it," said Brian.

They all looked up as Hayley came in. "Talking about me behind my back?" she asked with a smile.

"Er, no, I meant Queen Freya actually," said Brian.

"We are discussing our strategy for recapturing the regalia," added LC.

"Without me?" asked Hayley.

"Sorry," said Tamara. "We would have waited, but we didn't know how long you'd be."

Hayley shrugged, pretending not to care. "Whatever. You carry on, I'll put these away."

Hayley sloped to the airing cupboard and hid the cans under a pile of towels. She had no idea how long everyone would be staying, so she would need to ration their supplies. Passing by her gran's bedroom, she was shocked to see Freya perched on the end of the bed combing her hair.

"Uh-uh, no way!" blurted Hayley, flying inside.

"What's the big deal?" replied Freya, not even looking at her.

"Sorry, princess," said Hayley. "You ain't sleeping in here, I don't care how big and green you get."

"You sure about that?" said Freya, looming over her.

Hayley was about to grab the Norwegian queen by her stupid silky hair and pull her out of the room when a pungent smell assaulted her nostrils.

"Ugh, what *is* that?" Hayley gasped. "Smells like burning plastic or something."

Freya rolled her eyes, squirting the air with perfume.

"You're not going to make a fuss too, are you? I'll have you know that where I come from I get compliments for my very mild half-troll fragrance."

Hayley smirked, then giggled, then guffawed. "On second thoughts, you can have the room. Might be better for everyone else," she gasped through the tears of laughter rolling down her cheeks. It felt weird to be laughing again, but she knew her gran would have approved. She backed into the hall and composed herself. In the darkness she almost trod on Tony, who was doing sit-ups.

"What are you doing?" she asked.

"Trying to get a six-pack," replied Tony. "Don't tell anyone, but there's a lady I'm trying to impress."

"Your secret's safe with me, Tony," Hayley said, smiling.

"It's good for keeping warm too! Want a go?"

"No thanks. Where's Alfie?"

"Oh, he popped out with the dog."

"He WHAT?!"

After a frantic search, Hayley finally found Alfie, sitting on the tower-block roof, gazing out at the frozen city, Herne lying by his side.

"Really like what you've done with the country while I've been away," said Alfie when he saw her.

Hayley took a seat next to him, legs stretched out towards the edge of the roof. "Yeah, well, I've had a bit of grief with some uninvited guests. They're real monsters."

They looked at each other and smiled.

"You know it's too cold to stay up here all night, don't you?" Hayley asked.

"Yeah, but it's better than listening to that lot arguing," said Alfie.

GRONK!

Hayley squealed in surprise and grabbed hold of Alfie. Gwenn and the other ravens were dotted around the icy roof, feathers puffed up to keep warm.

"Sorry about that, they kind of follow me around now."

"Well that's not creepy at all."

Realizing she was still clinging to Alfie's arm, Hayley let go and shuffled away from him again. They sat together on the roof, snow falling on them like confetti as the sun tried and failed to break through the veil of black snow clouds that hung heavy over the city.

"Weird being back here, isn't it?" said Alfie. "Our fateful meeting place."

"Not quite," said Hayley. "This is where I met the Defender. Well, your first attempt at the Defender, anyway."

She laughed, remembering Alfie face-planting on the roof that night as he tried to dismount from Wyvern.

"I didn't meet you – the real you – till we got back to the Keep," she added.

"Yeah, I remember how pleased LC was that I'd brought a civilian back with me!" Alfie laughed. "Hard to believe that was less than a year ago. What with everything that's happened..."

"Yeah, I meant to say before, I'm sorry about your brother," said Hayley. "I can't believe what he did."

Alfie nodded. "And I'm sorry about your gran. I can't believe she's gone."

"Me neither," said Hayley.

She moved closer to Alfie and put her hand on his. He looked up at her.

"Listen, Alfie, when I saw you tonight, I—"

She never finished the sentence, as in the space of the next two seconds, Herne growled, the door behind them flew open, and Herne leapt past them, downing the emerging figure. Alfie and Hayley rolled away from the edge of the roof and scrambled to their feet to see the dog standing over the prostrate form of Fulcher, nose to nose, teeth bared.

"It's her! That government spook!" shouted Hayley.

"There isn't a government any more, in case you hadn't noticed," mumbled Fulcher, trying to move her lips as little as possible in the face of the slathering hound.

"I don't care, you nearly killed me and my gran. Herne, bite her head off."

"I'm not here to hurt you. I'm here to help," said

Fulcher, craning her thick neck as far away from the growling dog as she could.

"Stand down, Herne," commanded Alfie.

Herne instantly bounded off Fulcher and returned to his master's side.

"Alfie! What are you doing? We can't trust her!"

Alfie eyed Fulcher as she sat up and rubbed her head.

"She's unarmed," said Alfie. "Let's hear her out."

"Thanks, kid," said Fulcher. "The enemy of my enemy is my friend and all that."

But as the giant woman studied Alfie's face, realization dawned slowly.

"Wait a minute. You're him. That daft little king."

"Er, thanks," said Alfie.

"But you're supposed to be dead," said Fulcher.

"I get that a lot," shrugged Alfie.

"And *you're* not supposed to know any of this," said Hayley, arms folded. "So if you really expect us to believe you're on our side now, you better make this good."

Fulcher looked from Alfie to Hayley, furrowing her Neanderthal brow, and suddenly burst into tears.

"The truth is, I don't know whose side I'm on any more," she blubbed. "I mean, one day I'm working for the secret service, then next thing I know there are Vikings everywhere and the whole world's gone crazy!"

Alfie and Hayley looked at each other, bewildered. Alfie edged over to the weeping agent and patted her on the shoulder.

"Careful, it might be a trap," said Hayley.

But Fulcher was in full flow now, snot bubbles and all.

"And then Turpin – my partner – he turned into this horrible thing, and I know we never got on that well, but underneath it all I really cared about him. . ."

Hayley looked to Alfie and shrugged. "It's true, I've seen him," she said. Fulcher blubbed again, and Hayley rolled her eyes. "Oh come here," she said, handing Fulcher a tissue and putting an arm round her gargantuan shoulders.

Fulcher blew her nose so loudly that the nearest raven flew away and circled the tower block. Finally, she brought her sobs under control.

"Thanks. Reckon I've bottled all that up too long. Haven't spoken to anyone since it happened."

"You said you wanted to help us?" Alfie asked.

"Yeah. The thing is," sniffed Fulcher, "Whatever you've got going on here, you want to be careful. They're on to you."

"Who is?" said Hayley, worried.

"That little oik, Earl Barron," she replied. "The one who's got my Turpin chained up like some stinking dog. No offence."

Herne didn't look like he was offended.

"Anyway, that's why I came," continued Fulcher, "Figured I owed you after what we did to you, you know, before. I'm not the brightest spark in the world, but I found you easy enough. I don't expect it'll take them as long. That's if they're not here already."

The corridor outside Hayley's flat was jam-packed with undead Vikings: a drooling, stinky SWAT team of draugar warriors led by Guthrum, who had to bend low to fit his mighty frame inside the tight space. Dean Barron scurried to the front, pulling Turpin, his pet berserker, on his leash.

"That's the one. They're in there," he hissed, pointing eagerly at the door to the flat.

"Mun þat þér vel at hafir rétt fyrir þér,"* Guthrum snarled in Dean's face.

Dean didn't know what the Viking Lord had said, but he figured correctly that it was a threat.

"Yeah, yeah, you'll find the girl and her Resistance mates in there," he said, adding a thumbs up to try to keep it friendly.

The door to the flat exploded inwards, along with most of the wall either side, as Guthrum and his men smashed their way in, bellowing their war-cries.

---

* "You'd better be right."

They stampeded into the kitchen, which was empty, then they stampeded to the living room, which was also empty, then back to the kitchen to double check. There didn't seem to be anyone at home, but from the look of the plates of half-eaten food left lying around, they hadn't been gone long. Roaring with rage, Guthrum felled the bedroom doors with his axe. They were empty too. But in Hayley's room there was a cartoon of a dumb-looking Viking scrawled on a piece of paper and stuck to the wall along with a note. If Guthrum had been able to read, he'd have known that it said: "Better luck next time, deadheads."

Guthrum tore the cartoon to pieces and thundered back into the corridor, looking for Dean. Rather wisely for such an idiot, Dean was making a beeline for the lifts, pulling Turpin with him. The Viking spotted him and pointed.

"Haltu! Skaðask skaltu fyrir að taka á lopti veizlunna!"*

Dean whimpered and stabbed the lift button again. Unfortunately for him, when it opened he found himself plucked off the ground by Fulcher, who was already inside. She took Turpin's leash from him.

---

* "Halt! You will pay for wasting my feasting time!"

"I'll have that, ta muchly."

Fulcher shoved Dean back into the corridor. The last thing he saw before the lift doors closed was the massive woman holding the irate Turpin at bay and telling him off.

"Uh-uh, no biting! I can see we're going to have to start some training with you, pal."

Dean was so confused he almost forgot to scream as Guthrum arrived and yanked him off the ground by his ear.

Meanwhile, out on the streets, miles from the tower block, Hayley led the others through the shadows, eyes peeled for Viking patrols. She and Alfie had been smart enough to take Fulcher's warning seriously, and it wasn't hard to persuade everyone to pack up and leave. The idea of another minute crammed together in the flat didn't appeal to any of them. Besides, raiding the Tower of London sounded much more fun.

IG

RETURN OF
THE DEFENDER

Holgatroll was already enjoying herself hurling
Vikings off the drawbridge into the moat, where
they were set upon by what she would have
eventually worked out were giant vampire eels,
if she'd bothered to hang around and watch. But
the rampaging she-troll wasn't stopping. She head-
butted the Byward Tower gate off its hinges and
pounded over it, much to the disappointment of the
squad of berserkers pinned underneath. Ahead of
her, a band of fearsome draugar emerged on to the
cobbles of Water Lane. Their leader, an unusually
scrawny Viking called Eohric, who was only in
charge because Guthrum was his father, laughed
at Holgatroll.

"Sjáit! Fǫlt trǫll er undan komit hellinum sínum. Færit mér hǫfut sitt hit ljótt."*

Holgatroll smiled. "My family's been bashing Vikings since before you were dead," she boomed.

She bounded high into the air, spinning her arms up to pummelling speed, and fell on to the shocked draugar like an angry, green meteor.

While Holgatroll was attracting as much attention as she could at the Tower, a couple of miles away at Buckingham Palace, Alfie and Tony were squeezing as quietly as possible through the bent and broken gates. At the main entrance there were no guards to stop them, no soldiers standing to attention, no Royal Protection Officers sizing them up through their shades. Alfie took out the Scout Orb and tossed it through the door. He closed his eyes and let the images of the inside of the palace come into his mind as the Orb floated through corridors and rooms.

"So how does it work exactly?" asked Tony, before Alfie shushed him.

"I need to concentrate!"

After a couple of minutes, the Orb floated back out of the entrance and landed in Alfie's hands. He opened his eyes.

---

* "Look! A stinking troll has escaped from its cave. Bring me its ugly head."

205

"All clear," he said.

Inside it looked like a hurricane had blown through. Paintings lay trampled on the floor, furniture and vases scattered in pieces, whole rooms scorched by fires that by sheer luck had not claimed the whole building. Even though he had lived here most of his life, Alfie had never liked the palace very much; it always felt more like a workplace than a home. And yet as he and Tony picked their way over shattered glass and through wrecked rooms, he found himself growing angry.

"I've always wanted to visit your place, Alfalfa," said Tony.

Alfie marvelled at how his friend's mood always stayed so sunny no matter how grim their surroundings.

"Sorry, you'll have to come back if you want the full guided tour."

Footsteps. A shadow at the end of the hallway. Before Alfie could even react, Tony engaged his robes, touched Alfie's shoulder, and blink-shifted them through a doorway into an empty ballroom. Swiftly they hid behind a smashed grand piano, peeking through the cracks in the lid to see who was approaching. Richard paused by the doorway, holding a candle. He turned and looked back down the corridor, as if sensing he was not alone. Alfie was shocked by his brother's stooped, hunchbacked appearance, and grey, scaly skin. He wanted to reach out and ask Richard if he was all right. But he had made that mistake once before, and it had cost him his kingdom and very nearly his life.

Richard shuffled away like an old man heading for bed. It was only then that Alfie noticed his brother was barefoot, his long, hooked toenails scraping the floor like a hawk's talons.

In his old bedroom Alfie was relieved to find that the dressing table, though damaged, was still in its place against the wall. He reached beneath it and clicked the concealed release switch. Tony squealed with excitement as the dressing table slid aside, revealing the tunnel entrance behind.

"That's why I wish I had a palace and stuff: look at all the gadgets you get!"

"Tony, you have a magical hoverboard and you can teleport," said Alfie.

"Yeah, but apart from that. . ." muttered Tony as he followed Alfie down the dark stone staircase.

There was no sign that anyone had been down here in months, and Alfie was optimistic as they reached the bottom of the steps and the carriage chamber.

"Where are we?" asked Tony.

Alfie smiled as he recalled asking LC the very same thing the first time he was shown the tunnel.

"About a hundred and fifty feet beneath street level," he said, putting his hand into an alcove and feeling around till he found the lever.

The flagstones slid apart and the stagecoach rose out. Alfie hopped on board and the carriage rolled forward, its wheels gliding out from underneath and travelling up the sides till they found their grooves in the wall of the exit tunnel. Tony's mouth was hanging open.

"Now you're just showing off," said Tony as he climbed inside.

"Oh, hang on, almost forgot!" said Alfie.

He leaned out of the carriage and rooted around inside one of the wheels' spokes until he found what he was looking for. He yanked, twisted and pulled until, with a crack, he came away holding a curved block of metal, sparking with magical energy where it had been severed from the wheel.

"What's that?" asked Tony.

"I'm hoping it's the brakes," said Alfie, repeating the process on each of the other wheels.

Tony frowned and secured his guard rail. As soon as Alfie had done the same, the carriage set off into the dark, accelerating with tremendous power.

"I'll signal when we're close," Alfie called over the din of rushing air. "You'll have about a second's line of sight to blink-shift us out of here before it crashes."

Tony nodded, serious, but soon he was whooping and hollering, getting more and more excited the faster they went. Alfie laughed at his hysterical friend.

"OK, relax, this next bit kind of takes your breath away!" yelled Alfie.

The carriage whipped to the vertical and shot up, pinning them back in their seats with tremendous G-force and in Tony's case rendering him instantly unconscious.

"Stop messing about!" shouted Alfie as they levelled out once more. "We're nearly there! Get ready to blink-shift!"

To his horror, Alfie realized that Tony wasn't joking and the very next moment heard the wheels clicking and clacking as the mechanism tried and failed to find the brake pads. Any moment they would crash into the antechamber outside the Keep at approximately three hundred miles per hour.

"TONY! *TONY!*"

Tony stirred, but still his eyes remained closed.

"Sorry, mate," said Alfie, as he kicked Tony as hard as he could in the shins.

"YOWW!" yelled Tony, eyes springing open.

Alfie grabbed Tony's arm and twisted him towards the window. The blackness of the tunnel walls was replaced with a blur of lights outside as the carriage rocketed into the antechamber.

"NOW, TONY! NOW!"

Tony whipped his mask on, focused his eyes and the next moment they were sliding to a halt on the antechamber floor, while the carriage hit the end of the tracks, bucked and flew through the air, smashing through the doors to the Keep. Alfie groaned and sat up, nursing the bruises on his arms and legs.

"I really need my armour back."

Tony hovered over him, beaming. "THAT was wild!"

Inside the Keep, the carriage had done its job, not only gaining them entry, but taking out three Viking draugar guards on its way towards crashing into the broken ops table. Tony gazed in wonder at the huge underground hall.

"You never told me you had such a cool base! Needs a tidy up, though," he said.

"Yeah, thanks, I'll have a word with the cleaners," said Alfie, leading him past the unconscious Vikings, towards the entrance to the Arena. "Come on, the regalia is kept in here."

They ran on to the dirt floor of the wide, oval training arena, eyes on the regalia cases that lined the wall on the far side. Alfie was relieved to see that even though the glass had been smashed, most of the swords, crowns, sceptres and other items of regalia seemed to be intact. Lock must have ordered that they be left there for the new king to use. What Alfie and Tony failed to notice till it was too late were the six Viking draugar who had been left to guard the real Crown Jewels waking up on the benches either side of them.

"ÞJÓFAR!"* yelled one of the Vikings, rallying the others to their feet.

The growling Viking squad surrounded Alfie and Tony, circling them like a pack of wolves.

"OK, Qilin," said Alfie. "Time to do your thing."

The red-robed superhero disappeared, throwing the meathead Vikings into confusion, then reappeared by the regalia cabinet. Another split-second later he was back next to Alfie handing him the tiny Coronation spoon.

Alfie looked at it, unimpressed. "The *spoon?* What did you pick that one for?"

"Sorry, I thought it looked useful," said Tony.

"Not for fighting Vikings!"

They both ducked as the first axe swing whooshed past. Alfie scooted through the nearest Viking's legs and rolled clear.

"GET ME SOMETHING TO FIGHT WITH!"

Tony blink-shifted back to the cabinet and returned with the Sword of State. Alfie grabbed it

---

* "THIEVES!"

and the blade burst into light with a blinding flash that had the Vikings stumbling back, arms raised.

As the glare dimmed, two of the draugar charged again, but this time Alfie was ready for them. Sparks flew from his blade as it crashed into their onrushing axe heads, sending the pair spinning into the benches. The rest of the Vikings were more wary now, muttering Old Norse curses under their breath as they lunged and withdrew. Alfie spun round, parrying each blow in turn, but he knew he couldn't keep this up for long.

"Some armour would be nice!" he yelled at Qilin, who was back by the regalia.

"Armour, armour..." said Tony, running his fingers over the jumble of bejewelled items. "I don't see any!"

Alfie ducked as an axe gave his hair a trim. "The Shroud Tunic! Looks like an old T-shirt!"

Tony saw the dirty white tunic and picked it up. "Really? Oh well, if you say so."

He materialized next to Alfie, who blocked a Viking's axe an inch from his nose.

"Whoa! Thanks. Here."

Qilin grabbed him and blink-shifted him out of harm's way, behind the startled Vikings.

"GEFÐU STAÐAR VIÐ ÞESS!"* yelled a frustrated-sounding Viking.

"JÁ, ER EKKI RÉTT!"† complained another.

Alfie took the spurs out of his pocket and spoke to them gently. "Ready to have some fun, girl?"

He tossed them high in the air and pulled the tunic over his head. A white tide swept over him from head to toe as the magical armour enveloped his body. The Defender was back in the Keep. He rolled forward, letting the spurs lock like magnets into his heels as they fell.

"SPURS!" shouted Alfie.

The Arena was filled with fearsome whinnying as Wyvern uncoiled from Alfie's heels like a giant butterfly bursting from its chrysalis. She reared up at the Vikings, clattering them with her front hooves, then took off, diving at the panicking draugar and chasing them in circles round the arena. Tony clapped his hands.

"Wow, your ride really hates Vikings, huh?"

Once Wyvern had redecorated the arena with knocked-out Vikings, Alfie recalled her into his spurs and took as much of the regalia as he could carry, packing the rest in the portable regalia case.

---

* "STOP DOING THAT!"
† "YEAH, IT'S NOT FAIR!"

The Swords of State and Mercy, sceptres and armill bracelets, each shimmered with a golden glow, as if comforted by the touch of their rightful owner. Finally, he was relieved to see that the diamond, sapphire and ruby-adorned Ring of Command was there in its place – he had feared it had been lost for ever when he had taken it off during the battle on the oil rig. He slipped it on to his finger and turned round to find Tony giggling at him.

"You are so bling, Super Alfie."

As agreed, Alfie headed down to the dungeons, while Tony slung the regalia case over his back and climbed up the nearest tower. Holgatroll's full-frontal assault had drawn most of the Vikings and berserkers outside, so Alfie didn't meet anyone as he raced downstairs. He was surprised how much he'd missed the feeling of power he got from wearing the armour, but he reminded himself that they weren't out of trouble yet. It was only when he ran into the dungeon antechamber and was faced with the dozens of doors that he realized there was a problem. He had no idea which cell Ellie was inside, if any.

"Ellie? Are you here?" he called out.

Big mistake. A cacophony of hoots, shrieks and growls erupted from the cells as every inmate decided to make their presence felt. Some even tried to trick him into opening their cells by shouting, "I'm Ellie! In here! Let me out!" – but their low, gruff voices rather gave them away. Suddenly Alfie felt his spurs twitch. He summoned Wyvern.

"What is it, girl? You got a hunch?"

Wyvern whinnied and trotted straight to one cell door, touching it gently with her head.

"Well, OK, but if I find some giant sugar-lump monster in here, you'll be in trouble."

Alfie recalled Wyvern into his spurs, unsheathed his sword and ripped it into the door, cutting his way inside. He stepped back, ready to be attacked if he'd got it wrong. But as his eyes adjusted to the gloom, he saw a small figure hunched on the bed with her knees pulled tight to her chest. She looked up through strands of lank, greasy hair, shielding her eyes.

"Ellie!" he called out.

"Who are you?" she muttered through cracked lips.

"It's me, Alfie."

Ellie chuckled a bitter laugh. "No, you're not. Anyway, he's gone."

Alfie realized he was still wearing his Defender armour. He reached up and pulled it off, the armour transforming back into the tunic and coming to rest in his hand.

215

"Ellie, it is me. Look."

His sister's eyes grew wide as she stood up from the bed on shaky legs and walked over to him. He reached out and caught her as she fell into his arms.

"Alfie? But how...?"

"I'll explain later. Right now, we need to leave."

Alfie pulled the tunic back over his head and, with his Defender armour restored, he carried Ellie out of her cell.

Outside on Tower Green, Viking devil dogs were swarming over Holgatroll like wasps on jam. She had at least two on every limb, biting and clawing at her tough green hide. Every time she threw one off, two more Vikings would transform into the monstrous canines and take its place. Suddenly, to her surprise, Qilin appeared from thin air, clinging to the only free spot he could find – the top of her head.

"Get off me, imp!" roared Holgatroll, shaking her head. "I can't see!"

"I thought you might like a hand," shrieked Tony, gripping hold of her bushy eyebrows.

"I don't need help from you!"

But just then a devil dog's dagger teeth found their way through the troll's skin and sank into her leg. She howled and shook off the devil dogs in her fury.

"You could have fooled me!" shouted Qilin, clinging on by his fingertips. "Let's take this somewhere quieter!"

And with that he blink-shifted them away from the devil dogs, which fell into a heap, biting each other in their confusion, and reappeared with Holgatroll on top of the White Tower.

"Fine!" huffed Holgatroll, grabbing hold of the weathervane and bending it over in her attempt to balance on the roof. "Where is King Alfred?"

Tony scanned the towers anxiously.

"He'll be here soon. I hope."

Alfie was inside the tower, making for the light above. As soon as he reached the roof, he would summon Wyvern and fly them out of there. That would be Qilin and Holgatroll's cue to make their retreat too and meet up at the rendezvous point. But as he passed an archway off the staircase, a familiar voice stopped him in his tracks.

"Your Majesty. . ."

He tried to ignore it – he had to get Ellie to safety. He climbed up another couple of steps. But the voice came again.

"Alfie. . ."

Alfie eased Ellie on to the steps and helped her to find her feet.

"What are you doing?" she asked, half delirious.

"Keep going," he answered. "I'll be right behind you."

The Defender stepped through the archway into a small, whitewashed cell, with a single thin window in the shape of a cross high on one wall. Soft light from a dozen black candles dappled the ceiling. At the far corner was a stand covered with a dark velvet cloth, next to a small desk.

At the desk sat Cameron Lock, writing in a book. "This was Sir Thomas More's cell," he said, and looked up, smiling.

Alfie's hand gripped the hilt of his sword.

"You're not my history teacher any more, remember?" he said through gritted teeth.

"Nevertheless, you might learn something, Alfie," said Lock. "Lord Chancellor More was a wise and powerful man. Some said it was he, rather than the king, who really ran the country. But if you ask me, his greatest achievement was this."

He threw the book he had been annotating across the cell to Alfie. As it landed with a loud *clap*, Alfie could read the title: *Utopia*.

"It's another word for paradise," Lock continued. "More imagined a land where nobody disagreed with each other, everyone got along and no one had any secrets. There was a darker side, of course – slavery, executions for the smallest crime, and so on, but, well, nowhere's perfect."

"Sounds like a snore-fest to me," said Alfie, kicking the book back to him.

"People assumed he'd made the whole Utopia thing up, of course," Lock persisted. "But actually he'd been there himself; pan-dimensional travel was a hobby of his. He was quite a guy."

"Aren't you forgetting something?" asked Alfie. "Like, how he died."

He unsheathed his sword, illuminating the cell. But if Lock was worried, he didn't show it.

"Executed on the orders of his king and master, Henry the Eighth," said Lock. "I'm delighted to see some of my lessons sank in after all. Now, let me teach you something else."

He pulled the velvet cloth off its stand, revealing the seeing mirror. The buzzing of flies instantly filled the cell, burrowing through Alfie's helmet and into his ears, making him feel woozy. Somehow he knew he shouldn't look into the mirror, but he couldn't stop himself. The black glass rippled like an oil slick and through the darkness came the woman's face. Lock didn't have to tell him who this was – it was Hel, the Norse Goddess of Plague. The half of her face that he could make out was radiant, drinking him in like she was looking right through his superhero armour at the child beneath. Alfie opened his mouth to speak, but nothing came out. It felt as if the mirror was sucking all the oxygen from the air.

"At last, you bring me a king." *Had she spoken out loud, or had her words merely appeared in his mind?* "I can feel your fear, young Alfred. Fear for your friends, your family, your people. Fear that you will let them down. Yes, you worry that you lack courage."

Alfie shook his head – there was no difference between the buzzing of the flies and the lilting music of Hel's voice. He could feel her pulling thoughts from his mind, guiding him closer, like his mother's hand around his when he was little. The Defender took a step towards the mirror.

"I can help you, Alfie. I can help you find your strength. I can help you save them all. I can help you. . ."

Alfie felt like he was floating through a dream. He was a passenger in his own body. All he could think of was her voice. He didn't even feel the spurs digging themselves into the floor, trying to hold him back as he stepped closer to the mirror. He reached out. He wanted to touch her face.

"Alfie?"

A voice cutting through the fog. Not hers. But familiar.

"Come to me. Come. . ." Hel spoke close, hard, a command now.

"Alfie, don't!"

His sister's voice. Ellie. His sister. His—

Alfie snapped out of the trance and yanked his hand away from the mirror. Hel's face turned fully towards him, the skeleton half revealed, screaming at him. He stumbled back to the doorway. Ellie grabbed his arm.

"What are you doing? Alfie?"

Lock was out from behind the desk, running at him. But the spell was broken. Alfie swung Ellie on to his back and, pointing his fist at the staircase wall outside the room, focused his mind through the Ring of Command. The Defender ran at the wall as the ancient stones answered their monarch's call, scattering outward like windblown leaves. Alfie and Ellie hurtled through the gap into the waiting night's air, falling for a moment before Wyvern unfurled beneath them and carried them high and away. All Lock could do was watch from the open wound left in the tower's side and think about how he would calm his angry mistress in the mirror.

Seeing the Defender flying from the tower, Qilin stretched his hand out to Holgatroll.

"It only works if you hold my hand," he said with a shrug.

"I'm good, thanks," said the troll.

Holgatroll bent her knees and leapt clean over the Tower walls, bounding off across the rooftops. Qilin scratched his head.

"Girls are so hard to talk to sometimes," he said and blink-shifted after the others half a mile at a time.

17
CRYSTAL PALACE

If Hayley stopped running, she would die. Her legs felt like lead and her breath was coming in short, sharp stabs. She was built for sprinting, not the marathon. All her energy spent, she slowed to a walk and clutched her sides.

"KEEP GOING!" Brian shouted, waving her on urgently.

Behind Brian was a sight she'd never forget. A yowling, screaming mass of enraged berserkers, led by a handful of fearsome Viking draugar, who vaulted over parked cars and pushed over phone boxes in their relentless pursuit. A black-feathered arrow whistled past her head and embedded itself in the wooden fence she was leaning against with a deep *thunk*.

"MOVE!" Brian yelled, grabbing her arm and dragging her on. Hayley sucked in more air and forced her legs to work.

"How ... much..." Hayley gasped but couldn't finish the sentence. But Brian knew what she meant.

"The park should be right around this corner."

They had to make it. They couldn't fail on their part of the mission. And to think, earlier Hayley was feeling annoyed that she was going to be left out of the action while Alfie and his new, shiny superhero buddies were busy doing all the fun stuff at the Tower. Instead she and Brian were on a mission to break into the Crystal Palace transmitter. The huge radio mast towered over the south London park, and it was their job to switch it back on and start broadcasting again.

"This will be a message of great comfort and cheer to those who hear it," LC had told them before they left, solemnly handing them a flash drive.

"Do you even know what this thing is called?" Hayley had laughed, holding the USB stick.

"I confess I do not, Miss Hicks. But you need to ensure it is delivered," LC had said, his face stern.

Hayley and Brian had set off south across London in good time before the curfew, keeping to quiet back streets, and had only occasionally glimpsed distant berserker patrols. The blizzard was particularly thick today, which helped them to stay concealed. They'd used the sub to travel west along the river and disembarked at Vauxhall before setting off again through the deserted streets of south London. All they had to do was reach Crystal Palace Park by nightfall, hide out and then turn on the transmitter. But as bad luck would have it, when they emerged from an alley in Dulwich, they'd ran slap bang into a party of Viking draugar from the Swanage fleet who were enjoying some shore leave. Brian and Hayley had tried to pass by the rowdy rabble unnoticed, as if they were just locals heading to the market, but one of Vikings, a huge brute with part of his skull breaking through the green skin of his forehead, had caught Hayley's eye, and grabbed her.

"Heu! Sjáið andlit á henni!"* he had yelled to his mates, turning her head this way and that, while Brian tried to reach her.

"Já, ötul er hún í alvöru!"† another Viking had guffawed, sending the rest into fits of belching laughter.

"Nei, fávitar – HÚN er sú sem höfumaðurinn leita at!"‡

---

* "Hey! Look at her face!"
† "Yeah, she's an ugly one all right!"
‡ "No, you idiots – it's HER, the one the chief is looking for!"

At this, the other Vikings had stopped laughing and started pulling Hayley back and forth between them, trying to see her face and arguing in their strange language about whether she was the infamous Resistance fighter.

"GET OFF!" Hayley had yelled at last, wriggling free and putting her hands on her hips defiantly. "If you just asked politely I might tell you. Yes, it's me."

And with that, she'd darted past them and run off with Brian. The startled Vikings had looked at each other for a moment, then roared with anger and barrelled after them. The chase was on.

"See? Fame isn't all it's cracked up to be!" Brian had yelled as they ran.

But that had been the last of the jokes as they realized these Vikings weren't going to be shaken off so easily. One of the zombies blew into a bone horn and dozens of berserkers were summoned to join the hunt.

Hayley and Brian rounded the corner of a row of shuttered houses, sprinted across the empty road and into the dark trees of Crystal Palace Park. They dived behind a snowdrift and sucked in lungfuls of air. Somewhere behind them, the Vikings howled and raged, but at least it sounded like they were moving away.

"Have you still got the laptop?" Brian asked when he'd caught his breath.

Hayley patted her backpack by way of a reply.

"And the USB stick?"

Hayley rolled her eyes and patted the backpack again. She was about to tell Brian to quit being such a control freak when the pitted blade of a battle axe sliced down from above and buried itself in the snow right next to Hayley's head. Standing above them was an undead Viking, a straggler who had chanced upon them. The creature's rusty, torn chainmail clanked as he raised the axe again. Hayley was frozen in place with terror as she stared at the Viking's face, which was pretty much a skull with no eyes. *How can it even see me?*

Brian reacted first and expertly rolled away, kicking out his legs and tripping the Viking over as he did so. But the draugar warrior landed on top of Hayley in a tangle of jagged rotten bones and stinking leather, knocking the wind out of her. The next thing she knew, Brian had grabbed the backpack and its precious cargo and hauled her to her feet.

"I'm going to need a bath!" she managed to say as behind them the downed Viking brought a horn to his lips. The deep *honk* sounded across the park and once again the chase was on as the rest of the Viking pack charged back in their direction.

"Let's go!" Brian yelled, but Hayley was limping.

"Brian ... I can't run!" Hayley gasped as she slowed down again, rubbing her thigh.

"Are you injured? Cut?" Brian asked, frantically checking her for wounds.

Hayley shook her head. The Viking had just given her a dead leg when it fell on her, which was ironic but didn't seem that funny to her at that particular moment. They had to find somewhere to hide, right now. The Vikings closed in and hammered their weapons against their shields. Brian slung Hayley over his shoulder in a fireman's lift and charged on.

Suddenly, a megalosaurus loomed out of the fog, its fearsome fangs bared.

"Dinosaur!" Hayley managed to squeak, uncomprehending. Soon they were surrounded by yet more extinct lizards: long-necked iguanadons perched on rocks and a crocodile-like telesaurus bathed in an icy pond.

It took a few seconds to realize that they were only old, life-sized models of dinosaurs, which was still a pretty odd thing to find in the middle of a park, Hayley thought. Brian gave her a boost up into the mouth of the megalosaurus and together they scrambled inside and out of sight in the giant model's belly.

"What is this place?" Hayley whispered.

"Dinosaur Court. Been here for a hundred and fifty years. Victorians were mad for them," Brian said as he peeked out of the mouth.

The pursuing Vikings had stopped hollering and were huddled at the edge of the dinosaur area, like they were daring each other to go first. It was hard to tell with all the rotten flesh, but they looked scared.

"They think these are real monsters!" Brian whispered to Hayley.

"RAAAARRGHH!" The dinosaur's hollow belly echoed Brian's bellow nicely.

"GRAARGHHHHHH!" Hayley yelled and slapped the side of the iron model for good measure.

The Vikings instantly formed a shield wall and retreated, snarling and cursing at the gathered dinosaurs. Soon Hayley and Brian could only hear them as they chased shadows in another distant part of the park.

"Saved by dinosaurs. As if my life couldn't get any weirder," Hayley sighed, rubbing her leg.

"Can you walk on it? We're not done yet." Brian said.

"Don't worry about me. You just try and keep up." Hayley smiled.

A little while later, they were standing at the base of the radio tower transmitter, which rose over seven hundred feet into the air, dominating the surrounding park. Not that you could see the top; it was shrouded in the thick, swirling snow. The tower's perimeter was surrounded by a tall fence topped with razor wire and a few bunker-like brick buildings. Checking the coast was clear, Brian produced some bolt cutters and hacked his way through a padlocked door. Inside, Hayley flicked on a torch. The beam picked out banks of computers and processors standing idle; they hadn't been used in months. A coffee cup full of mould sat on top of one of the monitors and nearby a table was smashed in half. Hayley wondered if the engineer who worked here had turned into a berserker when Lock's magic hit all those weeks ago.

"It's all yours. Do your computer-y stuff," Brian said.

"OK. We have two options. I can run a bypass with the generators, but I'd have to override the primary phase circuits and see if I can get the backups on line. That's if – and it's a big if – if the whole thing doesn't kick off a massive electricity surge with all the dirty power and cause an unstoppable overload."

"That sounds bad. What's the second option?"

"I flick this switch right here to 'on'," said Hayley and did just that.

With a rush of processor fans, a multicoloured constellation of lights appeared all around them as the transmitter station came back to beeping, whirring electronic life.

"All right, clever-clogs, well done."

Hayley grinned at Brian, retrieved her laptop from the torn backpack, and plugged it in. She was confident she could get her computer talking to the transmitter and boost whatever message they had to play.

"How do we know anyone's listening?" she asked, slotting in the USB stick and tapping away at the keyboard.

"Trust me, they will be. This might just be the spark that starts a revolution. A rallying cry."

Hayley nodded and leaned in to a microphone. "OK, listeners, this next track is something special," she said, impersonating her favourite radio DJ. "I don't know what exactly, but my friends tell me you're going to love it!"

Excited, Hayley pressed play and turned the laptop's volume up. A posh lady's voice came on and spoke calmly:

"North Utsire, South Utsire, variable three or four, becoming southwesterly four or five, occasionally six, rain later... German Bight, Humber, northeast four or five, occasionally six at first, becoming variable three or four later. Slight or moderate. Showers at first. Good..."

"What's this supposed to be?" blurted Hayley.

But as she listened to the lady's soothing stream of what sounded like nonsense, she realized she'd heard it before.

"Wait a second, I know this – Gran used to listen to it on the radio sometimes late at night, said it helped her nod off to sleep. What's it called again?"

"This," said Brian, with a knowing smile, "is the shipping forecast. Every day it tells fishermen the weather in the seas around Great Britain."

"Are you telling me I risked my life to broadcast the weather forecast for a bunch of fishermen? How's that going to bring down the Vikings?" yelled Hayley.

"It wouldn't, if that's all it was. You never heard of a coded message before?"

"*Rockall, Malin, Hebrides. Southwest gale eight to storm ten, veering west, severe gale nine to violent storm eleven...*"

In a cottage in the small village of Barnack in Lincolnshire, Yeoman Warder Stangroom trudged up the attic stairs as he did every day at 5:59 p.m. sharp. He was in a bad mood. A raiding party of Viking draugar had steamed through the village at lunchtime, taken over the Millstone pub and drunk it dry. It was so stupid, what did zombies want with beer? They didn't have any guts to absorb the beautiful stuff and most of it passed straight through their ribcages and ended up on the floor. Not only that, they'd scared the village half to death before moving on.

Thinking about it, Yeoman Warder Stangroom had been in a bad mood ever since he had gone into hiding after the battle at the Tower of London. He hated being so helpless.

He checked his watch and flicked on the radio, expecting to hear nothing but static as usual. But when the shipping forecast came through, he leapt into the air with joy – and banged his head on a low hanging beam.

But he didn't stop smiling.

"Southeast Iceland. North seven to severe gale nine. Heavy snow showers. Good, becoming poor in showers. Moderate icing."

On the Holy Island of Lindisfarne, Yeoman Burgh Keeper Roderick "Sultana" Raisin danced around his fisherman's cottage with delight, scaring Imp, his cat.

"Oh yes, you beauty!" he shouted and then put his hand over his mouth. He couldn't afford anyone to hear. Lindisfarne had seen the first undead Viking raid when all the trouble started, and it was still crawling with smelly Norsemen who, like the brain-dead idiots they were, still searched for the gold the abbey used to contain. But now he'd heard the message from London he was hopeful he'd soon see the back of them.

"Imp, my lovely, looks like we're going on a little trip!" he said.

"Tyne, Dogger. Northeast three or four. Occasional rain. Moderate or poor."

All around the country, the surviving Yeoman Warders and Burgh Keepers tuned in and heard the secret message. Some were hiding in flats, others in houses, and there were more than a few sleeping rough, camping in isolated woods, caves and snow-covered hills, but all of them scrambled to find a pen and note down the map coordinates that were hidden in the forecast. Some of them yelled out in triumph, others nodded grimly.

It was time. The fightback had begun.

18

THE TYBURN TREE

"That's super annoying, you know," said Tamara.

"What is?" LC asked and continued tapping his umbrella impatiently on the ground.

Tamara briefly considered snatching the umbrella out of his hands and throwing it into the bushes, then thought better of it. She was feeling tense as well. They were huddled in the shadow of a ruined medieval gate at the end of a small bridge in the middle of a park, nervously waiting for Alfie, Hayley and the others to return from their separate missions. *If they make it,* Tamara thought and shuddered. She and LC had been standing in the snow for what felt like hours. Conversation, never exactly flowing between the two of them at the best of times, had dried up ages ago. Even Herne became bored and was now busying himself biting chunks of ice from the edges of the frozen stream below the bridge.

To the east, the ever-present dark snow clouds glowed with the faintest light of the rising sun. Tamara had just started to say, "Surely they'd be here by now..." when there was a startling *WHOMP* of air that made her ears pop and, with a flash, Qilin appeared in front them. He whipped off his robe and mask, and was followed a moment later by the thundering approach of Holgatroll, who bounded in and transformed back into Freya.

"I win! You owe me a tenner," Tony said to Freya.

"What are you talking about, you simpleton? We never had a bet," she replied.

Tony scratched his head. "Oh, yeah. Well, if we had, I'd totally have won."

Freya shook her head with exasperation and turned to LC and Tamara. "Mission accomplished," she said, straightening her clothes and checking her hair.

"Awesome!" Tamara exclaimed with relief. "Where's Alfie?"

Tony pointed to the sky. "Joyriding."

Above them Wyvern circled around low over the roofs of the surrounding town, then dived to

236

ground level and galloped full pelt through the park, slaloming around trees, towards them on the bridge.

"INCOMING!" Tony shouted.

While everyone else braced for impact, LC stood firm. Wyvern slammed to a dead stop inches from his nose and gave him a friendly nibble.

"Good to see you again, old girl." LC smiled as the horse disappeared with a happy whinny back into the spurs. "And you too, of course, Majesty. You look splendid."

"Ellie!" Tamara gasped and rushed forward to take her unconscious daughter from Alfie's arms.

"I think she's in shock," said Alfie, removing his armour.

"We need to get her somewhere safe," said Tamara, looking to LC.

Hayley and Brian, exhausted and footsore, emerged from the shadows.

"Sunrise in five minutes," said Brian. "London's going to be crawling with angry Vikings searching for us. We need to hide."

"If you'd all care to follow me. I thought Waltham Abbey the perfect rendezvous for one very special reason," LC said.

Brian carried Ellie as LC led everyone through the ruined gate, across a graveyard dotted with faded headstones and towards an old but modest-looking church. But instead of leading them inside, he stopped at a plain stone marker that poked out of a snowdrift.

"Here we are," said LC.

"We don't have time for your theatrics, LC," hissed Tamara.

Alfie knelt, wiped the snow away from the headstone and read the inscription carved on it.

"Harold, King of England. Obit 1066. I take it this is where he's buried?" Alfie said.

"Indeed – after his defeat by the Norman invaders at the Battle of Hastings, killed by an arrow through his eye," LC replied.

"Yyyeah, bit of a buzz-kill, to be honest, LC," said Alfie, scanning every inch of the headstone. "So is there a button, or what? Lever? Secret password?"

"Merely place your hand on the stone, Majesty, if you will."

Alfie did as he was told, and immediately his hand tingled as the stone glowed with familiar, blue-blood magic. Something ancient was waking up.

As they all gazed in wonder, the ghostly outlines of round columns, magnificent stone arches, stained-glass windows and a grand roof appeared out of thin air as the original abbey that once stood there was rebuilt around them. Soon the medieval building seemed to solidify, although, every once in a while, it would glitch and shimmer and they could glimpse the outside world through the walls. That wasn't all; it felt warmer now, and there was the smell of incense in the air.

"We call it a 'royal peculiar'. There are a number dotted around the country: sanctuaries for the Defender in times of trouble," said LC as the others began to explore the magical hideout.

"Nice. So can anyone see us in here?" asked Hayley.

"No, no," said LC, finding a bench to rest on. "We are quite safely hidden away, as long as you don't venture outside the walls. Anyone out there would just see a field." He turned to Alfie. "The magnificent abbey that now surrounds us is the place that King Harold came to pray before he defeated the Vikings at Stamford Bridge earlier in his reign."

Alfie could only nod. An invisible abbey. He was lost for words.

"Pretty neat trick, LC," Hayley said, gazing around in awe. "It's beautiful."

The mournful, haunting sound of plainsong echoed softly around the pillars and arcades of the ancient, ghostly building, but there was no sign of the monks singing it.

"Echoes of the past," LC whispered and closed his eyes, listening. "Now, about Princess Eleanor. . ."

Brian laid her down gently. Her skin was grey and clammy, her breathing shallow. Alfie opened the regalia case and took out a sword with a blunt, square end.

"What does that one do?" asked Tony.

"You'll see," said LC. "It is the Sword of Mercy."

Alfie pressed the flat edge of the sword against Ellie's chest and she reacted at once, arching her back, gasping as colour flooded back into her cheeks. She opened her eyes, taking a moment to register the crowd of faces looking down at her, until she saw Tamara.

"MUM?!" she croaked.

Tamara stroked her face. "Yeah, it's me. You're safe now."

Brian turned to the others. "Been a long day. Everyone, get some shut-eye," he ordered, and then stretched out on a pew using a backpack as a pillow.

But sleep was the last thing on Alfie's mind. He, Hayley, Freya and Tony moved away from everyone else to fill each other in on the details of the raid on the Tower. Freya and Tony argued about how many Vikings they'd each taken out. The current score was Freya: sixty-eight, Tony: fifty-two. Hayley listened patiently until they were finished then told them about the number of Vikings she outwitted at Crystal Palace. Even Freya seemed grudgingly impressed.

"Not bad, I suppose," the queen sniffed.

"Not bad? Listen, death breath, I did it all without any magic powers. Just what's in here. And here." Hayley said, tapping her own head and flexing her bicep.

"Yes, that's what I meant: not bad *for a commoner*," Freya said.

"Commoner?!" Hayley bristled and was about to launch into another verbal assault before Alfie headed it off.

"So, Freya, has your family always had, you know. . ." he began.

"BO problems?" interrupted Hayley.

"Troll's blood?" said Alfie rapidly.

"Yes, ever since ancient times," replied Freya. "Our land was once ruled by pure trolls, a noble, intelligent race. But when the first Ice Age thawed and foreign invaders arrived, they were afraid of them and, in a great war, drove them to the edge of extinction. My family were the trolls' only allies and soon our two tribes became one. We drove out the invaders and ruled in peace ever since. I got my troll powers when I was thirteen, so I had a little time to adjust before I took the throne."

Alfie pointed at the sparking green necklace that Freya always wore. "And is that part of your powers?"

Freya smiled, caressing the jewel. "It is much

more than that. It is called Brísingamen, forged from two rocks. One is an emerald – my human ancestors' greatest treasure. The other is Troll's Ice – the same for the troll side of my family. When I took the throne, I bonded with it for life. It will only be removed from my body when I die."

Tony was watching her, doe-eyed. "Wow, we have *so* much in common it's not even funny," he said.

Freya looked at him askance. "*You* have troll's blood?"

"Well, no, not that exactly," said Tony. "But my ancestors were way into all that nature conservation stuff too. The legend goes that thousands of years ago my homeland was ruled by an evil and greedy king who starved his own people. So one day my great-great-great-great-great-great-great-great-great—"

"We get the idea, Tony," said Alfie.

"All right, well, lots-of-greats grandmother, who was still a young girl, was hunting in the forest to feed her orphaned brothers and sisters when she accidentally shot the last Qilin – the Chinese Unicorn – through the heart with an arrow. The young girl cradled the magical creature as it lay dying and wept tears of regret. The gods of the forest were so touched by her grief that they transferred the Qilin's powers into her. She used them to get rid of the unjust king and took his place. Her descendants inherited her powers, all the way down to little old me."

"Good story, Tony," said Alfie.

"Sounds a little implausible if you ask me," quipped Freya.

"Says Miss Half-Troll," said Hayley.

As they laughed, Alfie noticed that Ellie was wandering around the abbey. He caught up with her near the altar as she gazed at the old stained-glass windows.

"How's it going, sis?"

"Oh, you know, pretty typical day. Found out that my loser big brother isn't dead like I thought and is actually a superhero and so are all his mates. Oh, and I forgot to mention, turns out my other brother is an evil monster who wants to destroy the world. So yeah, everything's just fine." Tears welled in Ellie's eyes. She looked at Alfie with such a look of desperation that he hugged her and, amazingly, she didn't even try to wriggle away.

"This feels really weird to say, but thanks for rescuing me from the Tower," she said, then seemed to remember something else. "Oh yeah, and from the Dragon at the coronation, and when I fell off the bridge before that. I think I need to sit down."

Alfie sat her down on a step.

"I'm sorry I couldn't tell you about all this before.

You wouldn't believe all the rules LC makes me follow," said Alfie.

"Yeah, I would," she said, then pointed at the regalia case, which sat open nearby. "How does all this stuff work, then?"

"It's complicated. Ancient blue blood, a mystical crown from the gods. . ."

"So magic, basically."

"Basically, yeah."

"So, do I have this magic in me, then?"

"Yep, afraid so. Although it follows the line of succession so it would only activate if Richard and me weren't around."

Ellie shook her head and laughed. "This is nuts."

Their mother came over to join them. "Are we having a family meeting?" she asked.

"It's a little overdue, wouldn't you say?" said Ellie. "Just let me ask the questions and don't stop answering unless I look like I'm going to faint again, yeah?"

And with that Ellie was off, like a determined detective on the trail of the answer to a long-buried mystery. The secret, magical history of the monarchy. The faked divorce between King Henry and Tamara. The disagreement with LC. What they knew about Lock and his diabolical plans. Alfie thought Ellie took it all in pretty well. Bit by bit, he could see her hostility to her mum ebbing away and, by the end, her main issue was that she was kept in the dark for so long.

"It's just so typical; I'm the youngest so I'm the last to know."

"I'm sorry, Ellie. Really," Tamara said. "If I could go back, I'd do things differently."

"Why don't we make a promise?" said Ellie. "From now on there's no more secrets between us." She offered her hand to shake.

"Sorry, I'm more of hugger," Tamara said.

"Take it or leave it," Ellie said. "We'll see about a hug later." Alfie smiled at his sister's no-nonsense way of dealing with the world.

"Just like your father. All right, have it your way." Tamara laughed, conceding defeat. She took Ellie's hand. "No more secrets."

"Do you think there's any hope?" Ellie said as she looked at a stained-glass window above them. In it, Saint George, depicted as a knight in armour, fought a green dragon that had wrapped its tail around his white horse, trying to drag it down. "For Rich, I mean?"

"Honestly? I don't know," Alfie said. "But I'll try everything I can, I promise."

"Chief? Think you'd better see this," Brian called from the far end of the abbey, waving his mobile phone. "I was just checking that the shipping forecast was still playing when this came on. We're not the only ones broadcasting something."

Alfie watched the phone as Hayley and the others peered over his shoulder. The screen was broadcasting images of Lock standing on some kind of wooden platform and addressing the camera.

"People of Britain. This is your Lord Protector Cameron Lock speaking to you from Marble Arch in London."

The camera panned around to show the silent, snow-shrouded city and the white stone of the famous London landmark.

"It has recently come to my attention that the so-called 'Defender' is once again at large. Rest assured, this trouble-making criminal and his gang will be found and punished."

"Cool! We're gangsters!" Tony said. Everybody shushed him as Lock went on.

"Once, they called this place I am standing on the Tyburn Tree. It is high time we raised it again to show how we deal with traitors. Anyone giving help or shelter to the Defender will pay the ultimate price."

The camera angle suddenly widened to show a heavy wooden arch above Lock's head.

"It's a gibbet," LC said darkly.

Alfie was just about to ask what that was when a rope, tied in a hangman's noose, dropped down next to Lock. Everyone gasped.

"Bring the prisoner forward!" Lock ordered.

Two hulking great undead Vikings climbed the scaffold, dragging a Yeoman Warder in a tatty uniform with them. As they heaved him to his feet, he turned to face the camera and they could see the wizened, scruffy features of the Yeoman Jailor.

"It's Sid!" gasped Ellie. "He helped me escape."

Sid the Jailer stared defiantly at his captors as they looped the noose over his head.

"They're going to kill him! Alfie, do something!" begged Ellie.

Alfie grabbed the Shroud Tunic from the regalia case and put it on, transforming into the Defender. "Spurs!" Alfie yelled. Wyvern appeared in an instant and reared up, ready for action.

"No, Majesty! You can't go!" LC ordered. He was waving his hands in the air like a man flagging down a taxi. "Lock is trying to draw you into a trap!"

"They're going to hang the poor guy!" Alfie protested. Wyvern stamped on the floor of the abbey as if agreeing with her master.

LC took the phone from Brian and turned it off. "Yes, sir. They will, and for that I am deeply sorry. But if you go now like this, in anger, without a plan, all you are doing is endangering the lives of millions more."

Alfie steadied Wyvern and recalled her into his spurs. He kicked the wall in anger, then took off his armour and flung the Shroud Tunic back into the regalia case. "I should never have come home," he said.

"I thought the same at first," said LC. "That your presence would play into Lock's hands. But perhaps I was wrong. Your return has also started something else. Defiance. Rebellion. Hope."

The others looked to the floor. Tamara hugged Ellie as she wept.

"We can't just let him get away with it," said Alfie quietly.

"Oh, we won't, Majesty. But joining battle before we are at our strongest, before we are truly ready? That's not courage. That's foolishness. If history tells us anything, it is that fighting evil comes at a price. The Yeoman Jailor knew that, and he made his choice. More will do the same before this is over."

"Is it worth it?" asked Ellie, drying her tears.

"That depends on all of you. Monarch, soldier or 'commoner'. It's not your title, nor your powers that make you a hero. It's what you do when all seems lost and the night is at its darkest."

19
CAPTURE THE FLAG

Lock's angry yelling could be heard echoing through every corner of the Keep. The Viking Lord standing before him might have been capable of snapping his neck like a toothpick, but that didn't seem to worry the ex-teacher as he scolded Guthrum like he was a naughty schoolboy.

"You and your incompetent friends have let the Defender slip through your fingers AGAIN! How you ever terrorized half the known world is beyond me. You can't even capture a teenaged boy when you have his address!"

"Gáðit at orðin ykkr hin næstuna, Engilsmenn,"*

---

* "Careful what you say next, Englishman."

snarled Guthrum, pointing a mighty finger at Lock's red face.

"I'll say whatever I like! I dug you up and I won't hesitate to bury you again – one Norse spell and you'll crumble to dust!"

Guthrum didn't know if Lock really had a spell that could do that, but he had enough brains left not to risk finding out the hard way.

"Sveinkonung þinn skulum vér finna. Þá endask með oss. Nú er mér nog boðit að heyra boðinum þinum."*

Guthrum raised his axe and with a roar stamped out of the hall.

Richard shuffled out of the shadows. He was deathly pale and sweating, pulling a blanket tight around his shivering body. Black ridges pushed through his scalp beneath his thinning hair and his teeth seemed to be pointed rather than square.

"Do you think they'll find Alfie?" he rasped. "He didn't like the way you spoke to him."

Lock waved a dismissive hand and pulled the velvet cloth from the scrying mirror which stood nearby, polishing its frame with it.

"What do you know about Vikings? The only thing they respect is strength."

---

* "We'll find your boy king. Then we're finished. I've had enough of taking orders from you."

"Yes, but if they don't catch him soon. . . I don't know how much longer I can take this," said Richard, coming closer and turning Lock to face him. "Look at me."

"Get your hands off me," snapped Lock. "Don't forget who's in charge here, boy."

"Who, you?" scoffed Richard. "I thought she was." He nodded to the mirror.

Lock grabbed him by the scruff of the neck. "You ungrateful brat! After everything I've done for you!"

"What you've done for me?!" yelled Richard, eyes flashing scarlet.

He lashed out, throwing Lock to the floor. Scales erupted over Richard's skin and, in an instant, he had transformed into the Black Dragon. Wings burst from his back, sending the broken halves of the ops table spinning into the wall. Flames licked round his jaws as he spat his words at Lock. "YOU'VE CURSED ME! I SHOULD BURN YOU FOR WHAT YOU'VE DONE!"

The Dragon's throat glowed deep orange as flames crackled inside.

"Your anger serves you well." The words swam through the Dragon's skull. The voice from the mirror was talking to him again, accompanied by the constant drone of flies.

Hel's face appeared from the black soup of the

mirror's surface, this time both halves: the living and the long dead. The Dragon recoiled at the sight.

"Can't you look at me, young prince?" Hel asked. "I wasn't always like this. But it is so much better to be powerful and a monster than beautiful and weak, don't you agree? This world was never meant for mortal men," she went on, her words slithering into the Dragon's ears and coiling round his brain like a snake. "Once I have risen, we shall return it to the way it was before they infested it. And you will reign by my side. That is, if you still have the stomach to be a king."

The Black Dragon looked up at her, eyes burning red.

"I am with you," he said.

Lock stepped forward, wringing his hands nervously.

"There has been a slight delay, but the rebel king will be captured soon enough," he said.

Hel's terrible eyes flicked to Lock, scowling with menace. "I am growing impatient with your promises," she hissed. "Without king's blood given freely, we cannot complete the ritual. If you cannot bring about my return, Professor, I will find someone else who can. Theirs will be the glory and the reward, not yours."

"It will be done, my mistress," said Lock with a bow.

Hel's image faded from the mirror and Lock covered it with the cloth. Agitated, he paced up and down.

"We cannot leave the hunt for Alfie to the Vikings alone," he muttered. "I have a feeling this time he hasn't gone far. England is riddled with bolt-holes used by your family over the centuries."

Lock strode over to the large hatch in the floor, beneath which lay the Archives – the cavern of scrolls holding the secret true history of Britain.

"What are you doing?" asked the Dragon.

"What I do best – uncovering the secrets of the past!"

He heaved open the hatch and no sooner had the stale air rushed out into the Keep than a berserker came screaming at him out of the darkness. It was Yeoman Brenda Box, who had been trapped in the Archives ever since Hayley had booted her down there just before the Vikings took the Keep. The Black Dragon grabbed her by the leg before she could reach Lock and lifted the shrieking maniac off her feet.

"Get lost," the Dragon growled into the berserker's crazed face, hurling her across the hall. He turned back to see Lock already climbing down into the

Archives and slinging scrolls out. "And what do we do once we've found their hideout?"

"We smoke them out," said Lock.

Brian lifted the powerful binoculars to his eyes and scanned the windows of the Palace of Westminster once more. He had found his way into the abandoned Treasury building on the far side of the square several hours earlier. Being careful not to make any noise or allow himself to be spotted from outside, he had positioned himself at a high window and begun his surveillance. The gothic spires of the Houses of Parliament were dusted white, like an ornament inside a snow globe waiting to be picked up and shaken. Brian was no sun worshipper – his army years in the Middle East had provided him quite enough baking heat for a lifetime. But now he missed the warmth of the sun on his skin, the same way he missed a lot of other things about his life before... He shook his head and focused on the job in hand. He'd counted Viking draugar in and out of St Stephen's Porch, the main entrance to Parliament, all day and thought he was starting to get a handle on their routine. It was dark now and the streets were quiet. A squad of six draugar came stomping out of the entrance, grunting and muttering at each other, and disappeared into the mist. Brian lifted his radio from his belt.

"The day shift just left. Estimate nine to twelve of them left inside. Hard to be sure, but recommend you deploy now."

High above the Houses of Parliament, Wyvern hovered in the cover of the cloud bank. Alfie heard Brian's transmission inside his Defender helmet.

"Got it, thanks. See you later," he replied.

He turned his head to Freya, who was sitting behind him, and Tony who was behind her, his arms round her waist, a cheesy grin plastered across his face.

"Time to get your property back, Your Majesty," said Alfie.

"Good," said Freya. "Another minute and I would have yanked your friend's arms out of their sockets."

"Like I said before," said Tony cheerfully, "it's purely a matter of horseback safety. I don't like it any more than you do."

Alfie smiled to himself. "Well, hang on, this is going to be quick," he said.

The Defender gripped the reins and kicked his heels, sending Wyvern into a steep dive. They plummeted from the clouds and a second later landed on the roof of the Houses of Parliament. Freya shook off Tony's arms and jumped down. Alfie recalled Wyvern into his spurs and together they edged their way along the slippery tiles until they reached the right spot.

"Ready?" asked Alfie.

Tony activated his Qilin outfit "Steady!" he said.

Freya's necklace glowed green and muscles sprouted all over her body as she transformed into Holgatroll. "I'm not going to say GO, if that's what you're waiting for," she said.

"You totally did just say it though," sniggered Tony.

With a growl of irritation, Holgatroll leapt thirty feet straight up into the air. As she started to fall back down again, the Defender and Qilin looked at each other and then tried to jump out of the way.

CRASH!

Holgatroll smashed down through the skylight in a shower of glass, tiles and plaster and landed at one end of the Commons chamber. The Defender and Qilin tumbled after her, Alfie summoning Wyvern just in time to fly above the benches and Tony spinning upright into a hover just above the floor. The three invaders braced themselves for the Viking onslaught.

But there was no one there.

"What's your status?" It was Brian, over Alfie's radio.

"Er, better than expected, actually. No one's home," replied Alfie.

"Nobody at all?" Brian sounded confused.

The Raven Banner stood in the centre of the

256

chamber, right where Lock had planted it, radiating its evil blood-red lines out through the scorched carpet, cracked floor and smashed green benches.

"You see?" grumbled Holgatroll. "Don't know what you wimps were so worried about."

She crossed the floor to the flag in three mighty strides and reached out to grab it.

"Get out of there! It's a trap!" yelled Brian through the radio.

Alfie looked to Holgatroll and shouted, "Stop!"

But it was too late. The troll's fingers passed through the flagpole as if it wasn't there.

"What?" she said, and grabbed at the banner itself. But the hologram of the flag and the red lines coming from it flickered and disappeared. In the same instant, a cage sprang up around Holgatroll, its bars made from pulsing, glowing beams of energy. She roared and punched at it with her fist. Sparks and smoke filled the cage and she withdrew her burned hand with a yelp.

"I'M COMING!" shouted Qilin.

He tried to blink-shift into the cage, but rematerialized outside it, rebounding off the pulsating bars with a flash and a loud bang. Qilin groaned and got up, trying to reach through the cage to touch Holgatroll, but every time he did the bars would shift position and he had to pull his fingers away. Hearing the main doors of the chamber burst open behind him, Alfie swept Qilin up and flew on Wyvern high into eaves of the ceiling.

"What are you doing?" Tony protested. "I nearly had her!"

"Look!" said Alfie, pointing to the entrance.

Ten draugar warriors marched inside, an escort guard for Lock and Guthrum, who was carrying a bulky silver-and-black laser pulse rifle. It was the Cyclotron Particle Accelerator, which the Prime Minister had used to capture the Defender before the invasion.

"Amazing the high-tech gear the government left lying around," said Lock, his voice echoing around the chamber. "The Cyclotron energy has so many useful applications."

Guthrum aimed the Cyclotron at the cage and fired it. A lasso of fizzing blue energy shot through the bars and wrapped themselves around Holgatroll's neck. She transformed back into Freya, screaming in agony as the beam tore her emerald necklace off and carried it out of the cage.

Lock waved at the Speaker's Chair and Guthrum directed the beam to drop the necklace on to it. Freya fell on all fours, moaning with pain. He peered at her through the fizzing bars. "Apologies, Majesty, but I'm going to need to hang on to your banner a little longer. Don't worry, though, it's nearby and quite safe."

The Defender whipped out his nunchuck-sceptres and hurled them at the cage. The impact caused a flash, but instead of cutting through the bars, the weapons fell to the floor. Alfie commanded them to fly up and return to his hand.

Lock gazed up at the Defender and Qilin hovering high above him. "So nice to see you making some friends at last, Alfie. You never were very popular at school, were you?"

"Let her go, Professor," said Alfie, unsheathing the Sword of State in a burst of light.

"It's Lord Protector these days, if you don't mind. And no, I won't release Her Majesty, I'm afraid. But I will allow you to join her."

He nodded at Guthrum, who shouldered the Cyclotron rifle and emitted a ferocious blast of snaking blue energy straight up at them. Qilin grabbed Alfie and blink-shifted them both to the opposite side of the chamber. The Viking Lord roared his irritation and swivelled around, sending another blast their way. They disappeared once more, reappearing back where they started.

"Enough party tricks," barked Lock. "Surrender now, and perhaps I'll call off your brother. He should be arriving at Waltham Abbey any minute now."

The Defender looked to Qilin, eyes wide with alarm. "They know," said Alfie. "We have to warn the others!"

He nodded at the gaping hole in the ceiling. They hovered nearer so Qilin could get a line of sight to blink-shift through. But Guthrum was too fast for them, shooting a third wave of Cyclotron energy in their direction. Alfie just had time to deploy the shields from his armill bracelets, but the impact sent them both spinning into the wall and crashing down on to the viewing balcony known as Strangers' Gallery.

"Close it," said Lock.

Guthrum adjusted the settings on the Cyclotron and blasted a web of energy at the hole in the roof, which sealed it with a spider's web of impenetrable beams.

"Now bring them to me," commanded Lock.

The Viking squad swarmed up the walls like giant cockroaches, closing in on the gallery from all sides, singing their oddly musical song as they climbed. Guthrum shut his eyes as his body responded to the Norse incantation, bulging and growing by the second, till he had doubled in size. The Defender and Qilin lay sprawled on the balcony.

"I can keep shifting us, but it won't buy much time at this rate," panted Qilin.

Alfie looked round for ideas, but all he could see were Viking fingers clawing their way over the lip of the gallery, and the top of giant, fifteen-feet-tall Guthrum's head rising into view. Suddenly gunshots rang out and the double doors at the far end of the gallery flew open. Brian stepped inside, tossed a smoke bomb into the chamber and beckoned to them.

"THIS WAY!"

As one, they made for the door through the smoke, Qilin scattering a handful of silver fireballs behind them, which blasted the incoming Vikings off their feet. For good measure, the Defender commanded every bench he could muster to fly at Guthrum, knocking him off balance just as he lunged for Alfie and Tony with his gargantuan hands. Moments later they were outside and flying clear on Wyvern. But there was no triumph in their escape. They were in a race against time. Holgatroll would have to fend for herself, for now.

They had to reach Waltham Abbey before the Black Dragon.

20
FIRESTORM

Thump.

The noise echoed around the ghostly abbey. Tamara woke from a light and troubled sleep. Was Alfie back already? Was that the sound of Wyvern's hooves?

Thump.

"Everyone else is hearing that, right?" Ellie said, as she ran down the cavernous nave to find LC and her mum glancing around.

Thump.

"I thought you said this place was safe?" Tamara whispered.

"It is. Perfectly," LC snapped.

"Even so. Maybe one of us should go outside and check it out?"

"Step outside of these walls and you'll become visible for all to see. I forbid it."

"You *forbid* it?" Tamara said, exasperated. "Where's the front door of this place?"

"Don't be foolish!" LC said as Tamara stormed off.

"What are you arguing about this time?" Hayley asked as she joined them. She held her longbow in one hand and had a quiver of newly sharpened arrows on her back. Next to her, Herne stretched and yawned, unconcerned.

"There's something thumping around out there. Didn't you hear it?" Ellie said.

"Oh, you mean this?" Hayley laughed, drew back her bow and fired an arrow at the ornately carved wooden partition wall of one of the abbey's side chapels. *Thump.*

"Need to keep my eye in." Hayley shrugged.

While Ellie giggled with relief, LC fumed.

"This abbey has been here for over a thousand years, Miss Hicks. I ask you kindly to not shoot arrows indoors!"

"It's not real. It's just a – what did you call it? A royal peculiar. A mirage."

While LC muttered something about "priceless rood screens" and the youth of today having no respect for history, Ellie helped Hayley retrieve her arrows, levering them out of the wood.

"We could have used you on my school's archery team," Ellie said as she admired the tight grouping of arrows.

"Seriously? What kind of school has an archery team?" Hayley asked.

"The stupid, posh kind. Hockey, lacrosse, water polo. . . You name it, we had it," Ellie said with a sigh and sat down on a wooden pew. "I was captain of gymnastics, swimming and table tennis. I was going to give women's rugby a go this term, but then some undead Vikings decided to wreck the country, which was very inconsiderate of them."

Hayley couldn't stop herself laughing. "You posh people just take everything in your stride, don't you?"

"You don't think much of us blue bloods, do you?" asked Ellie.

"I didn't used to. But you're growing on me." Hayley smiled as Ellie studied her, unashamedly sizing her up. "It's Queen Troll who has the serious attitude problem."

"She's really not Alfie's type, you know," Ellie said.

"Why does everyone think I fancy Alfie?!" Hayley said and tore one of her arrows out of the wood.

"Oh, sorry," Ellie shrugged, "I thought you were cross because he'd gone off with her tonight."

"What I'm mad about is that I had a perfectly good plan to get rid of the Raven Banner, but no, Alfie promised Queen Blondie that he'd help her get it back, so off they go. Didn't even ask me to help! Must be hard to think clearly when she bats those big stupid eyelashes and waves her long hair around."

"But you're definitely not jealous, though?" Ellie smirked, then held up her hands as Hayley glared at her.

She yanked the last arrow out of the wall and sat down next to Ellie. "He can be such an idiot sometimes. He says the stupidest things and his jokes are the lamest jokes in the history of lame."

"Agreed." Ellie smiled.

"But even so . . . all right, I suppose I do. . ." Hayley searched for the right word. ". . . *care* for him. A bit."

"How did you guys even meet in the first place?"

Hayley told Ellie everything – slowly at first, trying to remember the exact sequence of the many events that had brought her to the point of talking to a princess in a magical, ghost abbey. From Alfie and her first frantic moments on the roof of Gran's block of flats when he came for the dragon scale, and the early days of her hiding in the Tower, to gatecrashing Glastonbury; from her gran to her rows with LC. By the time she'd reached the battle at the Tower of London and the dark days that followed thinking Alfie was dead, Hayley was in full flow and Ellie was grasping her hand.

"You and Alf have been through so much together," said Ellie.

"I guess we have," said Hayley.

At their feet, Herne growled.

"And you too, Herne," Ellie joked, giving him a stroke.

But Hayley wasn't laughing. Something was wrong. "What is it, boy?"

Herne growled and bared his fangs. He was looking at the ceiling.

"The town is on fire!" Tamara shouted.

Ellie and Hayley ran over to join Tamara and LC, who were peering out of one of the stained-glass windows. Sure enough, the night sky was glowing orange. The houses of Waltham Abbey were ablaze. As they watched, a jet of bright yellow flame shot down from the sky like a fiery tongue, licking the densely packed rooftops.

Screeeeeeech!

Ellie clamped her hands over her ears and tried to block out the terrible noise as the hulking, bat-like shadow skimmed the rooftops.

"The Black Dragon! He's found us," LC said, shocked.

"Richard!" Ellie screamed in disbelief.

People in pyjamas and dressing gowns poured on to the streets, some pointing at the Black Dragon and others at the flames consuming their homes.

"We've got to help. Let's go!" Hayley yelled and ran for the abbey's great doors and threw them open. Ellie pelted after her along with Herne.

"NO! THAT'S WHAT HE WANTS! HE'S TRYING TO FLUSH US OUT!" LC shouted, but his words were drowned out as the Black Dragon made another pass over the town, screeching and belching fire.

Out on the streets, in a row of houses and shops near the church, Hayley and Ellie joined a bucket brigade of townspeople as they tried to extinguish one of the burning buildings. LC, alongside Tamara, elbowed his way into the line.

"We must protect the line of succession!" LC hissed and tried to pull Ellie away, but she wouldn't budge.

"Let go of me!" Ellie said.

"He's right. Back to the abbey, we're safe there!" Tamara said.

"Then we take everyone here too!" Hayley snapped and passed another bucket down the line.

"Impossible—" LC said and was about go on when he was interrupted by a girl, running up and down, frantically pulling on people's arms.

"Someone help me!" she shouted. She was wrapped in a winter coat but her feet were bare in the slush and ice.

"What is it?" Hayley asked.

"My gran! She's trapped inside!"

Hayley shot through the smoke-filled front door before the girl had even finished talking, Ellie hot on her heels.

"WAIT!" shouted her mother, but they were separated in the melee of panicking people outside the burning house.

Inside the house, the air was already full of dense black smoke. Hayley and Ellie crouched low, covering their mouths as they checked the living room and kitchen. Both were empty.

"She's got to be upstairs!" Hayley shouted over the loud crackling of the fire.

Ellie took off her jumper and ran it under the kitchen tap, then clasped it to her face. Hayley did the same with her own. They took the stairs two at a time. On the landing, the smoke was so dense they had to crawl along the floor, feeling the way with their hands. The first bedroom was engulfed with flames, forcing them back, but in the second one, they found an old woman huddled under a duvet, groaning.

"Help . . . me. . ." she croaked.

"You're going to be all right!" Hayley said, coughing hard as smoke filled her lungs.

Together, Hayley and Ellie tried to move the

woman, but she clung to her mattress like it was a life raft. They were running out of time. The roof above them was burning white hot.

"Give me a hand with this!" Ellie shouted, grabbing hold of the mattress and pulling it off the bed. Hayley followed suit, and together they heaved the mattress like a stretcher, with the old woman still on it, across the floor and towards the stairs.

Outside, Tamara was frantic, trying to reach the house. But as the flames rose higher, people held her back.

"NO, LET ME GO! MY DAUGHTER'S IN THERE!" she yelled, to no avail. But just then, through the crowd, Tamara saw Hayley and Ellie emerge from the house with the old lady, people hurrying to help them. They were exhausted and smoke-blackened, but unharmed.

She started to move towards them, but LC stopped her.

"What is it?" she asked.

LC nodded and she saw what had alarmed him. A squad of draugar Vikings were marching down the road towards them. The commander pointed directly at the Lord Chamberlain.

"We've been seen. We must draw them away," he whispered.

With a last, pained look back at her daughter,

Tamara nodded and followed LC away from the house, down the street. The Vikings quickened their pace.

"ÞÉR! LÉTTIÐ!"* shouted their commander.

Suddenly another draugar squad turned into the road ahead of them. LC stooped to pick up a handful of rocks from the side of the road.

"I don't think those are going to stop them, LC."

"They're not for them," he replied, arranging the stones in a circle on the pavement.

The Vikings advanced on them from both directions now, sending the street's residents fleeing in renewed panic. LC and Tamara stayed put in the stone circle; there was nowhere to go. They braced themselves to be cut down by the Vikings, but their attackers stopped a few yards short and looked to the sky.

"Oh no," uttered LC.

Talons descended from the darkness and lifted them both off the ground.

Outside the burning house, Ellie and Hayley watched in horror as Tamara and LC were carried away into the night sky by the Black Dragon.

A short while later, after the Vikings had departed and the town's residents had abandoned the smouldering ruins of their homes to find shelter

---

* "YOU THERE! HALT!"

elsewhere, Ellie and Hayley remained on the street near the abbey, shell-shocked. In a rumble of hooves, Alfie, Tony and Brian arrived, and both groups had to share the terrible news of their losses.

"You don't think Richard would really hurt Mum, do you?" Ellie asked Alfie, her eyes pleading.

"I don't know," replied Alfie, downcast. "I didn't think he'd hurt Dad, but..." He prepared to put his armour back on. "We'll make for the Tower right away. We have to save them."

"The Lord Chamberlain wouldn't want that," said Brian, who was some distance away, crouched over something in the road.

"How do you know that?" asked Alfie.

"Because he left us a message, that's why," Brian said, standing back to reveal the ring of stones still standing where LC had placed them.

"What does it mean?" asked Hayley.

"It means we should carry on with the plan," said Brian. "Continue to the rally point and await the Yeoman Warders."

"You got all that from a bunch of rocks?" asked Tony.

"Where is it?" asked Alfie. "Where are we going?"

"Can't you tell?" said Brian, pointing to the circle of rocks at their feet.

21

PRISONERS

The Lord Chamberlain lay in the dim light of the glowing keys that hung at the centre of the dungeon antechamber. Tamara leaned over him, holding his hand.

"That's it, just breathe. . ." she said.

LC closed his eyes and willed his heartbeat to slow its gallop. He felt Tamara's grip tighten for a moment and opened his eyes again to see her looking into the shadows, scared. A scrape of talon on rock, a gust of hot air, the flap of a leathery wing. So the Black Dragon wasn't done with them yet. It was still here, watching.

"Why don't you come out?" coughed LC. "Or are you too ashamed to be seen?"

"Don't," Tamara whispered to the old man. She

272

didn't want to see the thing that had carried them here. Her son. Her Richard.

"The only shame here is yours," hissed the Black Dragon, circling them in the gloom. "You let our family become weak, a laughing stock. If people have suffered, it's your fault, not mine."

"Is that what your keeper tells you?" continued LC. "It's funny, I don't remember you being such a gullible child."

The Dragon shot from the darkness, its jaws open, fire whistling around its dagger teeth, inches from LC's face.

"NO!" yelled Tamara.

The Dragon's eyes flicked to her. Then it withdrew, as if remembering what it must look like to her. LC squeezed Tamara's hand and whispered. "Talk to him. He'll listen to you."

Tamara swallowed hard and mustered a smile through her tears.

"I would like to speak to my son," she said in a level voice.

The Black Dragon snorted and flicked its tail across the dungeon doors behind it.

"That makes a change. I thought you were more interested in your horses than your family."

"I shouldn't have left; I'm sorry. But I did what I thought was best. Can I speak with Richard?"

The Dragon recoiled, as if stung by his own true name.

"Please," continued Tamara, "I'm still your mother. I love you. I want to help you."

For a moment the beast met her eyes and she thought she could see a fleeting glimpse of the son she remembered. A furrow in the brow, a softness in the eyes. LC watched with awe. She was getting through to him.

"Richard. It's me. Show me Richard," she urged, reaching out her hand to the monster's face.

The heavy clunk of a bolt being slid open and the sound of footsteps approaching shattered the moment. The Black Dragon shook its body and opened its wings.

"There is no Richard. There is only the Dragon. Your son is dead," it sneered, then turned and crawled away up a staircase into the dark.

Tamara put her hand to her mouth, giving way to the grief that swept over her.

Across the room, Cameron Lock stepped down into the chamber, flanked by his Viking guards. "How the mighty have fallen," he chuckled.

"You monster!" shouted Tamara, lunging at him, only for the nearest Viking to pick her up and fling her back to the floor.

"Careful now," said Lock, "I may have decided to

keep you alive for the time being, but if you push me, I'll gladly send you to the Tyburn Tree."

"You should be the one hanging," spat Tamara, "for what you've done."

"Is it really me you're angry with?" asked Lock. "Or is it the former Lord Chamberlain here?" He turned to LC. "How many kings and queens have you let down over your many, many years of service?"

"I don't answer to traitors," said LC, refusing to meet his eye.

"Or perhaps, Queen Tamara," continued Lock, enjoying himself, "it is yourself you blame, for abandoning your children to their fate? Still, at least you brought Alfie back. He's going to be very useful to me."

"If you harm a hair on his head, I promise you, I'll—"

Lock waved an arm dismissively. "You're in no position to promise anything. You are relics of this kingdom's pathetic past, both of you. A new age is coming, something glorious you'll never live to see." He turned to the Viking guards. "Throw them in a cell. If they resist, kill them."

He turned and made for the stairs. The Vikings heaved LC and Tamara to their feet.

"You're a fool if you think you can control her, Lock," shouted LC. The professor stopped for a moment but did not turn around. "Hel will destroy you along with everybody else."

Lock carried on up the staircase, out of sight.

Later, in the pitch darkness of their cell, the prisoners spoke in hushed, defeated tones.

"What he said about your long service, all the kings and queens... Does Alfie know?" asked Tamara.

LC let out a laboured sigh. "No. His Majesty knows only what he needs to."

"Then I hope he was paying attention to his training. Because Lock was right about one thing. You and I can't do anything now. It's up to the kids. Everything depends on them."

High above them, Lord Protector Lock caressed the edge of Hel's mirror. Even shrouded with its velvet cover, the sound of impatient flies coming from it was constant now. It was no longer a mere object; it was a living thing, like a mad dog straining at its leash. Lock smiled.

"Soon, my mistress, we will have what we need to release you, and you will turn our enemies into dust."

22

FAMILY TIES

Alfie had never liked hunting. Despite his father's attempts to take him grouse shooting or deer stalking when he was old enough, he'd always made excuses not to go. He could tell his father was disappointed, even though Richard was only too keen to join in. It wasn't just that Alfie felt faint at the sight of blood, it was more that it didn't seem like a fair fight to him – some defenceless animal against a bunch of fully-grown men armed with guns. It sounded more like a massacre than a sport. But tonight he truly understood for the first time what it must feel like to be that animal, hiding, running for your life, waiting for the end to come at any moment.

Lock had ordered every undead draugar and every berserker to join the Black Dragon in the hunt for the Defender and his Resistance allies. London and its sprawling suburbs were swarming with rampaging Vikings, terrorizing the streets, searching every house, leaving a trail of destruction in their wake. Brian had decided they should avoid the city entirely and strike west. They could turn south towards Stonehenge once they'd put some distance between themselves and their pursuers, he'd said. Even with Alfie, Ellie and Brian keeping airborne on Wyvern as much as possible and Qilin blink-shifting with Hayley, it took several hours of dodging Viking patrols before they could even begin to relax.

Wyvern glided into a smooth landing at the edge of a small wood on the edge of the Chiltern Hills. Brian dismounted and lifted Ellie down. Alfie let Herne jump down and then patted his weary horse on the neck; she shook her head playfully in response. Even though he was sure Wyvern could understand the seriousness of their situation – on the run, hunted, loved ones left behind – he could still feel her joy at being free to fly through the skies again. Fair enough, after months at the bottom of the North Sea, he supposed.

In truth there was something about being away from London, out in the countryside, that always made him feel better too. Even though the skies out here were just as dark and the ground was frozen just as solid as it was in the city, he felt like he could breathe for the first time in days. Maybe LC's plan would work, he thought. Maybe once they had rallied their forces they could turn the tide against Lock before it was too late. Maybe he could still save his family and his friends and everyone else. That was a lot of "maybes", but that was all he had right now, so it would have to do.

"Can we walk for a bit?" asked Ellie. "I need to warm up."

Alfie looked down at his little sister. She was shivering inside her big coat, hair laced with frost and lips turning blue. He didn't feel the cold inside his armour, but for Ellie and Brian the series of fast flights they'd made had been hard to endure.

"Sorry, yeah, of course," he said.

Alfie recalled Wyvern into his spurs and took off his armour. The biting cold snatched his breath away for a moment.

"Any sign of the others?" he asked, trying not to let his teeth chatter.

Qilin had been blink-shifting with Hayley from high point to high point, across the landscape below them, but he'd lost track of them after a while.

"Ahead of us, I reckon," said Brian. He wiped the

snow off a stile, revealing a footpath sign pointing into the woods. "This way. If we march fast, we won't feel the cold so much. Old army trick."

The trio wound their way through the woods quietly at first, saving what energy they still had for the journey ahead. Icicle-heavy branches overhung the path like claws reaching out to grab them. There seemed to be no animals or birds here, as if the unnatural winter had driven all the life out of the place.

"It's nicer in springtime, to be honest," said Brian. "Carpets of bluebells and all that."

Alfie laughed. "Didn't think of you as much of a rambler."

"He's full of secrets, aren't you, Brian?" said Ellie with a cheeky grin.

Brian frowned and changed the subject. "This is part of the Ridgeway. Oldest road in England. Traders have been pounding up and down this path for thousands of years. Anyway, you should feel right at home."

"Why's that?" asked Alfie.

"Because we just crossed into Wessex, Alfred the Great's original kingdom. Funny place; always been a ton of magic here."

They tramped on and a short while later came out of the woods into a frozen meadow. On the other side there was a small hill, just below the top of which they could see Hayley being sick and Tony patting her sympathetically on the back.

"What's wrong?" asked Alfie when they caught up with them.

"Shifting sickness," said Tony. "It can happen when you do too much teleporting in one go. It'll pass."

Hayley stood up and wiped her mouth. "I'm OK. Anyway, we have bigger things to worry about," she said, pointing to the brow of the hill.

They crept up and peered over into the valley below. Campfires were burning, flickering flames illuminating the hulking figures of Guthrum and his draugar warriors. Some were resting, some sharpening their axes, others arguing and pushing each other around. Berserker slaves delivered a dead deer to be roasted over one of the fires.

"A Viking camp in Wessex. Well, that's a blast from the past," whispered Alfie.

A pair of devil dogs ran into the camp and transformed back into draugar as they reached their lord. The Vikings said some words to Guthrum, who yelled at them and then battered them round their heads till they ran off.

"They must have been tracking us," said Brian. "Looks like the trail's gone cold, for now."

Herne let out a low growl. He was looking up at the sky behind them.

"Er, what's that?" said Tony, pointing above the woods.

The others turned to see the clouds above the wood glow red. A jet of fire erupted across the sky, and a dragon's wingtips scythed down through the swirling fog.

Alfie looked at the woods. The beast had not yet emerged from the clouds, but they were too far away across the field to make it in time. Nor could they go down the hill towards the Vikings. If the Black Dragon was descending towards the camp, it would pass right over them.

"Everyone stay low," said Brian, looking around for cover that wasn't there.

"He'll see us against the snow – we're sitting ducks!" said Hayley.

Above them, the belly of the Black Dragon was breaking through the cloudbank. Desperate, Alfie looked at the blanket of snow that surrounded them and had an idea.

"Everyone lie down!" shouted Alfie, taking Herne's collar and pulling him close. "And hold your breath!"

Confused, the others nevertheless obeyed – it was too late to run anyway. Alfie extended his ring finger at the snow all around them and closed his eyes, focusing his mind. Suddenly the surface of the snow moved, as if shifted by a strong wind, clouds of it covering them all in an instant, until they became nothing more than five shallow bumps in the snow-covered field. The Black Dragon thundered low over their hiding place and swooped on, into the Viking camp.

A moment later, Alfie sat up gasping for air, followed by the rest. Ellie wiped snow from her face and looked around in a daze.

"I'm not even going to ask what just happened there..."

They shook the snow from their bodies and peered once more over the hill. The Black Dragon had landed in the Viking camp.

"What do we do now?" cut in Hayley. "We can't risk flying – not with Lizard-breath around."

"And it's too dark to blink-shift very far," added Tony.

Brian looked around at everyone's tired faces. Alfie was hugging Ellie, who was shivering again.

"We'll find somewhere warm to rest for the night," he said. "If the Vikings have gone by the morning, we'll carry on south."

"Are there any of those, what did LC call them, peculiar royals round here?" Tony asked.

"Royal peculiars," Brian corrected him. "No. But I know another place."

Being careful to keep below the brow of the hill, the tired gang followed Brian west.

Guthrum spat a thick ball of half-chewed meat on to the ground and rose to meet his visitor. His draugar men gathered around the Dragon, keeping hold of their axes just in case.

"Sjáðu! Engilsmaðrinn hefr sent oss skikkjurakkan hans til skemmtunar okkr,"* said Guthrum.

The Black Dragon didn't know what he had said, but he could tell from the guffaws of laughter all around him that he was being mocked. He opened his jaws and breathed a torrent of flames over the Viking that was laughing hardest. The draugar screamed and rolled on the floor, till his comrades kicked enough snow over him to put out the flames, and he sat up, blackened and smoking, but as undead as he was before.

"I have a message from Lord Protector Lock," growled the Dragon.

It was long after nightfall by the time the band of weary wanderers trudged towards the remote cottage. Brian had taken to carrying Herne because, despite the hound's size, the snow was too deep for him to walk now.

---

* "Look, the Englishman has sent his lapdog for our amusement."

"Where are we?" asked Alfie.

"Nearest big town is Chippenham, where Alfred the Great was nearly caught by the Vikings before he fled into exile," said Brian. "But that's still miles away."

"So we're in the middle of nowhere?" asked Alfie.

"That's the general idea," said Brian, quickening his pace.

Alfie could have sworn Brian was almost running up the path by the time they reached the quaint front porch of a little house. The curtains were drawn, but there was a dim light burning inside. Wherever this was, it looked like someone was home.

Brian put Herne down, took a breath and knocked on the door. They heard the latch being unlocked and the door swung open to reveal a middle-aged bear of a man, with a well-trimmed beard and a pot belly straining beneath a thick woollen cardigan. He stared at Brian, as if not believing what he was seeing, tears beading at the corners of his eyes. The silence was shattered by a four-year-old girl with long brown hair wearing a tiger onesie, who burst out past the man's legs and threw herself into Brian's arms.

"*Daddy!*" she cried with delight.

Alfie and Hayley looked at each other in astonishment.

The little girl's name was Willow, and she was full of questions.

"Why are you so cold? Where did you come from? What's your dog's name? Do you like unicorns?"

After she'd finally let go of Brian, her other dad, Greg, ushered them all into the warmth of the cottage. For a long time neither Brian nor Greg could say very much without crying or laughing or sometimes both at the same time. Alfie marvelled at how tenderly Brian hugged and caressed his family. The only thing he'd ever seen Brian treat that gently before was his gun when he was cleaning it.

Tony was now blink-shifting Willow from one side of the room to the other, which made her squeal with delight, while Brian piled logs into the wood-burning stove. Greg bustled through carrying a pile of dinner plates, which he nearly dropped when Tony and Willow appeared out of thin air right next to him.

"Again! Again!" shouted the girl, giggling.

"Do you mind if we lay off the magic until after dinner, just to avoid me completely freaking out," said Greg, depositing the plates on the table. He sounded much more well-spoken than Brian, Alfie thought.

"Yeah, sorry." Tony smiled, delivering Willow back on to the sofa.

By the time they had finished a hodgepodge dinner of potatoes, soup and a ham Greg had been keeping frozen outside for a special occasion, Willow had fallen asleep curled up on the floor next to Herne, and the others had learned all about Brian's family. He had met Greg years before in the army – Greg was his commanding officer, and they had had to keep their relationship a secret.

"I was his bit of posh totty," chuckled Greg, which made Tony spit a potato clean across the room with laughter. Herne was happy to clean it off the floor.

After they had both left the army and got married, they decided that Brian would keep working while Greg looked after their newly adopted baby, Willow. Brian's job involved protecting people and that's exactly what he did with his family too – by keeping them secret. The downside was that when the country was thrown into chaos by the Viking invasion, he couldn't let them know what he was doing and where he was going. And he wasn't going to risk putting them in danger by making contact afterwards, either.

"Weren't you worried that something had happened to him?" asked Ellie.

"Gosh, no," said Greg, squeezing Brian's hand. "If anyone knows how to look after himself, it's this chap. But the longer it went without word, yes, I've had some sleepless nights."

"And did you know what he really did for a living?" asked Hayley. "You know, all the superhero stuff?"

"Not at first, no. He's very discreet about his work – which is funny because usually he's a terrible gossip," said Greg.

"Oi," said Brian.

"Every time he had to work late they'd be some news story about a superhero averting disaster somewhere. At first I thought *he* was the Defender!" Greg continued, over everyone's laughter. "But after a while I put two and two together. It's nice to meet you all. I'm sorry I can't offer anyone seconds. The shops round here aren't what they used to be."

The laughter dwindled as everyone was reminded of what was happening in the world outside the cozy cottage. While the others helped wash the dishes, Brian carried Willow to bed and sat with Greg watching her sleep for a while, talking in soft whispers to each other.

Hayley found Alfie gazing from a window at the snowy night outside, deep in thought. "What is it?" she asked.

"I was just thinking how many more homes like this there must be out there. Families trying to carry on as normal, not knowing what's going to happen tomorrow," said Alfie.

"That's why we're doing something about it,

Alfie. We're going to help them – all of them," said Hayley.

Brian and Greg came out of Willow's room and pulled the door closed.

"Time to get some sleep, folks. We have a long journey tomorrow," said Brian.

"Yes, we do," said Alfie. "But you're not coming with us."

Everyone looked at Alfie, confused.

"Don't be daft, lad, what are you talking about?" asked Brian.

"We don't know what's going to happen when we go out there again, and I can't ask you to... You belong here, with your family," said Alfie.

Brian seemed lost for words. He looked at Greg, clearly torn. But it was Greg who spoke first.

"Don't forget, Your Majesty, I was in the army too," he said. "I took an oath of loyalty to crown and country, just like he did. And this is how I keep it – I tell him to go with you and do his duty."

"But what if he doesn't come back?" said Alfie.

Greg looked at Brian. Both had tears in their eyes.

"That's for me to deal with. You have a job to do, sir. You all do, same as me looking after our little girl in there," said Greg. "Britain doesn't lie down in the face of bullies – never has, never will – but people need someone to follow. King, Defender, doesn't matter, but courage inspires courage." Greg took a pile of towels from the airing cupboard and handed one to each of them. "I'll have breakfast ready for you at six. You'll be wanting an early start."

23

CELIA'S CHOICE

Celia Ogden dug her spade into the snowdrift. The Stonehenge Visitor Centre's roof had not been designed to have three feet of the white stuff dumped on top of it every few days. But, seeing as she was the only member of staff still around, the duty to make sure the whole structure didn't collapse fell to her. She puffed her cheeks out against the cold and worked hard, turning great shovelfuls of snow over her shoulder and on to the ground below. It was a strange thing to admit, but the Viking invasion of Britain had had one big upside for Celia: it had made her a lot fitter. Decades of working slouched over a desk had left her back seized up, her muscles prone to cramping and her waistline ever-expanding.

But clearing the roof every morning and feeding the café's wood-burning stove every afternoon had done wonders. Yes, democracy might have collapsed and Britain might be buried under a new dark age of snow and ice, but Celia Ogden had lost at least eleven kilos.

"Eleven kilos!" Celia shouted, trying to keep her spirits up. Her words whipped away on the cold wind that knifed across Salisbury Plain.

When the Raven Banner's evil magic had first hit Stonehenge a few months ago, there had been panic in the Visitor Centre as several tourists transformed into berserkers and went on the rampage. Instead of leading school children on a tour around the stones, Celia had found herself barricaded in an office, shaking in fear, the desk pushed up against the door. From the corridor outside had come the sound of terrified shouts, screams and berserkers roaring. When she'd finally found the courage to peek out hours later, what she saw had broken her heart: the brand new centre, with its high glass walls and polished wood, was a wreck. Smashed windows, splintered tables, bags and coats strewn around. Anyone else might have abandoned the place, but there was no way she could leave it in this state. So she started cleaning up and never really stopped.

Celia had only seen the Viking invaders with her own eyes twice after that: once when she'd hiked through the snow into Amesbury, the nearest town, to barter for some more food, and had witnessed a draugar gang hanging around outside a wrecked pub chucking beer down their rotten throats. And again when a small band of them had skirted the edges of the Stonehenge site. She watched them through some gift-shop binoculars as they stood and gazed at the old stones for a while, then backed away like they were afraid to get any closer. Celia wasn't sure why; it wasn't even like Stonehenge looked all that impressive any more. Even before the Vikings had arrived, there had been the freak earthquake that had levelled the stone circle as if it were a house of cards. She'd always remembered that date because it had been the same night King Henry the Ninth had died. Discussions about how best to restore Stonehenge had dragged on for weeks, but perversely visitor numbers had actually increased as people came to gawp at the damage. "Rubber-neckers", Celia called them.

She dumped one last shovelful of snow off the roof and straightened up. Night was closing in and dark clouds were gathering with the promise of yet more snow. Just then she glanced across the plain towards the main site and gasped. There were people there, five of them, in among the snow-covered stones! Even from this distance, she could tell they weren't Vikings. They were too strangely dressed, one in the pale armour of a knight and someone else all in red. There was a huge dog with them as well. What on earth were they up to?

"Hey!" Celia yelled and waved her arms but the wind was too strong, so she climbed down the ladder and set off through the snow up the hill as fast as her tired legs would carry her.

"There's nobody here," sighed Alfie, slumping down among the long, fallen stones.

Maybe it was too optimistic, but he'd been hoping they'd arrive to see the massed ranks of Yeoman Warders sitting around campfires toasting their return, cheering supporters – an army, perhaps. But there was nothing here except for snow, ice and the ancient grey stones, lying scattered like some giant's abandoned game of dominoes.

"Maybe they're hiding?" Tony said hopefully.

But Alfie found it hard to raise a smile. It wasn't just that their long cross-country flight had been in vain. He loathed being here again. It was where Richard had killed their father, and the scars of their epic battle were still visible on the shattered stones all around them. A sullen silence descended on everyone as the clouds closed in and it started to snow again.

"So why did we waste so much time coming all the way here?" Ellie asked. "My mum, our friends – they're all back in London!"

"The Lord Chamberlain was very clear," said Brian. "This *had* to be the rally point."

"Why?" asked Hayley. "What exactly did he say?"

Brian thought about it. "He said the king would find a new army and new power here."

"Well, the army is a no-show," said Alfie.

"What about the power part?" asked Hayley. "Did he say anything else?"

"LC's not exactly big on chit-chat, remember?" Brian shrugged.

"Whatever he meant—" said Alfie, standing up. Except he never got to finish the thought, because he was too busy wondering why his hand was stuck to the rock he'd been sitting on. He pulled and pulled, but his left palm was glued solid to the rock. "Well, *that's* odd," he grunted.

It felt like a thousand magnets were pulling his gloved hand towards them. The energy coming from the stone was so strong it was making him feel light-headed. The others tried to help prise his hand free, but it wouldn't budge. Alfie attempted to take his armour off with his other hand, but he couldn't.

"The exact same thing happened to me once with this tube of superglue and a fire extinguisher," said Tony. Everyone looked at him for a moment. "Yeah, it's not really the same."

"Try using your command power to separate it from your hand," suggested Brian.

Alfie closed his eyes and focused his thoughts through the Ring of Command. It felt like his hand was coming away, but when he looked up he saw that what he'd actually done was heave the entire stone upright. Suddenly as the stone settled in place, Alfie felt it release him and he fell back with a gasp of relief.

"Maybe it just wanted to stand up again?" Tony joked.

The others laughed. But as Alfie looked around at the fallen rocks he thought he could hear voices whispering on the wind, like they were talking to him.

"No, he's right," he said. "They do want to stand up. They want to be put back the way they were."

"And you know this, because. . .?" asked Hayley.

"They told me." Alfie shrugged.

"And that's it, today officially cannot get any weirder," said Ellie.

Alfie held out the Ring of Command towards another giant stone and willed it to move. A huge wave of déjà vu swept over him, so strong it felt like he was losing his balance for a second. Had his dad commanded the stones here to move when he fought Richard? A surge of energy swept back over him as the great grey slab reacted, floating into the air. Snow cascaded from it as Alfie slowly turned it around for all to see.

"Any ideas? Up? Down? Sideways?" Alfie asked.

"I wouldn't have started with that one," Qilin said, pulling his red cloak tighter against the blizzard.

"Really useful, thanks," Alfie said sarcastically.

"Put that down *at once!*" Celia shouted as she bustled into the middle of the stones, red-faced and out of breath.

She sounded so much like a school teacher that Alfie did just that, and the stone dropped out of the sky. It landed with an earth-shaking *crunch* on the ground and narrowly missed Qilin, who blink-shifted out of the way.

"Whoa, there, lady, step back. We're on important business," Brian said as he tried to usher her away. Herne growled. But Celia wasn't the sort to be intimidated by anyone.

"So am I! And take your hands off me! This is a scheduled prehistoric monument – you can't just throw these stones around. . ." Celia's voice trailed away as her mind suddenly caught up with what her eyes had just seen. A fifty-ton sarsen trilithon floating in the air as light as a feather. Impossible. She swayed on the spot like she was going to faint, until Alfie caught her and sat her down gently on one of the stones.

"Whoa, there. Have a seat."

"Oh, my giddy aunt. You're the Defender. But ... they said you were dead," Celia whispered.

"Nope, alive and well. I thought I could help put Stonehenge back together while I was here," Alfie explained.

"Well, I wouldn't start with that one," Celia said, pointing at the stone he'd just dropped.

"Boom!" Qilin said, snapping his fingers together.

"Is he quite all right?" Celia said as she watched the figure in the red robes and Chinese mask (*a Xiangdong Nuo mask, possibly Ming dynasty*, she thought) dance around.

"Don't worry about him. You know about this place? I mean, how it would have looked?" Alfie asked. Again, the certainty swept over him that he had to do this.

"Yes ... but ... the paperwork. Defender or not. I'd have to apply for permission from about a thousand different people."

"This has got to happen now," Alfie said. "I can't explain it, but I think it might be really important. Like, saving the country and maybe the planet important."

Celia closed her eyes and weighed up all the

298

crazy events that led her to be sitting in front of a legendary superhero. She stood up, proudly. "Celia Ogden, Professor of Archaeology, at your service."

And with that, they started to rebuild. Working through the night, Alfie raised the stones with the Ring of Command and flew them around the site as Celia directed them in ("Left a bit, right a bit, stop!"), like one of those people on the runway who guide planes safely to the gate. Ellie found the crunch of stones grinding their way into the frozen soil oddly satisfying. And with each standing stone that was put the right way up, with each lintel that was laid back where it used to be, Alfie could feel something ancient, immense and magical building, like a long-dead current of electricity had been switched back on. When the rebuilding work was done, everyone stood in the middle of the ancient stone circle and gazed about them in awe.

"Do you feel that? It tingles," Alfie asked Hayley, a little worried as he touched a stone.

"Nope," Hayley said, puzzled. "But then I'm not Defender of the Realm. Looks better, though."

Alfie didn't know if it was just him, but the air seemed to be shimmering with light. Somewhere, across the snowy plain, a distant hunting horn was blaring. Clouds formed themselves into the silhouettes of riders on horseback and chased each other through the night sky. There was no doubt about it, something strange was happening. The horn sounded again.

"Can't you hear that?" Alfie whispered.

"Alfie, are you OK?" Hayley said, but he barely heard her.

"I think you'd all better get out of the circle," Alfie shouted, and everyone did as they were told. Herne paced, restless, and the agitated ravens wheeled overhead, gronking. Alfie wasn't wearing a watch, but a strange voice was inside his head, counting down the seconds to midnight.

10, 9, 8...

"You feeling OK, chief?" Brian shouted from the edge of the circle.

"What's happening?" Tony asked.

7, 6, 5...

"Herne!" Ellie shouted as the howling wolfhound suddenly bolted away from her to be by Alfie's side at the very centre of the stones. Alfie gripped on to Herne as the air seemed to warp and vibrate around him. Stonehenge went in and out of focus like he was looking at it underwater.

4, 3, 2, 1...

Midnight.

24

THE WILD HUNT

When Alfie's vision cleared, it was daytime. Everything and everyone around him, except Herne, had disappeared. There was now no trace of Stonehenge at all. The snow was gone. All he could see was the grassy plain stretching towards the horizon, a vision of what it must have looked like in pre-historic times. The ground shook as, across Salisbury Plain, for as far as the eye could see, thousands of trees in full leaf burst out of the ground, sending explosions of black soil into the sky. Soon the barren landscape had been magically transformed into dense, green forest. The air was damp and the rich smell of rotten leaves filled his nose. Everywhere he looked there was a tangled mass of giant tree trunks and twisted, moss-covered roots, like something from the pages of a dark fairytale. Suddenly a dazzling white stag leapt through the clearing. Alfie and Herne dived out of the way as the magnificent creature stopped and looked back at them with a snort. From one of its impressive, many-pointed antlers hung a crown. Alfie recognized it at once.

"King Alfred's crown!" he gasped.

The last time Alfie had seen it was when the Black Dragon had fused the final part back into it at his coronation, making it whole again. Later they'd retrieved it from the rubble inside Westminster Abbey and LC had told him he would send it far away, to a safe place. Was this what the old man had meant? On a stag's antlers in some weird, enchanted wood?

The blast of a hunting horn started the stag running again, and it rapidly disappeared into the thick forest. Seconds later, hooves pounded the ground as riders crashed out of the trees and circled Alfie and Herne. The men and women were dressed in furs and mud-spattered cloaks, and their faces were craggy, scarred and weather-beaten. A large man with piercing blue eyes and a white beard neatly tied with a strip of leather raised his hand and the riders came to a stop. He was wearing a small crown made from antlers and riding a white horse a full couple of hands bigger than all the others.

"A new rider for my hunt! What is your name?" The man's voice was rich and low.

"Alfie."

"But you are dressed as a knight. Speak as one."

Alfie, throat suddenly as dry as sandpaper, coughed and said, "I am Alfred Henry Alexander Louis, King of Great Britain and Northern Ireland."

The bearded man nodded and smiled playfully, like he'd known it all along.

"This is not the first time your kin have come to seek my help against the Norsemen."

"You mean, Alfred the Great?" Alfie said. He remembered LC telling him ages ago that Alfred the Great had prayed to some ancient god called Woden to help beat the Vikings. He'd received the immensely powerful magical crown and that had been the start of his family's blue blood powers. Alfie's head was spinning. *Wait a second.* Could it be that this was Woden himself he was talking to?

"You must join us and ride with the Wild Hunt, young king. Catch the stag and you may keep the crown and use it to slay your enemies."

Is that the "new power" LC told Brian about? Did he know this would happen? wondered Alfie.

"But know this," Woden continued. "If you fail, you will ride with the hunt for ever."

A chill ran down Alfie's spine as he gazed at the

other riders. They did indeed look like they'd been on horseback for a long, long time, their wasted bodies wrapped in threadbare cloaks as they rested in their battered saddles. How many centuries had they been trapped here?

"OK, Mr Woden. Or is it just Woden?" asked Alfie. The ancient god stared at him, impassive. "Never mind. Sorry. But just before we start, I need to tell you, I'm really anti-hunting."

Ignoring him, Woden gave another blast of his hunting horn and led the Wild Hunt off again, leaving only a swirl of dead leaves in the air.

"Wait!" Alfie yelled, but the sounds of the hunt were already fading. He couldn't risk being lost in this place. But how was he supposed to keep up with them? *Oh yeah. Dur.*

"Spurs!" Alfie shouted, and Wyvern appeared beneath him, but something extraordinary had happened: Wyvern's usual ghostly form had been replaced with her *real* body. Alfie could feel every living sinew, every muscle under her white hair as it twitched. He ruffled his horse's mane and marvelled at the coarseness of it.

"Wyvern ... you're alive!" Alfie said.

By way of a reply, she whinnied and galloped forward at tremendous speed, ears pricked.

"Tally-ho!" Alfie shouted, and Herne barked happily as they sprinted after the hunters.

The woods flashed past. Ahead of them, the Wild Hunt was in full flow, but Alfie could see he was gaining on them fast. Wyvern leapt over a log and in seconds they were up alongside the riders. It was a melee of horses and elbows as everyone jostled for position. Alfie lost sight of Herne, but he could hear the dog barking somewhere in the enchanted forest. He couldn't afford to take his eyes off what was happening right in front of him. Branches appeared at warp speed, and he was ducking and weaving like a boxer dodging blows. But he couldn't avoid them all. Branches clanged against his armour, which to his surprise was getting dented and scratched.

Woden's hunting horn sounded again as the white stag bounded across their path and everyone tore after it. But Wyvern found yet more speed, broke away from the main pack and bounded on to another path in the forest. Suddenly they were free of all the jostling. He could see what Wyvern was trying to do: head the white stag off from a different direction.

"Good girl, Wyvern!" Alfie shouted, but suddenly the air was thick with missiles. Arrows glanced off his armour. The chasing pack was now hunting him too! A snarling rider, her face a mass of old scars and scratches, drew her sword and swiped at Alfie.

"Where did you get that horse, you cheating swine!" she yelled.

"I am not cheating!" Alfie shouted back and spurred Wyvern on till he was clear of the pack. It wasn't his fault that his horse was faster than all of theirs, was it?

Ahead, the white stag leapt over a gulley. Alfie remembered his Ring of Command – now, that really would be cheating, but he had no intention of being stuck in this forest for eternity. Would the ring work in the magical realm of the Wild Hunt? It was worth a shot. Alfie held out his gauntlet and commanded the trees ahead of the white stag to bend down, and to his surprise they did as they were told. With a deafening creak, the trees swayed low and knitted their branches together, forming a dense, green barrier. The white stag skidded to a halt and charged the other way, but Alfie commanded more trees and branches to move and the creature was cornered.

Wyvern reared up and Alfie tried to recall her into his spurs, but that didn't work, so he simply dismounted. Now he was close to the white stag he could see how truly magnificent he looked. Huge antlers towered from his head, and entwined among the many points of Alfred's Crown were leaves picked up from the endless chase through the forest. Behind Alfie, the rest of the Wild Hunt drew up their horses and watched in sullen silence.

"Easy there, boy. I don't want to hurt you. I just want the crown." Alfie said in his best stag-whispering voice.

Remarkably, the white stag seemed to calm down and even lowered his head. But as Alfie reached for the crown the cunning stag suddenly shied away and leapt over him! Behind him, the massed ranks of the Wild Hunt laughed and jeered as the stag once again ran free.

"No!" Alfie yelled.

The stag was off and running again through the forest, Alfred the Great's crown still dangling from its antlers. With a roar, the Wild Hunt set off after it and Alfie was back among them as he urged Wyvern on. But however hard he spurred her on, he couldn't move clear of the pack like he had done before. Tears of frustration stung Alfie's eyes. He was one of the Wild Hunt now, doomed to chase through these endless woods for ever. He would grow old and withered like the others, the memory of his life before and the friends he'd left behind fading as he slowly turned into just another wraith of the hunt.

But there was someone he'd forgotten, and the wily stag hadn't reckoned on him either. Herne. With a snarl and a flash of grey fur, Alfie's dog bounded through the trees and took the white stag down, clamping his jaws around his neck. He hadn't killed it, just stopped it in its tracks. Sensing its race was run, the stag went limp, at Herne's mercy.

"Don't feel too bad, it's what wolfhounds were bred to do," Alfie said to the gathered hunters who were grumbling again. But before he could get to the stag, someone had appeared at his side and put their hand on his shoulder. It was Woden, his eyes blue and fathomless.

"You are indeed worthy, young Alfred. Behold."

The thick woods around them had suddenly vanished and in their place was Stonehenge. Above it, the sky looked like it was rewinding. The sun, clouds, moon and stars looped past at a million miles per hour. And standing in the ancient stone circle was somebody Alfie recognized from the dreams and visions he experienced during his turbulent Succession.

Alfred the Great.

Dressed in a mixture of chainmail and leather armour, the king kneeled in the centre of the stones as Woden placed the crown on his head. Alfie knew what he was seeing was a vision from the ancient past, the day that Alfred the Great received the crown and the powers that had flowed in every king and queen of Britain ever since.

"With this crown you will defeat the Vikings and

drive them from your lands. All Albion is given to you and your sons and daughters," Woden decreed.

Alfred the Great nodded solemnly as the crown glowed blue. His body went taut as the magical power coursed through his body. Alfie winced; it was like watching someone receive a prolonged and painful electrical shock. Finally, Alfred the Great staggered to his feet, recovering from the jolt, fighting for breath.

"With the crown comes power. And power will corrupt," Woden said. "Unless you are well advised. Saint Cuthbert!"

Alfie gasped as a tall, thin man materialized next to Woden. It was the Lord Chamberlain! At least, it looked a lot like LC, wearing a fine, golden embroidered robe and holding a staff.

"Cuthbert will guide you and your kin, giving wise council for ever more."

Alfie gasped. He knew LC was old, but this meant he was immortal! No wonder he knew so much about every single invasion, war and plague that had ever hit Britain. He'd seen it all, literally. Alfie steadied himself against one of the huge stones and closed his eyes briefly. *Also, LC's real name is Cuthbert!* Alfie thought. He couldn't wait to tell Hayley, and he wondered if Brian even knew—

"ALFRED! Come forward." Woden's voiced boomed.

He's talking to me, Alfie thought and opened his eyes again. Alfred the Great and LC had disappeared, leaving only Woden, who beckoned Alfie into the centre of Stonehenge.

"A thousand years ago, Alfred the Great asked for my help. He too ran with the Wild Hunt and won his prize. Now a new King Alfred comes seeking power."

Woden raised his arms above his head. In his hands was the crown. Blue sparks rose off it like fire. It reminded Alfie of the time he'd gone on a hike as part of a Geography field trip: the air had still been damp after a sudden downpour, and when they had passed underneath a massive electricity pylon he had heard the thick power lines fizzing overhead, dangerous and immense.

"Kneel," Woden commanded.

Alfie figured he shouldn't argue with an ancient god and did as he was told. But something was bothering him, something about the crown that was now inches from his head, alive with magic. Alfie's mind worked overtime as he tried to figure it out. He was certain now that this is what LC had had in mind the whole time. Reach Stonehenge, beat the Wild Hunt and find the crown. With its extra power, he'd easily see off the Vikings, Lock and the Black Dragon. And it would even give him a fighting chance against Hel—

"Drive the Vikings from your land!" Woden declared.

"Wait!" Alfie said, but it was too late. Woden had placed the crown on his head.

Power.

So much energy, filling every inch of his being. His body shook with it. His hair stood on end. His teeth clamped together then chattered uncontrollably. Sometimes when Alfie touched the regalia, he would get a low-level shock like a static charge, but this was something else entirely: an ultra-high voltage, next-level power-up. With Alfred the Great's crown he'd be unstoppable. Forget the Defender armour, he wouldn't need it; Alfie could feel the surge of magical power toughening his skin so nothing could cut it. Forget the Sword of State, great arcs of blue electricity could flash from his fingers and fry anyone who stood in his way, whenever he wanted. Forget the Orb, Alfie's crystal blue eyes could see for thousands of miles. Alfie laughed with the thrill of it. The Vikings wouldn't last a second. Lock, *pfft*, he was nothing. And as for Richard, the pathetic Black Dragon would be made to kneel in front of the new King Alfred the Great. No, wait, Alfred the Awesome. Alfred the Unstoppable. Alfred the—

No... No... NO! Alfie mind was screaming. This was all wrong. *Hadn't Alfred the Great broken the crown and scattered its pieces for this very reason? It was too dangerous. Wasn't ultimate power what Richard had wanted? Look what had happened to him! Wearing it for a few minutes at Westminster Abbey had sent his brother mad and transformed him into a monster. This crown was the source of all the trouble they'd ever known. No mortal should be allowed to ever wield such power. It was better off hung on the Stag's horns and left to roam the wild woods for eternity.*

"Get ... it ... off!" Alfie stammered and groped at the crown.

He tried to tear it from his head, but the crown squeezed like a vice, fusing itself to him for ever.

"I DON'T WANT THE CROWN!" Alfie screamed, making one final attempt to rid himself of it. But he passed out into black nothingness.

"Wake up! Alfie!"

He opened his eyes to see Hayley's kind face hovering over him.

Then she slapped him.

"Ow! Hayley!" Alfie spluttered and she laughed, relieved.

He was dizzy and lying in the middle of Stonehenge, the shroud tunic clutched in his hand. Moonlight broke for a moment through the black clouds, glistening off the snow.

"He's alive!" Hayley shouted, and Brian, Tony and Ellie crowded around.

Just about, Alfie thought. He had the mother of all headaches, but overall he seemed to have survived.

"Welcome back, Alpha-bet," Tony said. "One second you were there then *pop*, wow, you just disappeared!"

"You've been gone hours!" Ellie said. "Spill the beans."

"Not before we get him warm," Brian said.

He picked Alfie up and sat him down next to a blazing campfire, set in the shelter of one of the standing stones. Celia poured him a cup of tea from a thermos and Alfie tried to tell them where he'd been and the incredible things he'd just witnessed: the stag, the Wild Hunt, Woden, his close encounter with King Alfred the Great's crown. It all came out in a big jumbled mess, but he thought they'd got the gist. If LC had meant for him to take Alfred the Great's crown back and wield its power, well, he'd need to explain to the old man why he chose not to. If he ever saw him again, that was.

"Ultimate power, though?" Tony winced. "Would have been handy to defeat Lock and Hel."

"I know," said Alfie. "We'll just have to find another way."

"Fair enough, you're the boss," Brian said, and everyone nodded in agreement. They were all silent for a few minutes, huddled around and staring into the fire.

"Hey, wait a second," Alfie said as he suddenly remembered something. "You'll never guess what LC's real name is!"

25
KING'S ARMY

Troll-song swam through her head like eels through a stream. It was the song of her ancestors calling her home to Fólkvangr, the eternal fields where she would spend the afterlife with them. Queen Freya knew what she was supposed to do. She was supposed to join in with the song and let her voice carry her spirit to that place as she died. It was an appealing prospect, leaving behind the pain that coursed through her body and drifting away from this cage. No Norwegian monarch could survive the separation from Brísingamen for long.

Though her vision was blurry, she could see the emerald necklace gleaming from where Lock had left it on the Speaker's Chair, as if to mock her. Freya knew it was only a matter of time now. And yet she resisted. She screwed her mouth shut tight, biting into her lip till she tasted blood. She would not sing. She would not leave here defeated. Because there was something she wanted more than an end to the agony. Revenge. The daylight that lit the chamber through the windows was weak, but she had to wait. Nightfall. If she could just make it to nightfall, then there was still a chance.

In another cell made not from particle energy but from good old-fashioned stone walls, deep beneath the Tower of London's secret Keep, the Lord Chamberlain and Queen Tamara also awaited their fates.

"I owe you an apology," said Tamara, a disembodied voice in the pitch darkness. "And in case they come back and I don't get the chance, I need to get it out, so don't interrupt."

Silence. Tamara could see and hear nothing.

"LC?"

"Yes, ma'am?" said LC, making her jump.

"What are you doing? I thought you were asleep or something!"

"On the contrary, I was merely following your instruction and not interrupting."

Tamara tutted. "Fine. OK, then. The thing is, I

know it can't have been easy for you, living as long as you've lived and seeing all the terrible things you must have seen. And I guess I was so wrapped up in my life with Henry, I never gave you enough credit. I know you were only doing your job. Sorry if I gave you a hard time..." She waited for a response, but none came. "You can talk now."

LC cleared his throat as if about to commence a long speech. "Apology accepted, ma'am."

"Apology *accepted*?" yelled Tamara. "That's all you have to say to me?"

"I thought your point was well made and I am merely agreeing with you. You were indeed too hard on me, from time to time."

"And...?"

There was a long pause. Tamara was glad she couldn't see him or she thought she might have started strangling him by now.

"Very well," said LC, at last. "I must, in turn, say that I was perhaps too fast to dismiss your point of view."

"And...?" said Tamara.

"And ... I ... apologize?" offered LC.

Tamara lay back on the bed, exhausted.

"Why do I get the feeling that's the first apology you've given anyone for a long, long time?"

"That's true. The last was in the year 1135, if I

317

recall correctly. I rather over-ordered the seafood. Poor Henry the First. Then again, His Majesty didn't have to eat it all himself."

Above their cell, in the Keep, the Black Dragon had returned to the hall to find it lit by tall black candles, and Lock dressed in red robes preparing the mirror for the ceremony.

"Is it done?" asked Lock when he heard the Dragon's talons hit the floor behind him.

"I delivered your message," said the Black Dragon. "The Norsemen didn't like it."

"Soon their part will be played and we'll have no further need for them," said Lock in a hushed tone. There were still some of Guthrum's draugar hanging around at the edges of the hall. Lock signalled to one of the Vikings, who shuffled forward, carrying Hel's covered mirror, looking uncharacteristically nervous. He placed it in the centre of the Keep and scurried away.

"And what about me?" asked the Dragon.

"You? You will be released from your curse." Lock smiled grimly. "If that is truly what you desire – and free to reign over your kingdom as you see fit."

The tiny part of the Dragon's mind that remained human – Richard – pushed against the overwhelming lust for power and revenge. But it was getting harder by the second. A kingdom. A throne. That's what he'd always wanted. That's what *she* would give him.

At Stonehenge, Alfie couldn't look at the fire without thinking of his brother. It was strange to associate something so primal with a person, he thought, as he stared into the burning embers, but maybe that was because Richard wasn't a person any more. And if he was the Black Dragon for good now, that meant Alfie would never see his brother again.

He felt the fur of a blanket fall over his shoulders and looked up to see Hayley sitting down next to him. She poked the fire and threw some more sticks on.

"You have to keep feeding the fire if you don't want it to go out," she said. "Don't they take you camping at posh schools?"

"I didn't know if we'd be staying much longer," Alfie replied.

Hayley pulled half the blanket over her and shuffled closer, till their arms were touching.

"I guess that's up to you, boss," she said with a smirk. "But there's not much point going anywhere tonight. You'd only fall into a snowdrift and I'd have to rescue you."

"Good point," Alfie smiled. "Hayley, can you tell me something honestly – did I just throw away our last chance of winning?"

"What are you talking about?"

"Not taking the crown. I was scared I couldn't handle that kind of power. Maybe if I was braver. . ."

"You're such an idiot sometimes, Alfie. Don't you see: what you did took a whole load more guts. Not taking the easy way out, deciding to do it the right way, even though it's harder. That's what I call brave."

"Oh, good. OK, thanks," Alfie stuttered.

"You're welcome," said Hayley, resting her head on Alfie's shoulder and hugging his arm. "Now shut up and chuck some more wood on before we freeze to death."

Alfie tossed another branch into the fire. The flames grew higher, bathing them in their warm glow.

"Listen, Hayley, I'm sorry about how it was when I first came back. I didn't mean to take over like that. I know you were doing fine without me, really. . ."

Hayley lifted her head off his shoulder and cocked her head to one side, studying his face.

"What?" said Alfie, frowning. "Why are you looking at me like that?"

Hayley sighed and smiled at him. "There you go being a colossal idiot again. Did you really think I was doing fine without you, Alfie?"

Before Alfie knew what was happening, Hayley leaned in and kissed him on the lips. Alfie's eyes popped wide as his brain exploded with surprise. He didn't know what he was supposed to do, so he opted for doing nothing at all. It turned out that being kissed for the first time by a real girl was actually sort of amazing.

"Hey! Hey!" Ellie's voice rang out as she rounded the massive stone, then stopped dead when she saw what was happening.

Hayley and Alfie sprang away from each other, embarrassed.

"Yeah, whoa, OK, whatever this is will have to wait," blurted Ellie, words tumbling over each other in her excitement. "Because there's something you both have to see. Right now."

Alarmed, Hayley and Alfie got up and ran after Ellie.

Across the plain, lights were approaching from every direction. Flickering torches held by figures that were dark against the snow.

"Who is it? Vikings?" asked Hayley, slotting an arrow on to her bow.

Alfie looked down at Herne, who was scratching himself behind an ear, apparently unconcerned. "I don't think so," he said.

Tony scanned for a possible landing spot. Then, seeing an exposed rock near the group of figures holding torches, he pulled on his mask. "Back in a sec," he said, and disappeared.

They saw him appear on the distant rock. Everyone held their breath.

Then, with a loud *pop* and rush of air, Qilin was back. He removed his mask, breathless and beaming from ear to ear. "You're never going to believe this!" he cried.

They had come. From north, south, east and west; from desolate cities, wrecked towns and hidden villages; by boat, by car till the petrol ran out; by foot through miles and miles of snow. The Yeoman Warders had returned. And with them had come an army of ordinary folk, heeding the rallying cry. Rumours of the Defender's return had spread through the countryside, whispered from neighbour to neighbour. The beefeaters had confirmed the news – a secret signal had been received, a force was massing in the south. Some said that the infamous Resistance fighter Hayley Hicks was leading them, some that the young King Alfred himself had returned from the dead with new allies from foreign lands.

"What did I tell you?" Hayley said to Alfie. "We're not alone any more."

That night the weary crowd of new arrivals made camp downhill from the stones. Alfie, Hayley, Tony, Ellie and Brian helped set fires and gave out what food and blankets Celia could plunder from the visitors' centre. At first, Alfie was nervous about what reaction he might get – after all, everyone thought he was dead. What would they say when they realized he had only run away? Would they think he'd abandoned them at the first sign of trouble? In the end he needn't have worried. The ordinary people who had joined the Resistance force were ecstatic to see their young king "back from the dead". As word spread that he was there, they rushed towards him, eager to set eyes on his face for themselves, to tell him they were glad to see him and determined to take their country back. Alfie was happy and relieved, but after a while Brian was forced to pull him away from the excited crowd before he got crushed.

Even better than the army's welcome were the many reunions they had with old friends – Yeoman "Sultana" Raisin was there, all the way from Lindisfarne, with most of his darts team and a dozen burly fishermen. Even Yeoman Gillam, the apprentice Armourer, had made it from his hiding place in the Welsh borders with a small group of soldiers he'd found defending Skenrith Castle against a horde of berserkers. From the south had come Yeoman Burgh Keepers Hein and Chambers of Bridport and Hastings. Yeoman Warder Stevens, who had been the last to leave the outskirts of the Tower after it collapsed, told them about the sad but brave demise of the Ravenmaster, Yeoman Eshelby, who had stayed behind to ensure his birds flew to freedom. Gwenn and the other ravens seemed to understand the grim news and took off from the stones, circling and calling with a mournful cry no one had ever heard them make before.

There were maybe eight hundred people in total camped around Stonehenge by morning, many armed with nothing more than what they could find in their garden sheds. Not exactly a huge force, but as Brian said, it was a decent start. They would surely pick up more on their way to London.

At dawn a single shaft of sunlight somehow found its way through the heavy clouds above Salisbury Plain to warm the stirring army. It felt like a good omen. Hayley found Alfie pacing behind one of the huge stones, passing his Shroud Tunic from hand to hand.

"They're waiting, Alfie. You should say something."

"I know," he said. "But what?"

"'Thanks' would be a start," said Ellie, joining them. "I can't believe so many people came."

Brian and Tony were close behind, carrying bowls of warm soup fresh from one of the campfires. But Alfie didn't take any. His appetite had deserted him. He lifted the tunic to put it on, but Hayley stopped him.

"What are you doing?" she asked.

"They want to see the Defender, don't they?" said Alfie.

"They want you, Alfie. Their king," she replied. "You saw how pleased they were to see you last night."

"Yeah, but this is different. I'm asking them to go into battle and risk their lives. . . I just think the Defender can ask them to do that better than me."

"Maybe it's time they knew who the Defender is anyway?" said Tony. They all looked at him, shocked. He shrugged. "It's just an idea."

"What do you think, Brian?" asked Ellie.

"I'm not sure what LC would say, but well, he's not here," Brian replied. "And under the circumstances, no one could blame you, Your Majesty."

Alfie peered round the stone, at the mass of expectant faces further down the hill. All he had to do was show them he was the Defender and he would instantly get the respect he'd never had before. They would know it was he who had saved the people at the coronation; it was he who had fought the Viking invasion: Alfie, their king and Defender. He thought for a moment, then lowered the tunic still in his hand.

"No, the secret has to be kept," said Alfie. "Yes, I want to take the kingdom back from Lock. But not for me, for them. I'm not supposed to be in charge of the country; I'm just supposed to defend it."

"I heard people talking about it last night," said Tony. "A lot of them already think it's you. Although some were still like 'that scrawny kid's the Defender? Yeah, right.'"

"Thanks, Tony," laughed Alfie. "I just wish there was a way the king *and* the Defender could walk out there. Then they'd never know."

"Bit late to rustle up a remote-control suit of armour, sorry," said Hayley. "You can't have two Defenders."

"Actually," said Brian, "that's not completely true..."

Everyone turned to him.

"Seriously?" asked Alfie, looking sceptical.

"Yeah, this is more LC's department than mine, but from what I recall, there was one reign when two monarchs ruled jointly," continued Brian.

"William and Mary!" said Ellie. "They called it the co-regency, seventeenth century."

Alfie looked at her, surprised.

"What? Some of us actually pay attention at school, you know."

"But, how would that even work?" asked Hayley, confused.

Brian scratched his head. "Well, normally you'd need an Act of Parliament to allow it, but seeing as there is no parliament right now, I suppose the monarch could just declare it?"

"It can't be that easy," Alfie said. "OK, I declare it."

"Better make it sound official," suggested Brian.

"All right. . ." Alfie stood tall. "I, Alfred the Second, King of Great Britain and Northern Ireland, declare that my sister, Princess Eleanor, shall henceforth . . ."

"Ooh, good word," said Tony.

". . . shall henceforth reign as my co-regent. Um, that's it," said Alfie with a shrug.

Thunder boomed out in the distance.

"That's probably just a coincidence, right?" said Hayley.

Ellie stepped forward nervously. "Wait a minute, did you really just make me queen?"

Alfie held out the Shroud Tunic to her. "Let's see, shall we? Sorry, I didn't have time to wash it."

Ellie took the tunic, sniffed it, pulled a face, then put it over her head, letting it fall down over her body. She was halfway through saying "I feel ridiculous", when it happened. The magical white armour appeared, covering her from head to toe until she stood there as the Defender.

"No . . . WAY." Ellie's excited voice squealed from inside the armour.

She lifted up the nearest huge trilithon stone.

"Look at me!" she yelled.

"Excuse me, put that down, please!" yelled Celia from afar.

327

"Sorry!" said Ellie, putting it back down.

Moments later, Alfie and the new Defender prepared to step out and greet the crowd. Alfie couldn't stop smiling every time he looked over at his sister, flexing her gloves and testing out her new superhero suit.

"Seriously, Alfie, I can't believe you didn't tell me before about all this," she said.

"OK, just don't get too comfortable," he replied. "And whatever you do, don't say 'spurs'. Wyvern is kind of tetchy with new people."

Alfie took a deep breath and stepped out in front of the waiting crowd. There was applause and some cheers. But clearly many of those watching were weary and uncertain about what to expect. He needed to say something inspiring.

"Good morning! Um ... how are you?" Yeah, that wasn't going to work. He cleared his throat and tried again. "Last night I'd kind of given up hope. We all felt very cold and alone out here. And it's hard to feel brave when you're alone. But then you all came. . ."

"God save the King!" shouted Yeoman Gillam.

There were nods and cheers from parts of the crowd. Alfie held his hands up.

"There are a lot more important things than me we need to save. There are countless families out there who feel like I did last night – scared, and like no one is coming to help them. We have to show them they're not alone. It won't be easy, but we have some good friends here to help us."

Qilin materialized next to him to gasps of surprise from the onlookers.

"You get used to it. This is Qilin. With a 'Q'," said Alfie. "And there's someone else you already know too."

He waved to Ellie, who strode out from behind the stones. Now the crowd erupted into cheers and yells of triumph. Some were in tears. The Defender waved at them, excited, and even pulled a couple of muscle poses.

"Hello, Stonehenge!" shouted Ellie.

"All right, take it easy," whispered Alfie.

"Oh, chill out, Alf," she replied. "Your problem is you never knew how to enjoy this enough. SPURS!"

Wyvern uncoiled beneath the Defender and took to the air. Alfie watched in horror – the first few times he'd tried to ride Wyvern, she'd almost killed him – but he needn't have worried, as the spectral horse didn't seem to mind its new rider and shook her mane with pleasure, pulling a loop-the-loop over the exhilarated crowd.

"WOOOOHOO!" yelled the new Defender.

Alfie shook his head and laughed.

"Wyvern *likes* her? Unbelievable. . ."

The rest of the morning was taken up with preparations for the army's next move: the march on London. While the Yeoman Warders organized the volunteers into different squads, Brian laid out the strategy for taking back the capital from Lock. He explained that when vastly outnumbered, as they were, the best military option was to "cut off the head of the snake". While they would try to rescue Tamara and LC and Freya if they could, the priority had to be taking the Tower of London and catching or killing Cameron Lock. If they could do that, then they could stop any chance of Hel's return.

"So how are we supposed to take back the Tower of London?" asked Hayley.

"Yeah, a hit-and-run raid is one thing, but taking it and holding it against that undead army is a whole different kettle of fish," said new Chief Yeoman Stevens. "They don't call it the Fortress for nothing."

Brian took out a map of central London, showing the River Thames snaking beneath Tower Bridge and the famous hexagonal outline of the Tower of London's walls on the north bank.

"It won't be easy, but I have a few ideas..." he began.

*

Later, Brian found Alfie standing in the middle of the tall stones clutching the Shroud Tunic, lost in thought.

"You finally got your armour back from Ellie, then?" he asked.

"Yeah, although she took some persuading," said Alfie. "I had to promise she could 'have another go' later."

Brian shuffled awkwardly. Alfie could see that there was something on his mind, but he was having trouble saying it.

"You don't think I should go back to London, do you?" Alfie asked.

Brian looked surprised. "Well, that's not exactly what I was going to say, sir, but..."

"You're worried about what happens if we lose and Lock captures me? Then we've given him exactly what he needs to bring back Hel."

"Yeah, something like that. LC might be a stuffy old coot, but he's pretty wise when it comes to this sort of thing. I've arranged a boat for you and your sister. If you want, you can take it."

Alfie took a deep breath. "Into exile again?"

"Just till we've got rid of Lock, and it's safe to return."

"But without the Defender, you'll have less chance of winning, won't you?"

Brian didn't need to answer – it was clear Alfie was right.

"Do you remember what Greg said when I wanted you to stay at home? He said we had a duty to do our jobs, to show leadership."

"Yeah, he's kind of annoying like that – always right."

"I know it's dangerous," Alfie said, "but I'm not running away this time, and I'm not letting others fight my battles for me. We're going to London and we're going to win."

Alfie pulled the tunic over his head and the Defender armour flowed over his body.

"Yes, sir." Brian saluted him.

"Did you just salute me, Brian?"

"Er, yeah, sorry."

"No, I liked it. You should definitely keep doing that."

26

MARCH ON LONDON

They were expecting to be attacked at any moment. All morning they trekked through the countryside, waiting for the ravens that flew high above them to sound a warning cry at the first sight of Vikings charging their way. Deep into the afternoon they kept one eye on the dark skies, waiting for the Black Dragon to swoop down and strafe them with flames.

But the attack never came. Instead the king's army travelled from Salisbury Plain all the way into London almost without incident. First, a former bus driver from Yeovil had led them to a depot untouched since the invasion, where they had found a dozen buses with full petrol tanks. The Yeoman Warders had tracked down a snow-plough and cleared a path for them up the motorway. It was slow progress, as the roads had not been salted and the Defender and Qilin had to act fast more than once to stop a bus skidding out of control on the ice. At the outskirts of the city the snow-plough had run out of petrol and with the roads increasingly clogged with abandoned vehicles, they'd decided to continue on foot. Alfie, in his Defender armour, was riding ahead on Wyvern with a disgruntled Ellie sitting behind him, while Hayley walked next to them, eyes constantly scanning the side streets for movement.

"I don't know why you get to wear it the whole time now," Ellie muttered to Alfie.

"Because I've had the training and I have actually fought a few battles, you know," replied Alfie.

"Yeah, I suppose so. Sorry, I keep forgetting that you're . . . him. Still seems ridiculous."

"Tell me about it."

A pop of warm air and Qilin arrived next to them.

"Message delivered," he said to Hayley, before disappearing again and blink-shifting from rooftop to rooftop ahead of them.

"What message?" asked Alfie.

But Hayley didn't have time to answer before Qilin appeared in front of them on top of a row of shops and whistled an alarm. She readied her bow, and soon a berserker came round the corner, frothing at the mouth and growling.

"That could be someone's dad or brother, remember," said Alfie.

"Chill out, I know," Hayley said and shot an arrow close to the berserker's feet.

The berserker must have had a trace of brains left because he wisely backed off and disappeared.

"Do you think they're stuck like that for ever?" asked Ellie. "Or can we still save them?"

"Only one way to find out," said Alfie, leading them on through the streets.

Aside from the odd berserker, they had seen very few people along their journey. Curtains twitched and faces appeared at windows, watching the strange sight of the ragtag army marching past, but only a handful came out of their houses and joined them.

"I thought we'd get more new recruits than this," Alfie said to Brian, who had caught up with them after his shift guarding the rear of the army.

"That's what months of living in fear will do to people," Brian replied. "They're not going to risk their necks unless they think it's worth it."

When they reached Southwark, not far from the river, the army split up as planned. After some hasty goodbyes and hopeful "see you laters", Brian and Qilin took several of the Yeoman Warders and a handful of ex-soldiers and headed west. Alfie and Hayley led the rest on towards the Thames, beyond which lay their target, the Tower of London. It was just after four o'clock that the first Viking attack finally came. The small army was picking its way down a wide street carpeted with rubble and wrecked cars and lined by tall office blocks, when they heard a sudden smash of breaking glass, and a photocopier crashed on to the road in front of them, shattering to pieces.

"Here we go," said Alfie, drawing his sword.

From the broken window a couple of floors above, four draugar Vikings climbed out and dropped into their path. The sight of the hulking, festering brutes with their dead eyes and blood-stained axes sent a wave of fear through the army of ordinary folk. A few broke ranks and fled into the side streets. Alfie couldn't blame them – he'd also felt like running away the first time he saw an undead draugar in the stinking flesh, and he wouldn't like to face them without his armour and weapons.

"STAND FAST!" shouted Hayley, calming the ranks behind them.

"NÝTT KJǪTT HANDA OSS Í KVǪLD, SVEINAR!"* yelled one of the Vikings, scraping his axe along the asphalt.

---

* "FRESH MEAT FOR US TONIGHT, BOYS!"

"Same to you!" Ellie yelled back, making Alfie jump. "Whatever you said."

"Ow! Bit of warning next time?" He winced, lifting her off Wyvern's back and placing her on the ground.

"What are you doing?" asked Ellie.

"Stay back, we'll handle this," said Alfie, nodding to Hayley.

Ellie folded her arms, annoyed, while Hayley nocked an arrow and stood by Alfie's side, facing off with the snarling Vikings.

"She's got guts, your little sister," Hayley said to him with a wry smile.

"Yeah, too much sometimes," he said, laughing. His eyes scanned the street. The Vikings were prowling from side to side like caged tigers, but they weren't yet attacking. It was almost as if they were waiting for something. "Why do you think there's only four of these guys anyway?"

"Search me," said Hayley.

Suddenly a shadow swept across them as the Black Dragon soared overhead, screeching. Another pair of Viking zombie warriors dangled from each talon. The Dragon banked low over the rear of the king's army, dropping his passengers on to the street behind them.

"Me and my big mouth. You got this end covered?" asked Alfie. Hayley nodded. "Herne, you stay with Hayley."

The dog stood close to Hayley, growling at the Vikings as they swayed their axes and moved closer. Several Yeomen Warders ran up to join Hayley and Herne, brandishing their long pikes.

"Time to kebab some Vikings!" said Chief Yeoman Stevens, grinning from ear to ear.

Meanwhile, Wyvern flew the Defender over the heads of his army, back towards the rear. Along the way, he called to them to move off the street – he knew that the Dragon was probably circling for another dive and he didn't want them to be exposed. The army obeyed, moving into the shadows of the office blocks. Just in time too, as the Black Dragon shot back along the road, filling it with fire from his throat. Alfie closed his eyes as the flames passed over him. His armour was a little scorched but he was unharmed and, looking back, he was relieved to see that everyone had made it safely out of the firing line.

At the front of the column, Herne led the first charge, leaping at a Viking and clamping his jaws around its arm. Hayley and the Yeoman Warders were close behind, firing arrows and poking the startled draugar with their sharp pikes. Encouraged by the anguished yelps of the Vikings, many ordinary people joined the fight, bashing the undead brutes with whatever they were carrying. At the back, Wyvern kicked the first Viking to the ground, then withdrew into her spurs, leaving the Defender to unsheathe the Sword of State and swing it at the rest. At first he forced them on to the back foot, but soon they were coming back at him hard and Alfie was parrying three axes at once, testing his swordsmanship to its limit. So Alfie was relieved when a large group of his citizens joined in, unfurling long nets and running at the Vikings with them. It was an idea Brian had come up with on the way to London – an old gladiator's trick – and Alfie was pleased to see it was working a treat, as the draugar became too tangled in the nets to fight back. The Defender recalled Wyvern and hung the nets full of dazed Vikings up one at a time from lampposts where they dangled like angry Christmas tree baubles.

With the army's rear protected, the Defender flew to the front to see how Hayley was getting on. He was proud to see that she was standing on top of a heap of four stunned Vikings as the others tied them down with ropes. Herne trotted over to Alfie and licked his glove.

"Nice work," said Alfie.

"Thanks," said Hayley. "Your sister's pretty handy."

Ellie looked up and grinned from the pile of Vikings, where she was busy securing one of the restraints.

"RAAAARGH!" yelled the Viking she was tying up.

"Oh, put a cork in it," said Ellie, shoving another Viking's foot in his friend's mouth.

Suddenly the blast of a war-horn filled the streets around them. The stamping of giant feet shook the ground as a gang of more than fifty Viking draugar appeared at the junction ahead of them. They were led by Guthrum's son, the gangly, sneering Eohric, who held up his war-horn for one of his underlings to blow through.

BLOOOOOOOOO!

Gripped by the magic command of the horn, half the Vikings – including the ones tied up at Hayley's feet – began to shape-shift into huge, shaggy, black-furred, slathering devil dogs. Herne howled his own battle cry in response, but Alfie's army was gripped by renewed terror at the sight of the fiery-eyed giant hounds. To make matters worse, the shadow of the Black Dragon could be seen circling high above, preparing for another dive.

"Hey, Defender! What do we do now?" called out a man brandishing a broken snooker cue.

Alfie turned to Hayley. "What do you reckon?"

"Me?" asked Hayley.

"This is your turf. You've led the Resistance longer than I have," Alfie replied. "What's your call? Fight? Run? Take it into the side streets?"

Hayley surveyed the streets, considering their

options. Ahead of them, the devil dogs stalked closer, preparing to charge. Suddenly she caught sight of something in a nearby alleyway. She smiled.

"I always find when in doubt," she said to Alfie, "hail a cab."

She put two fingers in her mouth and whistled loud. On cue, a convoy of black cabs drove out of the alley and pulled up alongside them. The window of the first cab wound down to reveal the ruddy smiling face of Ged.

"Hello, luv. Got the message from your funny friend in the red get-up," he said with a wink. "Where to?"

"Tower Bridge, please," replied Hayley, waving for everyone to get behind the cabs. "And if you could take out as many Vikings as possible on the way there's a tip in for you."

"Now you're talking," said Ged, gunning the engine. Hayley got in, leaning out of the window with her bow, while Ellie and the Yeoman Warders hopped on to the back bumper.

A hideous chorus of snarls rose up from the devil dog pack as Eohric ordered them to attack. The hellhounds barrelled forward en masse, just as the line of black cabs started to accelerate towards them. Hayley shot an arrow clean into the first devil dog's chest as it leapt at the cab. Ellie and the Yeoman

Warders whacked the hounds off their feet as they passed by. Soon devil dogs and Vikings were being thrown out of the road in every direction as the cabs ploughed a path through them. Those that managed to dodge out of the way were trampled by the citizen army stampeding behind. Eohric, seeing that his force was defeated, shrieked with frustration and retreated down an alleyway, an arrow sticking out of one buttock, care of eagle-eyed Hayley.

Above them, the Dragon streaked down from the clouds, gathering flames in his throat for another attack. What he hadn't noticed was that the Defender had concealed himself on the roof of the tallest office block, and as the Dragon dropped past, he threw himself into the air, ambushing him from above. Wyvern's hooves hammered into the Black Dragon's back, pushing him off his attack run and instead smashing through the side of a building in a shower of glass. Flames exploded from the hole where the Dragon had collided with the block as the Defender flew on, to rejoin his forces.

"Not a bad start," shouted Hayley from the cab as the Defender flew alongside.

"Yeah, but I have a feeling they'll be back. Let's hope Brian's having an easier time. . ."

27
BATTLE OF THE THAMES

The undead Viking lookout standing on top of the rebuilt White Tower didn't notice the Royal Navy cruiser till it was too late. He was too busy watching the smoke rising from the battle in the streets of the South Bank to pay much attention to what was happening on the river. *HMS Belfast*, the eighty-year-old, 11,000-ton battleship that was moored just west of Tower Bridge as a floating museum, was on the move again. The Viking frowned, unsure if his eyes were playing tricks on him (to be fair, he only had one – a family of rats was living in the other eye socket these days), as the six-hundred-foot-long, grey vessel floated to the middle of the river. A grinding of metal drew his gaze to the twelve main battery guns, which he was startled to see were now pointing his way. They had not been fired in anger since the Korean War, but, thanks to the stealthy work of Yeoman Sultana and a handful of Naval officers they had picked up on their way from Stonehenge, the ship's armoury was now very much back in business.

"Let her rip!" yelled Sultana from the ship's bridge.

BOOM! BOOM! BOOM! BOOM! Shells rocketed from the guns and flew across the river. The Viking lookout threw himself to the floor, but it didn't do him much good as the shells found their mark and he was swallowed up by the collapsing tower.

"I feel a bit bad about this," said young Yeoman Gillam, joining Sultana on the bridge. "I mean, couldn't we get the sack or something?"

"Rubbish – it was a horrible rebuild anyway," scoffed Sultana. "We'll do up the place nice and proper, once we've turfed out those stinking squatters. Fire again!"

Deep down in the Keep, Lock felt the impact of the shells shake the foundations and noted the clouds of dust falling from the ceiling. But he didn't seem concerned. He waved over a Viking guard.

"I think I'll go for some fresh air. Ask the Lord

Chamberlain and Queen Tamara to join me, would you?"

Furrowing his broad brow, the Viking nodded and stamped off to the dungeons.

On the river, *HMS Belfast* was just lining up another barrage against the Tower when a Viking longship burst from the water like a great white shark hunting a seal. It cleared the surface entirely, giving the Yeomen a good view of its blackened timbers and undead oarsmen, before crashing down on the surf in their path. At the helm stood Guthrum, beard thick with kelp, brandishing his axe and yelling across the water at them.

"Víkingar járnaskips! Búið þér dauðinum! Grafir þín verðr áráll!"*

"Engines, stop! Target the longship!" shouted Sultana.

Yeoman Gillam ran to help the crew reload the guns. But no sooner had they taken aim and fired than the longship submerged and reappeared a hundred yards to the right, now joined by two more. Then another group of three longships appeared behind those, and another and another, until the entire undead Viking fleet filled the river, all the way under Tower Bridge

---

* "Iron ship pirates! Prepare to die! Your graves will be the riverbed!"

and beyond. As one, they rowed in a V-formation, making straight for the *HMS Belfast*.

"What do we do now?" cried Yeoman Gillam, running back on to the bridge.

"Hold fast," said Sultana, scanning the water.

Suddenly the royal submarine surfaced between the *Belfast* and the onrushing Viking armada, forcing the longships into a hasty halt, the wake from the sub even capsizing one of them. The conning tower hatch opened and Brian and Tony stepped out. Guthrum laughed bitterly from his ship.

"Bátr þín er fǫgr, en hon hefir engi vopn!"* he called out.

"Show these deadbeats what we have, would you, Tony?" said Brian.

"Coming up, chief!" said Tony, donning his Qilin gear and disappearing.

Guthrum felt a tap on his shoulder and was surprised to find Qilin standing next to him on his longship.

"Special delivery," said Qilin.

He handed Guthrum something and blink-shifted away. Guthrum opened his large grey palm and looked at the small silver fireball sitting in it. Yelping like a startled dog, he tried to toss the fireball away,

---

* "Your vessel may be pretty, but she has no weapons!"

but it exploded, knocking him spinning into the river, and setting fire to the boat. Brian watched with a satisfied grin as Qilin teleported from longship to longship, leaving a fireball behind each time. Flames flashed from boat after boat like a firework display gone wrong, setting decks, sails and oars alight and sending their draugar crews tumbling overboard.

On the banks of the river, the cab convoy had reached Tower Bridge. Ahead, the road bridge was clogged with long-abandoned vehicles. Ged leaned out of his window as Hayley hopped out of the cab.

"Can't go any further, unless you have a way to shift that lot?"

"I might know a guy," Hayley said, waving the Defender down to them.

Alfie landed and Wyvern disappeared into his spurs.

"Qilin's doing quite the job on those longships," he said.

Sure enough, the Thames was turning into a grave-yard of burning longships before their eyes. Vikings were splashing about and sinking all over the river.

"Reckon you could clear us a path?" asked Hayley.

"I'll do my best," said Alfie, taking off once more and hovering over the bridge.

He pointed his ring finger to the rows of cars and

focused his mind. Within seconds, every British-made vehicle, except for one bus, had floated into the air and dropped on to the already beleaguered Viking boats below. Alfie then commanded the bus to ride across the bridge, ramming the remaining cars to the sides. He was just allowing himself to admire a job well done when the Black Dragon swooped overhead, screeching. The Defender banked away sharply and landed back with his army, but the Dragon wasn't attacking them. He was flying towards the *HMS Belfast*.

On the sub, Brian just had time to wave a warning at the ship, where Yeoman Sultana saw the incoming shape of the Dragon and sounded the alarm. The crew hit the deck as the Dragon dived at the gun battery, yanked it clean off the ship with its talons in a screech of rending metal, and dropped it into the river. Alfie was relieved that no one on the ship seemed to have been hurt in the attack, but he felt uneasy as he watched his brother fold his wings and dive behind the walls of the Tower of London on the other side of the river.

"Do you think he's coming back?" asked Ellie.

"I don't know. But we should hurry," Alfie replied.

Following Hayley's lead, the king's army started to pick their way across Tower Bridge, behind the black cabs.

*

Across the river, Lock had come up to the top of an undamaged tower to observe the battle. As instructed, the Vikings had brought the Lord Chamberlain and Queen Tamara up from their cell and they stood now, under guard, also watching the unfolding battle below. They could see everything from up here – the longships on fire, crashing into each other, and the mass of people being led across the bridge by the Defender.

"They're winning," Tamara whispered to LC.

"Don't be so sure. . ." LC replied.

"Wise words, Lord Chamberlain," said Lock. He took out his ancient book of Old Norse spells and read from a cracked, yellow page.

"Rán, Sjávargyðja, gef mér feldinn þinn til að glepja óvinar!"*

High above the river the black clouds swirled and billowed, spinning back and forth unnaturally.

"You meddle with such ancient powers at your peril!" shouted LC.

But Lock ignored him and continued casting his spell.

"Søkktu sálar dauðlegra manna, dragðu þeir í djúpið!"†

---

* "Goddess Ran of the Sea, send me your cloak to shroud my enemies!"
† "Sink the souls of mortal men, drag them into the depths!"

A bank of black fog rose like a wall from the river and rolled towards the ships. Guthrum sounded his horn and his longships submerged as one, putting out the flames, and returned to the surface. On the sub, Brian and Qilin watched the supernatural fog as it moved towards them.

"If I can't see, I can't blink-shift," said Qilin.

Brian looked towards the bridge – the army wasn't even halfway across.

"We have to give the others as much cover as we can," he said. "For as long as we can."

He signalled the advance to the *HMS Belfast* and together they made for the Viking fleet, as the fog rolled in behind them.

Deep in the Tower of London's dungeons, the Black Dragon eyed the gleaming ball of golden keys that hung by some unknown magic in the centre of the chamber. What Lock had told him to do seemed like madness, but then madness was all he had now – that and a boiling rage that trapped him inside this monstrous body. *What difference does it make now?* he thought. *Let chaos come.*

He inhaled and spat a torrent of dragon fire at the keys. They glowed red, then white, then they began to melt, molten gold pooling on the floor around his feet. *CLUNK, CLUNK, CLUNK* – one by one, the cell doors opened. The Black Dragon withdrew, leaving those inside to find their own way out.

Take every screech and howl of every beast and monster that has ever been imagined, put them together in one horrible cacophony, and that is something close to the noise that now drifted across Tower Bridge. It was the sound of centuries' worth of Britain's most vile and fearsome villains celebrating their freedom, and it was enough to stop the king's army in its tracks. Alfie looked over the side of the bridge and caught a final glimpse of the Yeoman Warders onboard *HMS Belfast*, and Brian and Qilin on the conning tower of the sub, all bracing themselves for battle as the Viking longships surrounded them before the fog bank tumbled in, hiding them all from view. But the blood-curdling shrieks and cackles were not coming from beneath them.

"Um, what's that?" asked Ellie, wide-eyed.

They were coming from the Tower across the river. Alfie peered ahead and was shocked to see creatures cascading over the walls like ants fleeing an anthill. Some were familiar from the pages of books on myths and legends – ogres, werewolves, vampires, what looked like a Yeti in a Nazi uniform and even a giant Cyclops wielding a club. Others were entirely new combinations so bizarre they didn't seem like they could be real – a giant bat with the head of a unicorn, a woman with a beautiful face and the body of a tarantula, a tall, lizard-faced man with webbed hands and feet, slime dripping from his green body. They slithered, climbed and flapped over the walls on to the streets outside. A red horned demon with long goat legs, who was called Spring-Heeled Jack, bounded across the rooftops. The enormous, snarling Beast of Bodmin, with shaggy black fur and three heads – a lion's, a wolf's and a bear's – smashed its way to freedom with a chorus of howls. Robyn Hood, a lithe young woman in a green hooded cloak, swung from wall to wall like an expert gymnast, firing arrows from her sleeves at a skull-faced vampire that tried to bite her.

"What's happening?" gasped Hayley, struggling to take in the nightmarish scene before them.

"It's Lock," said Alfie. "He's opened the dungeons."

Alfie looked back the way they'd come, ready to call for a retreat, but the end of the bridge behind them was blocked. A thousand grunting, drooling berserkers had gathered, barring any chance of an exit.

"We're trapped," said Alfie.

At the far end of the bridge ahead of them, the first of the dungeons' escapees had begun to appear. A pack of werewolves baring their fangs, a ghoulish skeleton armed with a spear, a giant snake rearing up and hissing. The army of ordinary citizens was beginning to panic. There was nowhere to turn.

"We need to make a defensive circle!" shouted Hayley to Alfie. "Yeoman Warders and trained soldiers round the outside. NOW!"

The Defender flew above the army, relaying Hayley's instruction. The army closed ranks until they were packed together in the centre of the bridge, ringed by the cabs, weapons pointing outward, ready for the attack. Alfie hovered ahead on Wyvern, sword drawn: a first line of defence. But the wall of monsters approaching along the bridge was almost too much to take in. He didn't know how long he would be able to hold them back. The faint outline of the setting sun disappeared behind the Tower of London and all was darkness.

In the Keep, the Lord Chamberlain and Tamara, still under armed Viking guard, watched with growing horror as Lock pulled the black velvet cloth away, revealing Hel's mirror. The buzzing of flies filled their ears as the dark waters of the mirror's surface swirled and bubbled, and the hideous face of Hel appeared.

"It is time, my mistress," Lock said.

28

TURNING THE TIDE

Most people like the sun on their skin. It makes them feel warm and full of life. But for half-trolls it's the other way round. Only when the sun goes down do they truly come alive. So it was for young Queen Freya as the muted light from outside finally disappeared from the House of Commons chamber, leaving her lying in shadow inside her particle-beam cage. The comforting darkness of the coming night awakened the troll within her and that gave her strength. Enough strength for what she had been planning next.

"You should take it before your friends come back..." she croaked in the ancient tongue of her motherland.

The single Viking draugar guard looked down at her from the bench where he was slouched.

"Geturðu ekki drífa þik ok deyast? Bardagi brestr,"* he grunted, wiping a thick rope of drool from his chin and flicking it against the wall.

"I'll be with my ancestors soon enough," replied Freya in Old Norse. "Which is why I want you to have Brísingamen."

The Viking flicked his dead, milky eyes to the necklace hanging nearby. He had been trying not to look at it for hours, trying not to think about its glittering gold and sparkling emeralds. Having such treasures within reach but not being allowed to touch them was torture for his kind.

"Go on," continued Freya. "You might as well pick it up, at least."

"TEGÐU!"† yelled the Viking, turning away and folding his arms like a grumpy toddler.

"Please yourself," said Freya. She wasn't sure how many more words she could muster. The effort to sound like she didn't care was eating up the last of her reserves. "I suppose your friends will just take it when they get back, then. I heard them whispering about it. They didn't want to share it with you. How

---

* "Can you hurry up and die? I'm missing the battle."
† "SHUT UP!"

foolish they will feel when they discover you don't care for priceless jewels."

A frown grew across the Viking's grey forehead until it had become a scowl and before he knew it, he was stomping over to the Speaker's Chair and lifting the necklace between his fingers. It was dazzling. Just holding it made his skin tingle in a way he hadn't felt since he was alive. He decided he would kill anyone who ever tried to take it from him.

"Try it on," whispered Freya. She was barely clinging to consciousness.

The Viking looked at her and laughed.

"Go on. Nobody is here. Feel what it's like to be royalty!" she urged him.

The Viking shrugged, opened the necklace and carefully placed it round his neck. Amused, he gazed at his reflection in the polished wood of the dispatch box that sat on the Table of the Commons.

Freya smiled. "I'm glad you like it," she said. "If only it liked you back. I've just remembered that non-trolls aren't supposed to wear it. Sorry about that."

The Viking could smell meat cooking. Yellow smoke filled his vision. He looked down, alarmed to see that it was him that was on fire! The necklace was burning through his dead skin like acid. He grabbed the chain and tried to pull it off, but it was stuck fast. Desperate, he stumbled to Freya's cage.

"TAKTU Í HANN, FLAGÐ!"* he screamed.

"I'll take it when it's finished with you, thanks."

The Viking punched and kicked the energy beam bars in agony, sending sparks flying and only hastening his own end. Finally the necklace brushed against the cage, overloading the energy-beam bars and evaporating the whole thing in a cloud of smoke and embers.

Once she had recovered from the explosion, Freya reached into the pile of crackling bones that had until a few moments ago been the gullible guard and plucked out her necklace. She hung Brísingamen around her neck and instantly felt her life force rushing back. The transformation into Holgatroll was like a rebirth.

It took her less than a minute to sniff out the real Raven Banner planted in a room just behind the chamber. She placed her immense green fist around it and heaved it out of the stone floor with a roar of triumph. The entire Palace of Westminster shook as if struck by an earthquake. The red lines of the banner's magic crisscrossing Big Ben like poisoned veins vanished in an instant. The crimson glow from the cracks in the earth that spread out like spiders' legs from the base of the tower dimmed to nothing.

---

* "GET IT OFF ME, WITCH!"

A group of berserkers hanging around in the square outside Parliament froze as if electrocuted, shaking and shrinking as the curse left their bodies.

Across the country, berserkers found the blue warpaint fading from their faces, their thick Viking hair receding and their eyes clearing as they returned to normal. It would take some time for them to understand how they had come to be where they were and why their clothes were in tatters.

In the garden of Number Ten, Downing Street, Sebastian Mortimer was trying to help his rather large father over a wall, as newly recovered secret service agents retook the building.

In a sewer somewhere beneath the streets of east London, Prime Minister Thorn awoke as if from a nightmare to find a half-eaten rat hanging from her mouth. Once she had stopped screaming, she made her way above ground, wondering where her chauffeur-driven car could be parked.

And in the shadow of Hayley's old block of flats, a restored Turpin was fighting off Fulcher, who was hugging and kissing him for some reason he couldn't begin to fathom. Soon families everywhere would celebrate the return of loved ones thought lost, unaware of the battle raging in London that could still doom them all.

Holgatroll bounded out of Parliament clutching

her banner and turned north. Soon she would be back in Norway and with it she would free her kingdom from the Viking chaos and return the undead to their eternal slumber beneath the fjords. At a troll's pace she could be home before sunrise. But as the wind changed direction, her keen nose caught the scent of sulphur. An evil stench was in the air and for once she was pretty sure it wasn't her fault. Her troll's ears were not as powerful as her nose, but she could still hear the distant screams of the battle. Holgatroll leapt up the side of Big Ben and on to the roof until she had a clear view downstream. She could make out the unnatural blanket of fog that hugged the river and the swirling mass of bodies on the bridge, along with the bizarre and hideous shapes of the monsters assailing it from every side. But there was something else she noticed. Everywhere she looked there were small groups of people moving through the streets, coming out of houses and offices, gathering and heading for the river – *towards* the battle.

She considered the banner in her mighty hand, then thought of Alfie and the others. Making a decision she hoped she would not regret, she turned and jumped down through the roof, back into Parliament.

On Tower Bridge the king's army was losing hope. At his last count, Alfie had fought off a sabre-toothed centaur, a black-bearded pirate and a swarm of giant bees armed with meat cleavers. Herne shadowed his master's every move, savaging any creature that came close and bravely ignoring his own injuries. Hayley had got the better of a stalking werewolf and a pair of hovering harpies with her longbow, but there were more monsters coming at them all the time. The outer ring of Yeoman Warders and soldiers were taking casualties, the injured being dragged back into the middle of the circle. But they couldn't hold out much longer.

The Defender spotted Robyn Hood just in time. She was perched on a strut high above them, aiming her arrow-sleeves at them, but Alfie flew into the arrows' path, parried them with his armill bracelets, then hurled his nunchuck sceptres at her, sending her tumbling into the foggy river below.

On the deck of *HMS Belfast*, Yeomen Sultana and Gillam were fighting the Viking draugar hand-to-hand with their pikes, while Brian steered the submarine into as many longships as he could to stop more invaders boarding them. Tony, frustrated by his inability to blink-shift in the fog, had taken to hovering round the ship, fending off the Vikings as best he could. But they were outnumbered.

A hand landed on the Defender's shoulder and spun him round. He was about to elbow whichever villain it was in the face when he saw it was Hayley.

"Look!" she cried.

She was pointing at the south end of the bridge behind them. Where there had been a mass of crazed berserkers moments before, there now was just a great deal of very confused people milling about and walking away. Alfie didn't have to discuss it; he knew what she was saying.

"Sound the retreat!" he yelled, flying up.

The cabbies started their engines and began to reverse slowly back the way they had come, providing some cover for the army to withdraw. The three-headed Beast of Bodmin thundered along the bridge through the riot of monsters, charging straight at them. But the Defender used the Ring of Command to lift a strip of asphalt under its paws like a carpet and flip to the side, sending the confused creature tumbling into the water below. Alfie was using his command powers constantly now, to wrap an attacking vampire with the metal walkway railing, to throw an ogre off balance with a well-timed flying bicycle – but it wasn't enough. More monsters climbed up on to the bridge or landed behind them until the attacks were coming from all sides. With their retreat cut off, Alfie knew his army was seconds from being overrun.

"What do we do?" cried Ellie.

"I don't know," he said, pulling his sister behind him, cursing himself for being stupid enough to bring her into battle.

Hayley joined them. She was out of arrows and had resorted to swinging her bow to keep the monstrous attackers at bay.

"We fight for as long as we can," she said between gasps.

Alfie looked at Hayley for a moment – he was sure it would be the last time he would see her face.

Suddenly a fierce wind blew across the bridge. A stale, hideous odour like a thousand rotten fish was carried on it, a smell so vile that every human and monster on the river stopped what they were doing and held their noses in disgust. The stinking gale swept away the thick fog, revealing the beleaguered *HMS Belfast* and mini-submarine covered with the marauding draugar undead below. It also revealed the source of the freak wind: Nessie. She was puffing out the intense wind from between her razor-sharp teeth. And sitting astride the magnificent beast was Holgatroll.

"BABE!" shouted Qilin from the deck of the Belfast, waving at her.

With his line of sight clear once more, Qilin blink-shifted around the boat grabbing Viking after Viking and delivering them one by one to the top of a distant crane until it collapsed under their weight. He only interrupted his Viking-clearing spree to appear next to Holgatroll for a moment and kiss her on the cheek, blink-shifting away again before her swinging fist could connect with him.

On his longship, Guthrum raged at his men.

"DREPIÐ SJÓORMINN, MANNSKRÆFUR!"*

But as Nessie bore down on them, he abandoned ship like the rest of his crew and within seconds the Viking fleet was reduced to driftwood by her mighty thrashing flippers.

In a single leap Holgatroll bounded up on to Tower Bridge and roared so loudly that several of the monster villains turned tail and ran away there and then. For a moment, the civilians of the resistance army assumed this was just another escapee from the Tower's dungeons come to massacre them.

"It's OK," shouted Hayley. "She's with us!" She turned to Holgatroll. "You are, aren't you?"

The troll cracked a smile. "Looks that way. Besides, I have something to return to you."

She heaved three large holdalls off her back on to the ground. Hayley gawped at them, amazed.

"My gunpowder!"

Qilin appeared next to them with Brian.

---

* "KILL THE SEA-LIZARD, YOU COWARDS!"

"Well, that could even things up a bit," said Brian looking at the bags.

"Where do you want them?" grinned Tony.

"I'll leave that up to you lot," Holgatroll said. She extended one mighty arm and grabbed a lunging werewolf by the throat. Then she reached up with her other hand and plucked a dive-bombing harpy from the air. She smashed the two struggling creatures' heads together with a sickening CRUNCH and barrelled headlong down the bridge, swinging their inert bodies like clubs at anything foolish enough to come near her.

Meanwhile, Hayley and Ellie carefully ferried generous scoops of gunpowder to Qilin, who blink-shifted from monster to monster, leaving the explosives and a fireball at each one's feet. Soon it was raining claws, fangs and other assorted monster parts as the king's army charged forward, filled with courage once more.

At the rear, the Defender had just dispatched a rampaging goblin with his sword when he felt a strange rumbling shake the bridge from side to side. And it wasn't just the vibrations passing through his body; it was a sound, so deep it was almost too low to hear, undulating like music. He steadied himself on the side of the bridge and saw that the Vikings who were being carried downstream amid the wreckage of their boats, were singing. Not the same strange tune he had heard before, but a throbbing powerful bass note that made the water around them bubble and froth like it was coming to the boil.

Suddenly a huge grey hand the size of a car shot from beneath the river and thumped down right next to him. The Defender staggered back and watched incredulously as a giant heaved himself on to the bridge. It was Guthrum, transformed into a truly mammoth form, a hundred feet tall. Black veins ran through his vast, bulging muscles. Huge dead eyes blinked down at the Defender from behind swaying ropes of red hair. Had LC been there, he might have explained to Alfie that he should feel honoured – each undead Viking Lord can only adopt its mega-berserker form once in its existence and will only choose to do so when faced with the most formidable enemy. As it was, Alfie was too busy figuring out how to stay alive for the next five seconds to feel very much aside from armour-wetting terror.

"NÚ SKALTU DEYJA, RIDDARINN INN LITILL!"* bellowed the gargantuan Guthrum, spitting foam over the Defender and hefting his equally enormous axe.

Clearly Guthrum had not taken the destruction

---

* "TIME FOR YOU TO DIE, PUNY KNIGHT!"

of his fleet very well, thought Alfie. A Viking underling suddenly clambered up on to the bridge and ran over to Guthrum, seemingly concerned about something.

"En Lock hefr sagt at hann skyldi ei at skaða! Hann vil fá honum kvika!"* he called up to his master.

Whatever he said, Guthrum didn't want to hear it. He swatted the Viking away with the back of his hand, flinging him back into the river. Alfie summoned Wyvern and hovered up to the giant's eye level. There was no outrunning him this time – he would have to deal with Guthrum once and for all.

"The last time you picked a fight with a king it didn't go so well, remember?" he said.

Guthrum's eyes flared with rage and he launched himself at the Defender, swinging his axe. Wyvern dodged the blows like a fly avoiding a swatter, each impact of the Viking's blade shaking the bridge so much Alfie thought it could collapse at any moment. He readied his sword to strike back, but Guthrum was in a full berserker fury, spinning and swiping with such speed that he couldn't deliver a clean thrust. Severed steel suspension chains whipped past the Defender like demented snakes, threatening to unseat him. Alfie held out his ring

---

* "But Lock told us he was not to be harmed! He wants him alive!"

finger and commanded a chain to wrap itself round Guthrum's axe-arm, which slowed him down long enough for Alfie to look around and figure out a plan. While Guthrum struggled to pull the chain from its mooring, the Defender flew to the centre of the bridge, hovering between the South and North Towers. At the far end of the bridge, Hayley had spotted what was happening and was rounding up Qilin and Holgatroll, who were mopping up the last of the remaining monsters, to come to the Defender's aid. But seeing them approach, Alfie signalled for them to stay back.

"What's he up to?" asked Tony.

"He's handling it." Hayley smiled.

Guthrum swung his axe, removing the top half of the South Tower in a shower of glass and masonry, clearing the way for him to make a grab for the Defender. Alfie held tight as Wyvern looped-the-loop round the giant's arm. Somehow she understood what Alfie had planned, the telepathic bond between rider and horse in full flow. The upper walkway, now untethered at one end, groaned as it fell past them, crashing on to the bridge below. Alfie knew he needed Guthrum to come closer for his idea to work. Close enough to kill Alfie if it went wrong.

"EK MUN HAKKA HOLDIT ÞITT!" yelled Guthrum. "OK ÞÁ SKAL EK SLÁ VININA ÞÍNA

OK PRÝÐA STORAN HQLLINA HAUSINUM
ÞEIRRA!"*

"Whatever you just said," replied Alfie, "you'll
have to catch me first."

With an ear-splitting roar, Guthrum pushed
past the remains of the South Tower, stomping into
the middle of the bridge, and lunged at Alfie. But
rather than striking back, Alfie pulled Wyvern into a
vertical climb. Guthrum anticipated the move, bent
his knees and jumped after them. Hayley and the
others watched in growing horror as the giant Viking
strained every fibre of his stinking body to grab the
Defender. Alfie clung to Wyvern, who shot up like
a rocket. Guthrum's grasping fingers were inches
from them, so close that they brushed the end of the
horse's tail. But now he had reached the apex of his
ascent and he began to fall. Seeing the giant tumble
back towards the bridge, the Defender pulled Wyvern
level and extended his arm downwards. Alfie closed
his eyes and focused – this command would have to
be faster and better timed that anything he'd ever
attempted before. In a split second he felt a response
from his target: the steel of the bridge's bascules –

---

* "I'LL FEAST ON YOUR FLESH! AND THEN I'LL SLAUGHTER
YOUR FRIENDS AND DECORATE MY GREAT HALL WITH
THEIR SKULLS!"

the two halves of the central section that were raised every day to allow shipping to pass through. The counterweights spun round at high speed to his command and the bridge flew open from the middle just as Guthrum plummeted past, hands flailing in vain to stop his fall. Then as quickly as he'd opened them, Alfie commanded the bascules to snap shut. A stifled howl of rage was all Guthrum had time for before the steel trap closed on his neck, severing his head from his body, which fell into the water below to be washed away on the outgoing tide.

The Defender landed on the bridge and recalled Wyvern into his spurs. The head of Guthrum – which, being undead, was still functioning despite the loss of its body – rolled a few metres down the bridge, shrinking back to its normal size. It stared up at him, eyes wide with shock.

"Hvað hefr þú gjört við mik, riddari svíkligr?"*

"I suggest you chill out here for a bit and think about what you've done. I expect someone will bury you later," said Alfie.

He was just turning back to join his friends at the other end of the bridge when he heard Hayley's scream.

"LOOK OUT!"

---

* "What have you done to me, treacherous knight?"

A wall of fire engulfed him as something hit him with the force of a train, knocking the wind out of him. As his vision cleared of smoke he looked down to see thick talons encircling him, pinning his arms to his side, and the bridge growing smaller below him. Like a falcon with its prey, the Black Dragon was carrying the Defender back to the Tower.

29
RAISING HEL

"Richard! Let me go!" gasped Alfie.

Despite his armour, the Dragon's vice-like grip was squeezing the air from his lungs. But no answer came from the Black Dragon except a screech of triumph as it banked towards the Tower of London's walls. Alfie could no longer detect any trace of his brother in the monster that was clutching him. It was as if Richard was completely gone, leaving nothing but the creature and its venomous rage.

Alfie summoned Wyvern, but caught beneath the dragon's belly, she flailed and whinnied in distress. It felt like he was being torn in half as his horse struggled to pull away. He recalled Wyvern into his spurs. The Defender was running out of time. Another few moments and the Dragon would deliver him into Lock's hands and everything they had fought for would be lost. There was no choice; he had to stop the Black Dragon any way he could.

Calming his mind, he commanded the Sword of State to unsheathe itself, unsure if it would even work. But sure enough the sword slid out, filling the night sky with light. Alfie felt the Dragon twist to see where the sudden glare was coming from and as it did he commanded his sword to turn its tip to the beast's belly and thrust upwards.

The Defender's sword found its mark and the Dragon squealed in agony, releasing its grip on him. Alfie crash-landed on the deserted street below, and a moment later the Sword of State speared into the earth beside him, its blade wet with black blood. He heard the anguished cry of the wounded Dragon and looked up just in time to see it spiral out of sight behind the Tower of London's walls. Alfie felt arms lifting him off the ground and looked round to see the concerned face of Hayley, and Qilin blink-shifting in behind her with Brian.

"Are you OK?" asked Hayley.

"Yeah. Bit winded, but I'll live," said Alfie.

Ellie and Holgatroll ran up to join them, the massed ranks of the army not far behind. Ellie looked at the sword as Brian pulled it from the ground and wiped it clean.

"Is that—?" she stammered.

"Yes," said Alfie, casting his eyes to the ground. "There was nothing else I could do."

"You said we could save him," said Ellie, her eyes filling with tears. "He's still our brother."

"There's still a chance," said Alfie. "We'll try, I promise."

Brian handed him his sword. The gates to the Tower lay open before them.

"Do you think your mum's still in there?" asked Tony.

"And LC?" added Hayley.

"I don't know. But whatever else we lose tonight, we can't turn back now. People like Lock don't give up. We have to stop him, for good this time," Alfie said.

"That's what I'm talking about," Holgatroll growled, cracking her immense knuckles.

Alfie raised his sword. The king's army raised a cheer in reply.

"Long live the Defender!" cried a woman at the front.

Alfie turned and charged over the drawbridge, flanked by his friends and followed by the rest. They streamed down Water Lane, weapons drawn, yelling their war-cries as they went, and turned left through the arch of the Bloody Tower and up the steps on to Tower Green.

Just a few months ago I was right here with Gran watching the Ceremony of the Keys, Hayley thought. She remembered that while they'd waited for the ceremony to start, she actually thought this place was boring. Not that Gran would have recognized it now. Dust from the bombardment hung in the air like a grainy, white mist. Parts of the old walls had been completely blown to pieces, forcing them to clamber over piles of rubble. There were blackened remains of campfires and stacks of Viking axes and swords, but there was no sign of the undead monsters, or anyone else for that matter. It was eerily quiet.

Brian beckoned Chief Yeoman Warder Stevens. "Sweep every corner, then lock down every exit. No one leaves till you see us again."

Stevens nodded and went to brief his men.

Alfie circled the ruins of the White Tower until he found a doorway still intact, but blocked with rubble.

"We might be able to get in here," he said, waving the others over.

"Allow me," said Holgatroll, charging past him and smashing through the doorway.

Alfie, Hayley, Tony, Brian and Ellie ducked after her and found themselves inside the wrecked shell of the Tower's ground floor. Alfie eased open a door to the cellar to reveal a spiral staircase leading down into blackness.

"Everyone ready?" Alfie asked and drew his sword. Ellie looked alarmed as she gazed at the silver blade. "Get behind me."

The siege had knocked out all the power, and the winding steps down into the Keep were long and dark, but Alfie's glowing sword lit the way. Huge cracks from the *Belfast's* bombardment had ripped their way through the stone even this deep underground. Water cascaded from broken pipes that jutted out of the walls, washing down the steps in front of them. No one spoke as they descended deeper and deeper beneath the Tower, only the gushing water and their breathing broke the silence – that and Holgatroll's occasional cursing as she bumped her head against the low ceiling. Finally the steps opened out into a hallway that led to the shattered remains of an oak door. Alfie recognized it. Behind it lay the Map Room and the Keep. He tried the handle and was surprised to find it unlocked. Wary, he stepped through.

The great hall of the Keep was filled with torn tapestries and overturned desks. Standing beyond the splintered map table at its centre were LC and Tamara, their hands bound.

"Alfie! Look out—" Tamara shouted.

A draugar warrior stepped out of the shadows and, with a yell, swung its axe at Alfie's head. But Alfie side-stepped easily and swung his sword upwards, knocking the Viking's axe out of its hands. Suddenly unarmed, the Viking nevertheless bunched its skeletal fists and came again at Alfie.

Whoosh! Thunk.

An arrow hit the Viking straight in the forehead, and it collapsed into a pile with a sound like dry kindling being dropped on to the floor.

"Stay down, bag of bones," Hayley said and lowered her bow.

"Are you all right?" Alfie asked as he cut his mum's and LC's hands free.

"Yes, somehow," Tamara stammered as Ellie ran forward and hugged her fiercely.

LC straightened what remained of his tie and brushed down his shredded, dirty suit before bowing to Alfie.

"Most obliged, Majesty."

"Any more of those Viking guards around?"

"I think it was the last one, sir. Lock and your brother—" LC stopped and corrected himself. "I mean Lock and the *Black Dragon* have retreated to the Arena."

"Last stand, huh?" Alfie said.

"If I may suggest something, Majesty? Leave

them. We can seal them down here for ever, find a new base for the Defender."

"And run the risk of Lock getting out again? No way, Cuthbert."

"So, you finally know my true name." LC's smile was warm and knowing. "You've ridden with the Wild Hunt and lived. I knew the extra power from King Alfred's crown would aid you in your battle."

"Yeah, about that. . . I didn't take it. No one should have that much power." Alfie shrugged.

LC gazed at Alfie in awe. Tears sprang into his eyes.

"Then you are a wiser man than me, and truly King Alfred the Great's heir."

A roar, thick with pain, shattered the silence and made everyone jump.

"The Arena," Brian hissed and drew his pistol.

Alfie signalled everyone to get behind him and advanced inside. The Arena had changed almost beyond recognition since his raid with Qilin for the regalia. Tall, black candles stood at intervals around the edge of the wide, oval chamber, casting an eerie glow up the high inner walls of the tower above. On one side, where the benches had once sat, animal bones now lay scattered. Norse runes painted in what looked like blood were daubed on every wall and across the velvet curtains that covered the regalia cabinet on the other side. Alfie thought it looked more like a temple for some evil cult than his old training ground. In the centre of the dirt floor on a raised plinth, stood Cameron Lock next to the scrying mirror. He wore black ceremonial robes and his eyes blazed with excitement. Behind him cowered the vast form of the Black Dragon. It roared again, but Alfie thought it – *his brother!* – sounded weak. One of its wings was crumpled, and the deep slash across its chest where Alfie had plunged his sword was black and raw.

"Richard, I'm sorry," called Alfie.

But the Dragon merely growled in response and returned to licking its wounds.

"*I'm* sorry, Majesty, your brother is no longer with us," said Lock. "Nevertheless, this is a happy reunion."

Alfie fixed Lock with a fearless glare and strode towards him. "A nation can survive its fools, but it cannot survive treason from within," he said, his confident voice echoing around.

"Cicero, I believe?" said Lock, a thin smile on his lips. "I'm glad you haven't been neglecting your studies, Alfie." Deep, dark blotches hung under his bloodshot eyes and his cheeks were sunken. His skin looked as dry as one the draugar.

He looks totally out of it. Crazy, Alfie thought.

"That's King Alfred the Second to you, Lock. Surrender or die," Hayley announced as the others entered and fanned out around the edges of the arena, weapons drawn.

Lock watched them with a faintly amused look in his eyes and cocked his head. "I obey only one ruler. Would you all like to meet her?" he asked.

Lock lifted the seeing mirror over his head and hurled it to the floor at the Defender's feet. It exploded in a shower of glass. But far from remaining where they fell, the jagged shards melted like molten steel, then merged together to form a thick, bubbling black pool, like an oil slick. It spread with lightning speed, racing to the edges of the arena.

"Get back!" LC shouted as everyone retreated. "Don't let it touch you!"

Alfie was already astride Wyvern, hovering safely above the pool. He gazed down into the foul, churning liquid. The air was filled with the deafening buzz of a million flies as Hel's half-skull face emerged from the surface. Wyvern flew clear as the plague goddess's head reared out of the pool, snapping her jaws at them.

"Come to me, king!" Hel shrieked, her voice like a thousand nails being dragged down a chalkboard.

At the edges of the Arena, everyone clamped their hands over their ears.

"Never!" Alfie yelled. "Without my blue blood, you'll never be free!"

And it was true. While Hel screamed in rage, tendrils of black liquid clung to her, dragging her back down into the dark pool.

The Lord Chamberlain stepped forward. "Stop this, Lock," he commanded. "The king's blood you need must be given freely for your evil ritual to work. You've lost."

"You're right, of course," Lock said as he clung to the plinth that was now surrounded by the raging, opaque water. "But perhaps all His Majesty needs is a little more motivation. Saving his sister, for example."

"Alfie?" Ellie said.

But as Alfie looked down to his sister, Qilin placed his hands on her shoulders and blink-shifted the two of them away. They reappeared across the Arena, by Lock's side.

"Get off me!" yelled Ellie.

"Tony! What are you doing?" shouted Alfie.

But Qilin, moving stiffly, held her firm. And when he spoke, it was not with his own voice. It was with the icy, tittering words of Colonel Blood. "There, there, princess. Don't struggle. Your travails will soon be at an end."

Both the Defender and Holgatroll flew at them.

"Get back, I implore thee!" Colonel Blood hissed.

They both stopped when they saw the Viking axe Qilin had pressed to Ellie's throat. In the corner, the Black Dragon seemed to notice and growled for a moment, before turning away again, wracked with agony.

Qilin's head jerked, puppet-like, to regard Alfie, who backed off, hovering above them on Wyvern.

"Well met, young king! As I foretold, our paths have crossed once more!"

"Don't you dare hurt her, Blood!" he said.

But with a giggle that was not his own, Qilin pushed Ellie into the pool.

"NO!" screamed Tamara.

Ellie thrashed around in the thick, stinking black liquid, but it was pulling her down.

Time seemed to slow down to a dead crawl. Without thinking twice, Alfie forced Wyvern into a vertical dive towards the pool. The Black Dragon roared in anguish. Lock's eyes grew wide with hungry anticipation. Hayley yelled at Alfie to pull up. Hel pressed up through the whirlpool like a screaming death mask wrapped in black cloth. LC shouted at Alfie to stop.

But Alfie and Wyvern splashed down into the churning black water and disappeared.

Beneath the surface of Hel's mirror pool, all was black. Alfie tried to swim, but it was like being caught in quicksand. He screamed noiselessly as he felt the blue-blood power leech out of him. Once at Harrow he'd caught a virus and had to have a blood test. He'd watched anxiously as the nurse had pricked his arm with a needle and drawn out a vial of blood. But this was a million times worse. It wasn't just his blood he could feel flowing out of his body; it was a thousand years of blue-blood magic being sucked away. His ancestry. His family. His power. His life. Next to him, Ellie writhed in panic – she was drowning. Alfie reached for her, but his strength was being sapped by the second.

The black liquid began to clear, turning to an icy, pale blue as it drained Alfie of his family's magic. Hel's seven-hundred-year curse was coming to an end. The plague goddess's head broke free of the pool's grasp and her shrieking laughter echoed around the arena.

"My mistress!" Lock shouted as Hel's long, skeletal arm suddenly exploded out of the water and grabbed hold of the arena wall. "A new age has begun!"

LC fell to his knees in shock and nearly tumbled into the magical pool, but Hayley picked him up and dragged him away. Brian emptied his gun into Hel as she emerged, but it was like throwing pebbles at an elephant. Tamara tried to dive in after her son and daughter but was grabbed at the last second by

Holgatroll. Qilin, still possessed by Colonel Blood, shrieked with insane laughter and clapped his hands with delight. And no one in the Arena could take their eyes off the terrible creature being birthed in front of them.

Behind Lock, the Black Dragon's eyes cleared for a moment as he watched Hel emerge from the pool.

"What about me, Lock?" the Black Dragon managed to say. "You promised me a cure."

"Oh, there's no cure for you. There never was," Lock said, barely giving him a glance. "Alfie's was the pure blue blood we needed all along. Yours is too corrupted with dragon rot. But never mind, dirty lizard, you've served us well."

Across the pool, Tamara saw the Dragon struggling to lift himself on to his haunches.

"Help them, Richard! *Help them!*" she screamed.

The Black Dragon watched as Alfie and Ellie thrashed around in the pool. Somewhere deep down, where the last part of Richard flickered like a dying candle, he knew they were dying and he was sorry. With a scream of triumph, Hel's other arm shot out of the water and grasped the side of the Arena wall with skittering, clawed fingers. She was halfway out. Her gibbering laughter was pure madness. Anger rose in the Black Dragon, but this wasn't the unthinking animal rage ready to breathe fire; this was entirely human and directed only at himself. Richard knew he'd killed his father. He'd betrayed the brother who had only ever wanted to love and save him, and his sister who he should have protected. He'd betrayed his family, his country, the world. This was all his fault.

The Black Dragon stumbled to his feet, grunting with the effort, talons slipping on the stone floor as he tried to stand. Lock turned around, eyeing the pitiful creature with irritation.

"Put that wretched thing out of its misery!" yelled Lock, signalling to the Viking guards, who charged at the Dragon swinging their axes into his hide.

The Dragon screeched in pain and fell back. But as the Vikings closed in for the kill, he suddenly swiped his tail, cutting them in half. Lock watched in growing horror, as the Black Dragon opened his wings and flew up with some effort, crashing off the walls, blood draining from the gash in his belly.

"STOP!" yelled Lock, ducking as the Dragon flew over him and dived talons first at Hel. "WHAT ARE YOU DOING?"

The plague goddess shrieked and grabbed the Dragon's throat, pulling him off her, diverting the jet of fire meant for her to wash over the arena's ceiling. But the Dragon fought back, thrashing her with his wings and sending them both down into the pool with an immense splash. The effect was instantaneous. The pool turned from blue back to a viscous black as the Dragon's blood gushed out. Hel released her grip on the Dragon and tried to heave herself from the pool once more. But black oily tendrils of liquid shot after her, latching on and pulling her down.

"What's happening?" shouted Hayley, who was pinned to the floor amid the animal bones.

"It's the Dragon's blood – it's poisoning the ritual," the Lord Chamberlain called back.

Lock crawled to the edge of the pool, watching in horror. Suddenly one of Hel's thrashing arms caught his legs and he toppled into the pool too, emerging after a moment, coughing and spluttering at the surface, a tiny figure next to the colossal, desperate goddess, trying to keep his head above the churning slime.

"Help me!" he pleaded.

But Hel's bony hands lost their grip on the Arena walls and smashed down on top of him.

At the edge of the Arena, everyone watched as the black pool receded, like the tide racing out, travelling back towards the frame of the seeing mirror. In a bubbling rush of black goo and with a final, ear-splitting scream, Hel disappeared into the mirror's surface like a spider being sucked down a plughole.

Lock was next, flailing around like a swimmer caught in a rip tide.

Holgatroll tapped Qilin on the shoulder.

"Sorry, but this is going to hurt," she said, took a mighty roundhouse swing and punched him square in the mouth. Colonel Blood's red mist shot out of Qilin's ears and with a splat, landed on the receding water's surface.

"Eww, what *is* this vile liquid? Nooooooo—" Colonel Blood's disembodied voice screamed.

But it was cut short as he too was sucked back into the mirror. All was suddenly still. The mirror, its glass intact once more, lay in the middle of the Arena. Nearby, the bodies of Alfie, Ellie and the Black Dragon lay next to each other, still covered in black slime.

"Alfie!" Hayley yelled and ran over to him.

He was still in his armour, but the normal brilliant white shine was gone, replaced with a coat of black slime and mud.

"Ged de gunk oud of der mouds!" Tony said. He had taken off his mask and was rubbing his jaw.

"He said 'get the gunk out of their mouths'," Freya translated as she transformed back to her human form.

Hayley did just that, scooping out the oily black substance from Alfie's helmet's eye slits, mouth and nose guard, while Tamara did the same for Ellie. Alfie suddenly sat up, removed his armour and sucked in a deep lungful of air. He blinked in the light.

"Ellie?" he coughed.

She sat up next to him and spat the last of the black gunk from her mouth. "Here," she said.

They looked at each other, surprised for a second, then fell into a group hug with their mum and Hayley. A sudden heaving sound drew their attention to the Black Dragon. The battered, broken creature was sprawled on the stone floor, its breaths coming in short, jagged intervals.

"He's still alive," gasped Ellie.

Tamara cradled his head. "Richard, can you hear me?"

Slowly the Dragon's eyes blinked open – they were human again, not the red and yellow of the creature.

A loud *SCREECH* filled the Arena as the mirror suddenly burst back into life and Hel's long, bony arm shot out and grabbed the Dragon. Tamara screamed as Hel pulled the dragon towards the churning black waters of the mirror. Alfie whipped his armour back on and dived at the Dragon, grabbing his arm.

"He's ... not ... yours!" he shouted, heaving with all his strength.

The others rushed to help, each grabbing hold of the Dragon and pulling with all their might. Hel's fingers scrabbled to keep their grip. His scales were coming off like dead leaves from a tree. The Dragon's whole body was cracking apart like a shell, revealing the limp figure of a young man beneath – Richard. Hel's hand came away with nothing but the shredded carapace of the Dragon; she screamed with rage as she was sucked back into the mirror. LC threw the velvet cloth over the mirror and all was quiet once more.

The Defender collapsed to the floor, holding his brother. There was a long gash across Richard's chest. His naked, scarred body was deathly pale.

"Bring me the Sword of Mercy! Hurry!" called Alfie.

Brian ran to the regalia case and pulled out the blunt-ended sword. He handed it to the Defender and the sword glowed gold.

"Only drawn in mercy, never in vengeance," Alfie whispered as he gently laid the blade across Richard's chest.

All was silent in the Arena as they watched and waited.

30

THE ORDER OF ST GEORGE

"Britain is back to the way it was. But we as a people have changed."

Prime Minister Vanessa Thorn was addressing the cameras outside Number Ten, Downing Street. It was two months since the battle at Tower Bridge, and much of what had been destroyed had already been rebuilt. Shops, offices and schools were all up and running again. The borders had reopened and people travelled around just as they had before the Viking invasion. Best of all, the weather had improved, and what had felt like an endless winter was now turning into a bright spring. Although everyone was still talking about what had happened, there was a feeling that life was getting back to normal at last. Alfie was watching a re-run of the speech on a large TV inside a palace drawing room. He noticed that Thorn's voice had changed, the sharp edges softened. There was also a streak of white in her hair that hadn't been there before: a remnant, he figured, from her time as a berserker.

"The things we used to take for granted – our homes, our families, our freedoms – we now cherish more than ever. Our eyes have been opened to a world beyond our imaginations, a world of fresh possibilities and, yes, grave dangers. But let us not give in to fear or turn in on ourselves. Let us instead work harder to strengthen existing alliances and to forge new ones. Above all let us show gratitude – for what we have and for those who gave it back to us. Not just the Defender – wherever he is – but to the many who stood with him in our hour of need, both those with special powers and those with none. Britain has always shown its best self when tested. Today we can proudly say we have passed that test once more. Let us never forget the sacrifice and the courage that won us this victory."

"What do you think?"

Alfie was surprised to see the prime minister standing in the doorway behind him, in the same pale yellow outfit she'd been wearing on TV.

"Bit too Churchill? Or just enough? I wasn't sure," she said.

"You're really asking what *I* think?" said Alfie, fumbling to turn off the screen.

"Call it the new humble me. It's funny how living as a slobbering monster for a few months can change your outlook."

Alfie laughed, then stopped, unsure whether it was a joke or not. He was relieved to see her smile. He couldn't remember seeing her do that before.

"Sorry, Prime Minister, I didn't think our weekly audience was till tomorrow."

"It's not, Majesty. Forgive me, but I wanted you to be the first to know. I'm going to resign."

"What? Why?"

"Like I said, people change. And when I came back from my little . . . break, I realized something. I couldn't remember why it was I'd wanted to be PM in the first place. I think if you're given power it helps to know what you want to do with it."

"I know what you mean," said Alfie.

Thorn frowned, intrigued. "Is that why you decided not to abdicate after all? What was it that made you come back?"

Alfie felt himself turning red. He hadn't meant to get into this. "I suppose I just realized I had more idea about what to do with the job than I'd thought."

The prime minister gave a slight bow and went to leave. But she paused and turned back.

"One other thing I've been wondering, Majesty. There are still so many conflicting reports about what really happened around the time the Defender returned, but I heard that you were seen with him at Stonehenge. Did you get any clue as to who he might be? I'd love to know."

"Search me," Alfie said with a shrug. "But I did get the feeling it might be better if no one ever found out."

Thorn held his gaze for a long couple of seconds, as if considering another question. But then she merely smiled, nodded and walked out.

Later that night, it was Alfie's turn to surprise someone. Queen Tamara, Hayley, Tony and Queen Freya – who was back in the UK under the guise of a royal visit – had all been asked to assemble at Windsor Castle. But they had not been told why.

"Honey!" cried his mum when she saw Alfie walk in, sweeping him into her arms and planting a big kiss on his cheek, much to his embarrassment.

"All right, Mum, take it easy," he said, glancing over at Hayley, who was looking at him with her arms crossed and a quizzical expression on her face.

"You're up to something," said Hayley. "What's the big secret?"

"Yeah, and is it going to take long?" asked Tony.

"'Cos I've got a date tonight," he added, beaming at Freya.

Hayley and Alfie looked at each other, astonished. "You do?" asked Alfie.

Freya rolled her eyes. "Not me! It turns out my little sister, Sølvi, has a thing for geeks. There's no accounting for taste, I suppose."

Tony nodded with pride. The others laughed and Alfie beckoned them to follow him.

"OK, OK, no more secrets. This way," said Alfie.

He was enjoying being the one with the surprise up his sleeve for once. Alfie had given the entire staff the night off, so it was quiet as they processed through the Lower Ward and into St George's Chapel. High above them on either side of the aisle, the heraldic banners of the members of the Order of the Garter hung in the candlelight. Medieval depictions of lions, falcons and unicorns gazed down on them as they passed beneath. Herne rose from where he had been sleeping by the altar and greeted each of them with a nuzzle and lick of the hand.

"Nearly seven hundred years ago, when the Defender, Edward the Third, was battling Hel the first time round, he made this place his base of operations," said Alfie. "The Order of St George, later known as the Order of the Garter, was a company of knights – men and women – drawn from every blue bloodline he could find, dedicated to stopping the plague goddess and keeping the world safe."

"Sorry to interrupt, sweetie," said Tamara, "but wasn't it us who told you about all that in the first place?"

"True," Alfie smiled, "but there's something else you don't know . . ."

He pulled back the altar cloth to reveal a carving of a blue belt, laid in a circle around the red and white cross of St George. On the belt was written an inscription in medieval French – "*Honi soit qui mal y pense*." It meant: "Shame be to him who thinks evil of it."

". . . the Order's still here."

Alfie placed his hand over the symbol and every candle in the chapel went out, plunging them into darkness. As the others watched in silent awe, the ghostly shapes of priests appeared, carrying a ringed table that was the exact same shape and detailing as the garter belt, complete with St George's shield at its centre. Two dozen chairs slid from the darkness to surround the table. And as the light slowly returned to the chapel, they could see that the rows of pews had been replaced with tapestries and boards showing maps of the world, the translucent priests monitoring them in much the same way the Yeoman Warders manned their desks in the Keep.

"It's one of those thingies," blurted Tony. "Royal particulars."

"PECULIARS!" said Freya, Hayley and Tamara in unison.

"Whatever," said Tony. "Anyway, it's all jolly impressive, Your Majesticals, but why are you showing it to us?"

"Because," said Alfie, taking his seat at the table, "Hel may be gone, but she's not the only one out there who would destroy the world if they got the chance. Next time, we need to be ready. So I have decided to reform the Order of St George and you lot are going to be my first knights."

A ghost priest appeared behind each of them, holding a long, dark blue velvet cloak embossed with the insignia of the Order, which they draped over each of their shoulders. They looked at each other and laughed.

"What's the catch?" asked Hayley.

Alfie gestured for them to join him at the table.

"There are still a lot of empty seats," said Freya casting her eye around.

Alfie bit his lip. "Yeah, that's the catch. I'm not sure if you're going to be up for this, but. . ."

"Spit it out," said Hayley.

"OK, the thing is my place is here," said Alfie. "There are still a bunch of escaped prisoners from the Tower dungeons that need rounding up. I can't risk leaving the country right now."

"So. . .?" asked Tony.

"So I'm asking you to help me," continued Alfie. "Mum, you began the search for the ancient members of the Order of St George. I think we should finish the job."

"It took us two years just to find Tony," said Tamara, looking uncertain.

"I know," said Alfie. "But you were doing it alone. I've instructed LC to determine which current monarchs can be relied on to become our allies. And I've issued orders to the Yeoman Warders to scour the Archives to find any clue that can help us relocate the bloodlines that are no longer on their thrones. We have to try. But I can't do it by myself."

He looked at their startled faces waiting for any hint of enthusiasm to reveal itself. Finally Tony broke the silence and slapped the table, laughing.

"Of course we're with you, Alfie-bet!"

"Yeah, sounds like more fun than trying to teach the Yeoman Warders how to use computers," said Hayley.

"Where do we start, Your Majesty?" asked Freya.

Alfie exhaled, relieved. "Thank you. I was thinking you could handle Europe, Freya. That way you wouldn't be too far from home if there was any Viking outbreak."

She nodded. He turned to Tony.

"I figured you could handle Asia and the Middle East – it's a lot of ground to cover, but that should suit you."

"Sun, sea and sandcastles, here I come!" said Tony. "And, ahem, tough perilous missions and all that."

"Let me guess," said Tamara, "I'm heading to Africa?"

"I remembered you went on tour there with Dad when I was little," said Alfie. "I'm guessing you were already working some leads even back then?"

"Smart boy," replied Tamara. "I'll send you a postcard."

"And Hayley," began Alfie. But she interrupted him.

"Wait, Alfie. I want to help. But I made a promise to my gran." She was holding the Zemi pendant that hung around her neck. "I need to take her back to Jamaica."

"Which is why," continued Alfie, "I thought that when you're done, maybe you could fly on to South America?"

Hayley looked relieved. "Sure thing. Wow, I'm going to need a guidebook."

Alfie surveyed his new knights of the Order of St George. "Thanks, guys. I wasn't sure what I was going to do if you said no."

"Do we have time to hang out a little before we leave?" asked Hayley.

Alfie felt himself going red again. His mum, Tony and Freya all pretended to look around at the chapel so as not to embarrass him any further. He and Hayley hadn't talked about the kiss at Stonehenge since it happened.

"I'm supposed to head back to the palace tonight," Alfie stuttered. "Bunch of engagements tomorrow, you know."

Hayley looked down at the table, "Yeah, of course, no worries."

Alfie was still thinking about Hayley and their hurried, awkward goodbye the next morning as he stood in the rain outside a new pork-pie factory he was opening in a little market town in the Midlands called Wellingborough. He wished he'd had more time to talk to her, but. . .

Duty calls, he thought, smiling at the cameras as he snipped the ribbon.

Hours later, back at Buckingham Palace, he padded down a long, dark hallway and stopped outside a bedroom door. Hearing laughter he recognized from inside, he knocked and went in. Richard and Ellie looked up from the bed where they were playing a card game.

"He's cheating again," said Ellie.

"I'm still getting better, I'm allowed," Richard shot back with a friendly nudge.

"You look fine to me, Rich," said Alfie.

It was true. Richard looked almost back to his old self, though not as muscly and broad as he used to perhaps. Over the last few weeks, Alfie had sometimes caught his brother staring into space with a haunted look in his eyes, but those moments were becoming more fleeting. He was talking about getting back into his studies, maybe even training for the navy again. Ellie kept telling him to take it one day at a time; she had moved back to the palace too and taken charge of Richard's rehabilitation. Alfie was glad to have them both close by – it had made the place feel like a home again.

"Fancy a game, Alf?" asked Ellie. "Harder for him to win against both of us."

Alfie looked at his watch. "I'd love to but. . ."

They waved him away.

"All right, super-brother, you go do your thing," sighed Ellie.

"Careful out there," added Richard.

*

Back in his room, Alfie rubbed Herne's belly as the dog sprawled, snoring on his bed, then headed into the secret tunnel and down to the underground State Coach. It had taken weeks to rebuild it and he was under strict instructions from Brian never to tamper with the brakes ever again.

Alfie was surprised to find the Keep in darkness. He squinted against the gloom, but couldn't see anyone there. All was quiet.

"Hello?" His voice echoed through the hall, but there was no reply.

Alfie's hand went to his belt, but of course his sword was not there. He started to edge towards the Arena, hoping he could find the regalia cabinet in the dark, before— Suddenly the whole place burst into light. Alfie shielded his eyes and spun around, just as the beefeaters sprang out from behind their desks, cheering.

"GOD SAVE THE KING!" they chorused.

Startled, Alfie looked to the wall to see LC and Brian unveil a huge new tapestry. It depicted Alfie as the Defender on Tower Bridge, doing battle with Guthrum the Viking giant.

"Whoa," was all Alfie could muster.

"Is that it?" said Brian. "I was up all night stitching that!"

Alfie laughed, catching his breath. "Nice to see you, Brian. How was the holiday?"

"Rained every day, sir. We were stuck indoors the whole week. It was bliss. The family says hello, by the way."

"How was your day, Majesty?" asked LC.

Alfie thought about the hours of travelling, the dozens of hands he'd shaken, the dull speeches he'd delivered, the ache in his cheeks from smiling constantly.

"Do you know what? It was good. Thanks for asking, LC. Or should I say, Cuthbert?"

The beefeaters stifled giggles and pretended they hadn't heard. LC frowned and trotted after Alfie as he headed for the Arena to start training.

"You did promise you wouldn't call me that again, Majesty," he muttered.

Suddenly a shrill alarm sounded. Yeoman Box, back manning the ops table, yelped in surprise. "Ooh, I nearly dropped my scones!" she said, putting down her plate and blowing crumbs off the map as she looked for the source of the alarm.

"It's the Exeter burgh!" she announced.

"I'd say the Beast of Bodmin's found his way home," said Brian.

"Ready, Majesty?" asked LC.

Alfie nodded. "Sorry all, tea break's over. Let's get to work."

*

Wyvern was flying low over the Devon countryside when Alfie's radio crackled into life.

"Call for you, boss," said Brian in his ear.

"Oh, right. Put it through," said Alfie, unsure who it could be so late.

"Hiya. Is this a bad time?"

It was Hayley's voice.

"Er, no, fine," said Alfie. "Got a few minutes before we land, I reckon."

"I couldn't sleep. Big trip tomorrow." Hayley was booked on a flight to Jamaica the next morning.

"Yeah, sorry," Alfie said. "I was going to call you, but you know..."

"You've been busy? Oh, and boys are useless and have no idea how to do a simple thing like ask a girl out?"

Alfie was so surprised he almost slipped off Wyvern's back, sending her into a steep dive straight through the branches of a tall oak tree, emerging from the other side with a face full of twigs and leaves before she levelled out again, whinnying in irritation.

"Everything OK out there?" asked Hayley.

"What? Yeah. Spot of turbulence," squeaked Alfie. "You were saying?"

"Listen, Alfie, I'm not sure what the protocol is for asking a king out, but I thought it might be nice to see each other later. If you're not too busy, that is?"

"Wow. I mean, yeah, cool." Alfie was wincing for England inside his armour. "Got some business to take care of first, but I could pick you up, say, ten-ish?"

"It's a date," said Hayley. "Just do me a favour and don't get killed or anything before then. See you later."

He heard the click of Hayley hanging up the phone. In that moment Alfie thought that even if he hadn't been sitting on a magical flying ghost horse travelling at a hundred miles an hour, he'd still feel like he was flying.

"Mind on the mission, please, Majesty," said LC over the radio.

"Oh, let the boy have some fun, you old killjoy," said Brian.

Alfie had forgotten that everyone in the Keep would have heard his whole conversation with Hayley. But he didn't care. He steered Wyvern into a dive, rocketing towards the bleak moorland below, ready for whatever awaited him there in the dark.

"OK, Wyvern, let's make this quick," said the Defender. "I've got a date to keep."

ACKNOWLEDGEMENTS

Once more, we need to thank our publishers, Scholastic, especially the tireless Linas Alsenas, Rachel Phillipps, Peter Matthews and their brilliant teams. Cover designer Tom Sanderson deserves a special mention – thank you. Thanks also to our agent, Cathy King at 42 Management, for her everlasting support, and last but not least to our wives, Melanie and Anna – for their event-managing, proofreading and everything else. Finally, we want to thank YOU, the reader, for taking a chance on something new and for accompanying Alfie and Hayley all the way to the end of their journey. And if you've told a friend or written a review or put this book in another's hands, then we thank you all over again.

Is this the end for the Defender? We hope not. But it is the end of the trilogy we first had in mind all those years ago. A story we first told to each other, then to our families, then to our first editor and good friend, David Stevens, and now to all of you. We wanted to recapture the feelings of wonder and excitement we first experienced reading the fantasy adventure novels we loved as children, and we hope we've succeeded. What we didn't expect was the journey we would go on ourselves as new authors, and the firm friends we would make along the way, from publishing professionals to fellow authors, teachers, librarians, booksellers, children, parents and at least one real-life beefeater. Thank you all and see you soon.

Mark & Nick

Photo courtesy of Sarah Weal.

Nick Ostler and Mark Huckerby are Emmy-winning and BAFTA-nominated screenwriters best known for writing popular TV shows such as *Danger Mouse*, *Thunderbirds Are Go!* and *Peter Rabbit*. They are currently head writers on *Moominvalley*, a new adaptation of Tove Jansson's classic novels coming soon to TV screens everywhere. *Defender of the Realm* is their first book series.

Follow Nick on Twitter @nickostler
Follow Mark on Twitter @Huckywucky

Visit their website
www.ostlerandhuckerby.com

www.instagram.com/defenderoftherealm